THE SEVEN DIDDLY SINS

TED WEST

To Henry N. Manney III, who had the grace to laugh last.

TED WEST

Cast

Checquers

Montgomery Overdale Rutt, the Duke, CEO, the planet
Proserpina "Proz" Rutt-Lombardo, the Duke's daughter, 29 and counting
Neddy Lombardo, whelmed husband
Burtie Balfour, his particular pal

Cañon Perdido Loyalists

Peregrina "Peevy" Palmtry, Proz's dearest schoolmate from 12 years ago
Twitty Conway, Proz's *other* dearest schoolmate from 12 years ago
Lissa Montenero, dangerously beautiful

Literary Lite

Julian Axel, N.Y. Times Swell-Seller, nice shoes
Gary Larry, City College Lecturer, regional poet, footballist
Gerald Schmidt Thermos, City College composer, male
Duane Snit, Abstract-Expressionist family portraiture

Santa Lola Irregulars

Vance Crankenfuss Esq., the Duke's counsel
Crusty Yamaguchi, Nisei Chief of Security
Chester Halimony, third-generation bystander
Clive O.E.M. Monogram D.S., living with mother
"Two-Paw" Coggins, graven image
Keita Mammady Fallo, African reactionary
Ken Stukud, corner Camino Carne and Sabado Bingo
Ahmed al Fakhr, City College student, film-noir savant

Fisherman's Grange

Eddie Boyle, commercial fisherman, activist
Aloysius "Mickey Moose" Lovely, Olympian, draft or bottle
Spider, Mambo, Billy, Jiggy, Marty, Veal ... 'nuff said

Dodgers

Doug the Thug, Tillary St., the Duke's man
Angus Cannizaro, Canarsie, middle management
Ski Kobalefffsky, Red Hook soldier

Part One

CHAPTER 1

Prozie

OCTOBER, 1984

LOVELY PROZ GLIDES HER PALM on the air streaming by out the window.

"Couldn't we, Neddy?"

And he's game.

"Speaking to me?"

"Go out to the Olde Lighthouse, I mean—"

But the glam young wife isn't finished.

"In the fog, for cassoulet and … oh well, oh well."

Now he has her drift.

She means some adult pass-punt-and-kick in the roomy velour backseat.

"Gives me indigestion," he says.

"*Neddy!*"

"… the cassoulet," he submits, clarifying the broth.

"Ah."

She ponders its various components.

Meantime, he's going like the clappers, the impossibly rare big 1948 Tucker Torpedo sedan weaving through midday Santa Lola traffic like an industrial loom—and no wonder. They're an hour late for the Great Party at the Duke's estate, good grief, *in her honor!*

"Seriously," she says, "couldn't we? It was nice. I thought it might be nice again."

"Proz, we never agree on *anything*—and your solution is cassoulet in the fog!"

He swerves violently passing a big Mercedes, and she takes it ill.

"Well, if that's how you feel—I can take a hint. Fine, then ... I tried. Oh, well, oh, well."

Oh, hell.

The big Tucker sedan hurtles past chi-chi ladies' boutiques, Royal Swedish Bedding & Bath, dueling wine boîtes, Panseer Persian Carpets ... *Everything Must Go!*, Santa Lola Precious Metals Exchange, Condor & Stimpley Estates & More ... and more.

All the while Proz is arranged on the broad blue-velour front seat like a cheetah, elegant, motionless, serene. When things go wrong no blame attaches to her, she isn't the sort. If she were ... well, she isn't. As the Duke's daughter and sole heir, Proserpina—Proz, to you—is as blame-free as the "Teflon" moviestar Fortieth President currently tenting in the Oval Office. He parlayed a leading-man smile to Cold War mega-clout, serial re-electability and regular visits to Checquers, the Duke's grand estate—but even "Dutch" can stand improvement. For a time, he took to calling her "Prozie," and she's asked him not to.

Neddy forces the big Tucker ever onwards, knowing his commission.

Yet it wasn't him, *he* didn't spend two and a half bleeding hours arranging one hair next to the other in the wife's Olympic-size Salon, Yogatorium and Spa! He peeked-in twice to gauge her progress, but it looked like Hurricane Imelda, raw-silk chemises from India, straw belts from Luzon, silk scarves from Florence and Phnom Penh, sunhats from Paris, Pakistan and Paramus, all flung high and low—closing time at Saks Summer Clearance!

The turquoise Tucker careens past Ritz-Carlton Santa Lola, a blur of palmettos and pink stucco—but they're still light-years from the Duke's grand estate up in the mountains! All the while Proz imparts astral calm. On the cusp of thirty, chic, tall and tony in her oh-what's-the-us*e* way, she has "good bones," spa skin and the inborn swank of a very few catastrophically rich young women.

And for the record, Miss Parker is mistaken, you *can* be too rich and too thin.

She will consult her gold Rolex—an Oyster the size of an abalone.

"Oh, poor Daddy..." she laments now.

"The Duke is many things," Neddy allows, "but poor he is not."

It's the groaner of the American Century, yet he tosses it off like a scoop of chum.

"You should've hurried me along," she complains.

"I practically set my hair on fire!"

"Darling, that's an exaggeration."

"Couldn't find a match!"

She smirks—all hunky-dory.

They're still unforgivably late.

Always!

And yet ... and yet ... all is not lost. The Santa Lola afternoon is in the upper reaches of sublime. Bright sunbeams cascade down crimson three-quarter-length shop awnings. Visitors lick melting gelati, strolling past a diamond-studded sea. Bentleys, Rolls-Royces, Aston Martins, Ferraris ... the occasional black Mercedes Grosser 600 Limo ... sally to and fro emitting stardust. It's a prospect of perfection familiar to children of all ages.

Santa Lola ... the Gem of the Platinum Coast. It has no peer. Other villes seek to compete—none is in second place. Since the last rude judder of the Quake of '26, Cyrus Rutt, the Duke's legendary father and Proz's Gran'puh-paw, determined that with right architectural codes and Draconian enforcement, he would transform this Olde California port town to something remarkable. Yes, revered. By this October p.m., any Santa Lola commercial edifice not meeting the minimums of Spanish Colonial rises to high Santa Lola Mission. The look is warm, wealthy, winsome as the sea at sunset, the despair of any who would imitate it—even in Texas.

And the Santa Lola climate slams the door. While the outer world droops in autumnal decline, Summer Carnival clatters down on Sunny Santa Lola. The avenue teems with moneyed yet sleekly disdained out-of-towners, for to be elsewhere at this, or any, season would be just too sad. The air is utopian, 84 degrees. Santa Lola sun is never hot—it is smart. Visitors value its wisdom on their skin. Like chrome on a Packard Twelve, it confers completion.

Then promptly at four forty-five, with strings, a sweet Pacific breeze bends gently onshore—the same Santa Lola zephyr endorsed by Coco herself, who had a nose on her.

*****

Bursting Santa Lola's municipal bonds now, the Tucker goes vertical.

Climbing hard, it scales the first high ledges of the Coast Range. In pan-searing heat better suited to improving Chilean sea bass, the overmatched six-cylinder clatters like ball bearings in a blender—and Neddy Lombardo suffers with it. He gnaws the sensuous Sicilian lower lip, the exact hue and texture of fresh beef liver.

He has dark hair. Dark eyes. Dark socks.

You have the picture.

But he never doubts the Tucker—it is everything Aldo "Patsy" Lombardo, his late pater and moral North Star, demanded of American industrial might. Underscoring the point, it outlived Big Patsy by seven round years.

The molten two-lane mountain asphalt out the twin-pane windshield leaps and writhes past sheer rock cliffs. Neddy grapples with the wheel. Noxious fumes trail out astern, intimations of New Jersey, The Garden State. Perth Amboy was Big Patsy's home and hearth. Someday Neddy knows he must step away from this automobile—yet whenever the thought comes in on final approach, he feels Big Patsy's breath on his neck...

DoanevunthingGaboudit.

Suddenly now, far beneath, a huge, essential black stovebolt installed by Tucker craftsmen during the Truman Administration ... breaks free.

Skims across searing asphalt—

ka-*dink!*

dink-a-*DINK!*

Skips into waist-high, joyously flammable underbrush...

SSSssphhhisssssss....

Unaware, the lovebirds motor ever higher to the Duke's unthinkable "Front Gate."

Featured on every Santa Lola souvenir calendar, this signal portal is a split-level ranch-style rendering of Bonaparte's Parisian triumphal arc. While conceptually faithful to the original, minus the Metro station, the Duke's model is built to modestly grander scale, inviting two eighteen-wheelers to pass through at once, one going in, one coming out.

But years ago, Neddy's random eye, the curse of the Stanford man, spotted a typo high up in the carved stone. Clint Hardwood, the Duke's master stonemason, and a City College graduate, bearing witness to the Duke's financial triumphs Down Under, saw fit to substitute an "s" for the preferred "u." Neddy mentioned this, but the Duke came down hard on the side of artistic freedom—he wouldn't change a thing.

Now every time Neddy arrives, "Asstralia" leaps to his eye.

Close enough for California.

The Tucker is waved through the grand gate by crisply uniformed Nisei Chief of Security Crusty Yamaguchi.

The golden couple motors along Checquers' majestic Grande Allée.

Overarching trees confer blessed shade.

Off to the right and 1500 feet straight down, a blue Formica sea broods. Pacific black kelp lazes and curls in its swells like slow-simmering french onion soup.

And far ahead through weeping, nay, sobbing willows is the astonishing mansion!

"So beautiful..." Proz muses now, as if seeing her birthplace for the first time.

Neddy checks his watch—sixty seconds.

She's on an egg-timer.

... kuh-*Ting!*

"Feeling better, peanut?" he ventures.

"Don't be silly, dear, I'm fabulous!"

Missed something....

"And really, I think we should," she says, "... cassoulet and fog."

Under the mansion's spell, her instrument is less cornet, more flugelhorn.

"It'd be fun!"

Neddy clicks his tongue.

"Giving the Duke a pink-belly ... now, that would be fun!"

"Oh *youuu*—" she says.

He smiles.

She smiles right back: "You're an ass—"

He awaits the caustic final syllable.

... no?

Well fine.

All her life, she's gotten everything she ever wanted for a frown.

But Neddy needs a vacation, and this is the day of the Great Party. Beautiful Lissa Montenero is on the loose somewhere up ahead. Today is going to change everything!

CHAPTER 2

Two Scoops, Pleeeze

THE TURQUOISE TORPEDO NEGOTIATES one last gracious mile of Checquers parkland.

(Oh come now—a mile?)

(Yes. One mile. Pay attention.)

Basking in the glow of her ancestral home, Proz opens like an orchid.

Not many California lean-tos justify the moniker ... but great Checquers is ancestral as hell! Beloved CBS anchor Charles Foster Brunch, who immortalized himself by blubbering aloud at Adlai Stephenson's interment, quipped off the record, but it spread like mashed garlic, "Checquers is to embedded American wealth what the Playboy Mansion is to exposed nipples."

And so it is.

Before Checquers' grandeur now, Proz waxes resplendent, yet with just a wee hint of *mystère* ... or so her waiting-a-bloody-hour! classmates from twelve years ago at Cañon Perdido Proper School will swear.

Seeing the Tucker, they begin swearing immediately.

Gliding past the mansion's main entrance, the Tucker's wide-whitewall tires part an inland sea of combed, individually lacquered white pea gravel.

Achieving at last the Duke's Mission-Style 40-vehicle Monte Lola Automotive Service Lanai, young Neddy performs a boulevard stop, and Henry of the Lanai staff steps forward. Yet seeing no open flame, Henry sets down the extinguisher. He will administer two brimming containers of 50-weight oil. It is the commitment of John Beresford Tipton, the Automotive Service Lanai's motor-pool factotum, to take all measures in aid of young master's unhappy auto. The Tucker will be washed, Simonized

6

and corrected in all feasible regards. They have no magic.

And Proz is out!

Instantly, the air is rent with a cornea-shearing ... shuh-*rieeeeeeeekkk!*

Sixty yards distant and closing fast is Peregrina Palmtry—beloved "Peevy"—squealing like her scalp was ripped off.

"*Peeeeeee-VEEEEE!*" keens Proz with matching corneal disregard.

Shoulders low, knees driving, they meet, a jarring impact—

... *TWWWEEEEEEEttt*-ing in idiomatic chickadee.

Neddy's toes make fists in his Charles Jourdan black-linen pumps.

But now heel impacts of greater moment reverberate on the Lanai tiles.

Balls, the Duke!

Respectfully, Henry puts down the second drooling canister of oil ... goooonk.

"Well, then..." nods the great man.

"Young Ned," he extemporizes.

"My lad..." he confirms, hemorrhaging verbiage.

The peroration winding down, they bow like Guardsmen at a funeral.

But beyond the corner of the great mansion now—

In they rush, a headlong stampede of designer young things sprinting for dear Proz, caterwauling like competing air-raid sirens.

Even the Duke steps back!

Impact after impact occurs, the scrum shoving, grunting, exchanging heartfelt head-butts.

"And Neddy!" banshees wee Peevy.

She knows the worst about Neddy and Proz ... gets it straight from the filly's mouth.

"Dearest Ned," she French-horns just the same, "wonderful-to-*SEE*-you-you've-*NO-IDEA-just-how-we've-missed*—"

"PEEVE!"

He's tripped her up—nicely done.

"Your dog—" he says, invoking what comes uppermost, "... how's your dog."

Grotesque, in fact, part Chihuahua, part hamster.

"Adorable!" she beams, beside herself, or very nearby.

Neddy's fused toes—he can't feel a thing below his knees!

Detecting a pause, the Duke delivers his signature pronunciamento: "Whatever you're after, we got it plenty!"

With a grand ducal wave, he bows, "Shall we...."

We shall!

They begin a leisurely stroll to the stupefying white-stucco Moorish manse.

*****

Mighty Checquers towers above, improbably taller than the tallest eucalyptus.

Yet for all its paralyzing dignity, the edifice is a miracle of Spanish-Californian grace and ease. And now, from high in its lofty Campanile, Checquers' great bell carillon peals Proz's joyous arrival. It is played with wild-ass abandon by "Dr. Rory" Rhodes, Organist and Music Director of the Duke's Episcopal house of worship, slightly farther down the mount, The Cathedral Church of St. Biff In the Trees. The carillon celebrates all fêtes, sacred and national, and July fourteenth, in particular. Also marking something or other in France, the date denotes the Duke's betrothal to his beloved Constance, Proz's mother, sadly departed this life seven years ago.

A few stories above the carillon, on the peak of the Campanile, towering above the mansion like a Saturn Five rocket, select dinner guests are treated to infarctional views of the blue Pacific, the Channel Islands, Pt. Moot and the Olde Lighthouse Bistro—where Proz and Neddy will take cassoulet in the fog and ... oh well, oh well.

The leisurely stroll to the mansion proceeds, Neddy, Proz and retinue furnished the News of the Day, the Duke reporting:

Burtram Balfour, Neddy's particular pal, has already been disgraced in the All-Comers Greater Platinum Coast Chess Tournament, by a youth of twelve.

In an intriguing incident at Connaught Saltwater Baths, a Patek Philippe Nautilus wristwatch went missing—located moments later under the aggrieved's sunhat. Also involving Burtie Balfour, the quick-to-accuse Ms. Gordon Nose administered a closed-fisted slap, just seconds before lifting her hat.

The Duke's eye twinkles.

In other news....

Up at Checquers' Santa Lola Invitational Raceway, masterful Chester Halimony won two preliminary Porsche heat races, while Mason Frampton's Jaguar XKE went ass-over-ten-spot in the track's Scilly Esses.

Medical bulletins have Frampton responding well to Laphraoig. He'll be at his post first thing in the ayem, selling annuities—give'im a call.

*****

Ski Kobalefffsky isn't on the Checquers guest list.

It may only be a question of spelling.

So much in Kobalefffsky's life has been.

A year before Ski's birth in Red Hook, Brooklyn ("The Point" as everyone knows), Ludmilla Anna Kobalewski, Ski's grandmother, had spent a long productive life with her entirely serviceable Gdansk shipbuilding and domestic-services surname ... but by age 61, she was sick to death of having to clout every greaser, spic and mick who pronounced it "Kobalooski."

With a note from her priest, she arranged to have the name legally changed, specifying three "f"s ... the Brooklyn equivalent of one good Polish "w."

She changed the "i" to "y" for looks.

Ski Kobalefffsky's being halted by Security at Checquers' overwhelming Front Gate is not surprising—he and Marlon Sneave don't look like Great Partygoers. True, Great Parties are notorious all-skates, welcoming a cast of thousands. Even still....

Marlon Sneave, for his part, is skinny, pale olive, with sharp-boned cheeks, slits for eyes and skinny brows that point up at the ends in a permanent scowl. At the jungle gym, the other children just naturally named him "Snake."

"Snake Sneave."

It was funny to say.

Waiting at Checquers' towering entrance now, Snake slouches in the passenger seat of Ski's Ford like James Dean with a chest wound.

Women seeking gratuitous abuse will shoot him a second glance.

All the while, the monster V-8 in Ski's sinister black-on-black Ford Gran Torino Coupe grumbles menacingly—a chain smoker. Snake smokes the same way, as if disgusted by his own fumes.

"Kobalefffsky—with a 'K,'" snaps Ski to Checquers Security Chief Crusty Yamaguchi.

Ski applies just the right tone of annoyance.

"We're invited personally by the Duke."

Yamaguchi nods politely, "One moment sir."

Ski nods, letting the annoyance ride.

Yamaguchi steps into the Gate's dark-windowed Security kiosk. He'll send a routine alert up to Security Red, but the Gran Torino won't be turned away. The Duke is a Westerner, and turning people away "isn't Great Party."

Ski's and Snake's names, time of arrival, description, even their Gross Vehicle Weight (a scale lurks under the rumpa-rumpa-ing Gran Torino's fat tires) are recorded. Polaroid color photos of the driver, included in the dossier, are shot confidentially through the security kiosk's one-way glass. The passenger photo is shot through a lens concealed in the brass plaque on the far side. The plaque quotation, from *All's Well That Ends Well*, reads, "Make the coming hour o'erflow with joy...."

The last "o" in "joy" is a Polaroid lens.

Security procedures are activated whenever something sets off

Crusty Yamaguchi's keenly tuned belly. Those who would object are invited to attend less secure events. Tonight, open to all, City College is offering an Advanced Sand-Painting Workshop.

Yamaguchi returns now, smiling.

"Good to go, sir."

Ski smirks.

Clunks the Gran Torino into gear.

The big V-8 gurgles.

Snake Sneave sneers out his passenger window, where no one can see—

Except a motor-drive Polaroid...

cllllikkk!

*****

Proz makes an entrance.

Seeing her, loud cheers and bully applause crash around the Casino walls like the *pelota* in a jai-alai *fronton*.

Checquers has a *fronton*—three, in fact, for tournament play.

No one doubts this ovation's heartfelt sincerity, in celebration of ... well, let's see—

It's not her birthday.

And it's not the anniversary of her carefully measured marriage.

Then ... in recognition of the ongoing wonder of her impossible excellence.

That's got it!

High-fives all around.

And in less time than it takes to count your blessings—all of them—gaming returns to full fury.

Oh, yes, Checquers has gaming. The estate is on "tribal lands," the Duke saw to it. There is gaming at Checquers as surely as there are corporate jets in Aspen at Christmas.

Proz, Neddy and the Duke are joined at their Casino banquette by the "better" half of Proz's graduating class from twelve years ago at Cañon Perdido Proper School. ("*Toujours La Finesse...*" pronounces sorely mourned Headmistress Pimblitzer, smiling down beyond the clouds.) All gorge on alpine expressions of frosty Kosmic Karamel, Proz's fave!

Beads of moisture trickle down the heavy cut-glass goblets, in a sweat to please.

Meanwhile, zany gaming surges all around, fortunes spiraling skywards, crashing, and spiraling skywards anew. Horace Bigg Memorial Casino is a source of intense pride to the Duke, the only gaming forum extant where the players' chances are *better* than even. Bigg Casino opens

10

several times a year, costing the Duke millions. But no matter. It delights him to see his winners wander off into the night, thunderstruck at their sudden command of chance.

Intriguing species, humans.

And it's no happenstance that Checquers' gargantuan, rightly famed County Pool adjoins Bigg Casino. This affords all gamers a graceful exit strategy. They can joust with Fortune straight through till dawn, or slip away at any moment, bagfuls to the good, "for a dip." It's an item of utmost delicacy to Duke Monty. Under no circumstances should a big winner be held up to undue scrutiny for quitting while light-years ahead.

Bigg Casino is neither large nor small, but "just right." This felicitous paradigm is heard often around Checquers.

The Casino walls are lined with handsome Santa Lola scenes in stained glass, of surfing, sailing, soccer, Monterey fishing boats, the world-acclaimed Santa Lola sunset. The venue accommodates 600 seekers, blackjack to craps to roulette. Those delegated to bring home the "bacon" head straight to baccarat.

Winnings there can be appalling.

And Bigg Casino's blue-orange-and-gold carpet will be subliminally familiar to a very few. It is the exact same carpet used in the U.S. Senate.

It tickles the Duke no end.

Casino croupiers are flown in from South Shore Lake Tahoe on Duke Monty's gleaming white utility Douglas DC-8. This isn't the latest jetliner—but to the Duke's eye one of the most graceful.

The Tahoe crew is paid handsomely not to damage the suckers. Seeing a big winner cash-in, pants on fire, is sure to warm the good host's heart.

But a few years back, at a Tuesday Great Party (the Duke tosses his mind-busting galas at midweek just because he can), young Neddy Lombardo, not yet a recipient of Proz's most precious favors, emerged from Bigg Casino after winning for three hours straight—and smelled a rat.

The Old Bat was giving away money!

This didn't restrain Neddy from filling a Neiman-Marcus shopping bag with hundred-dollar chips, sufficient to convert his disastrous short sales at Kidder Bidder & Vance, repave his driveway before people began to talk, and order three new double-knit leisure suits from Singapore—in robin's egg blue, tomato soup and cream of asparagus.

*****

On this Festal Thursday, Santa Lola stands tall—
But it isn't easy.

Bounded on one side by the sea and three sides by naked envy, this gilded, gated municipality is aquiver with paralyzing "concerns." First, there is "the planet," referred to ever and always as though it's "over there someplace." Spinning through an ill-lit universe, random Buick-sized asteroids hurtling to and fro in no sensible traffic pattern ... any minute a cosmic Roadmaster could come crashing in upcounty, playing hell with real estate!

And there is more.

Santa Lola suffers the full inventory of Eighties urban blight—the indolent, the useless, the out-of-it.

Weekenders check-in Friday night, share in local abundance, and with no regard for "the Ecology," phone Fresno on Monday, quit their job at Penney's and elect to stay.

But Santa Lola loves a challenge. The homeless and pointless are transported to public housing at the northern end of the county, up in dusty Umpton, dumpy Guadalavista, and points worse. Sheriff Mickey Bunt sees to it. Yet despite Sheriff Mick's best efforts, concern is rising over Santa Lola's leading headache, the grievously rich. We speak of Neddy and Proz.

At mere mention of their names, things go wobbly.

Will they split?

How soon?

Will it affect real estate?

Why such clangor over just one crumbly marriage?

Why, indeed!

Proz and Neddy, the Duke's heir and heir presumptuous, are in line for The Full Lode!

It isn't every day you see thirteen trillion—by countless multiples, the biggest fortune on "the planet"—change directions!

(But darling ... isn't it just thirteen "billion?")

(No, dearest—it is *not!*)

At the prospect of this conjugal catastrophe, coloratura manifestations of grief are rehearsing in dressing rooms all across Santa Lola. It would be a relief to all—and their spouses—to have these expressions of despair tried in open competition!

And there is hope.

In his 32 years on "the planet," Neddy Lombardo has famously "had it" with any number of people, places, and pairs of socks. Only last Saturday, he "had it" with chinless, living-with-mother Clive O.E.M. Monogram ... *né* "The Dumb Shit."

He told all his friends.

He even told Clive.

Yet at the Great Party today, Neddy is resolved to be guided by manly moderation. He will be civil to all, including the D.S. It's how it's done.

Neddy sees in this an invaluable lesson, to wit; having "had it" with Proz and her unquenchable taste for having her own way is no proper cause to deconstruct a sacred union ordained in Heaven ... and very warmly regarded nearer home!

The lad is no fool.

Still, change is in the air. At the party Neddy may well misbehave—his sovereign right. He sees no shortcut to Happiness. He needs a vacation, and her name is Lissa Montenero, cool as a cucumber sandwich, no crust.

But he won't be a beast about it. He'll freely offer Proz her own best shot at bliss. She's welcome to slip off into the Library with chinless, living-with-mother Clive Monogram, if she must, her option.

For his part, he'll get lovely Lissa under the weather on "beaucoup" Tequila Mockingbirds—it must be done!

*****

Even the blindest soothsayer sees them, dark clouds gathering.

Yet Santa Lola soldiers bravely on. At Juan Corona State Beach on Tuesday evenings, The Daughters of the Golden West, some of the oldest daughters drawing wind, continue to host consciousness-raising Anti-Fur Luaus.

Santa Lola is always just one tony step ahead.

Down in the harbor, meanwhile, the Fishermen's Grange goes out on strike every second moon, demanding shorter hours and better catches.

They seem to be making some headway.

And City Councilperson Hon. Harvey Moonfarm-X, New-Age Marine Biologist at City College, campaigns tirelessly in Santa Lola schools for PSL—Porpoise as a Second Language.

But with one eye on Neddy and another on Proz...

The civic perspective is shot.

The times are out of joint.

The stars are out of town.

Even the sea is changed.

These evenings when the Pacific breeze veers gently onshore...

It bears a foul pong.

Something's died out there.

CHAPTER 3

The Maine Coon And The Eagle

NEDDY GIVES BURTIE Balfour the look.

"I know what you're up to!"

The particular pal feigns innocence.

"Being nice and all..." Neddy nods. "C'mon, Burt, you're as subtle as Jimmy Carter riding a giraffe. What *time* is it, anyway!"

They're alone on the third tee of Checquers' Robert Trent Jones Championship Golf Course—just Neddy and Burt. Flawless turf stretches off to infinity, a carpet of green velvet, not a soul in sight. Until the next golfing President shambles in—can't be long—in Santa Lola golf is for Shriners.

Burtie B. has tried every stratagem to convert Neddy to manly action. They can go aloft in a pair of Checquers' *frrrraaaaazzz*-ing, oil-dripping Kajun K2-A "Peppercorn" ultra-lights. They'll dogfight, fly down to the beach, buzz topless sunbathers, drop water-balloons on Peevy Palmtry's pointy pate!

Or they can go out to Santa Lola Invitational Raceway and race Corvettes.

At the guests' disposal—the apt word—they'll choose from Porsche Speedsters, Triumph TR-6s, Jaguar XKEs and Chevrolet Corvettes. They'll race themselves carsick on the Duke's superlative private road-racing circuit. The Duke even has three lethal CSX Carroll Shelby 427 Ford Cobras, way down at the end convenient to the chaplain's tent. All Raceway competitors earn the coveted Constance Chalice ... winners' chalices are slightly larger. This prized trophy honors the Duke's beloved late wife Constance, who, against type, particularly valued a Ferrari V-12's burnished blare. The sterling silver Constance Chalice is courage's fondest emblem.

14

It is also redeemable, by weight, at Zootie's Treasure Cave, Old Commercial Wharf, Pt. Moot ... plenty of free parking.

But you look bewildered.

Stop!

Whenever the Duke elects to create a new amusement ... a Circus Maximus here or a Balkan War-Games there (up behind the football stadium) ... his man contacts adjoining property owners for additional *Lebensraum*. Santa Lola real-estate speculators, a flinty squad, vie vigorously for Checquers-adjoining parcels, with cause. To make "a killing in California real estate," you best be waiting, deed in hand, when the Duke's man comes to call.

He pays two dollars on the dollar.

It's only money....

"I said, what *time* you got!" snaps Neddy hypoglycemically.

"Third time you asked, Bongo," Burtie snaps right back.

He sees Neddy has something fragrant in mind—and it's not like the bosom pal to play things so close to the cummerbund.

"My watch stopped," Ned dissembles.

"Didn't."

"Did!"

"Twenty past two, ten minutes since you asked—why!"

Neddy whacks the traitorous chronometer—why won't today get going! In thirteen creaky months of marriage, he's never plotted anything like this!

... well, he's thought of it.

Burtie gazes up at the sky.

"Or we could go up the mountain and surf."

Neddy glares. "Are you trying to drive me totally crazy!"

"Dunno, old son," Burtie grins, "but if I am, I'm doing a half-swell job."

*****

Ski Kobalefffsky and Snake Sneave slide in through the Casino back door like wolverines.

They're looking for someone, but like wolverines, they don't want someone looking for them!

Their eyes scan the Casino's dazzling array of gaming tables.

Each other.

They really shouldn't....

"'Scuse, honey," says Ski, flagging down a speeding blonde cocktail waitress. She stabs the brakes, balancing a tray of brimming glasses.

Snake enjoys the action.

"Um, d'you know Lissa Montenegro?" says Ski.

"Sorry, sir."

She smiles like Santa Lola sunshine.

"I don't."

She's going 95 again, tray leaned into the wind.

Snake snickers. "What'd you think—they wear name-tags?"

Undeterred ... undeterred in the least, it's Ski's whole strategy ... he settles on a new mark over in the next aisle. The guy looks a little lost, but not as lost as he might.

"'Scuse..." says Ski. "I'm looking for someone."

"You need legal advice?"

"Whah?"

The man smirks. "I'm a lawyer. You say you're looking for someone?"

"Do you know a Lissa Montenegro?"

"Montenero."

"Montenegro."

"Montenero."

"Montenero ... have it yer way," Ski shurgs.

"Everyone knows Lissa!" the legal fellow says.

Ski proffers his hand. "Ski Kobalefffsky. My friend, Marlon."

Nodding to Sneave, the man's smile goes luminous. "Vance Crankenfuss," he says. "You boys from Ventura? Pacoima?"

"San Pedro Gardens ... you?"

"I'm local. I handle all the Duke's legal affairs."

"Oh?" "That so?" "Yeah?" "Interesting work I bet ... huh?"

Fresh out of handy chit-chat, Ski falls silent.

Crankenfuss nods.

"New to Checquers, are you."

Ski chuckles. "Isn't everyone?"

Crankenfuss chuckles back. "I take your point. Lookin' for Lissa— a friend of hers?"

"Friend of a friend."

"I bet."

He has Ski a bit swoggled.

"She around?" Ski says, homing in.

"She was," says Crankenfuss. "But that's been a while."

Ski sees the trail icing over.

Snake gave up hours ago.

And there's a hand of blackjack just an arm's length away.

And craps—arm's length! With all day and a lot of night to kill before things get rolling....

"If I see Lissa," Crankenfuss nods, "I'll let her know you asked.

San Pedro Gardens, you say ... L.A."

The stark municipal letters convey maximal chill.

"Can't ask for more'n that," beams Ski—an old pal by now. "Thanks, Lance."

"Vance."

Damn!

Snake's heat-seeking guidance is already locked-on....

The redhead blackjack dealer.

Beauty mark on her nose.

His eyes narrow—a Maine Coon stalking the mature golden eagle.

*****

Neddy and Burt ride up the massive mountain.

The Duke's high-speed electric tram, the Comet, makes eleven stops from the beach three miles up to Top-Forty. From up here, the blue-green Pacific, behind and far below, is panoramic, and today, more blue than green—a vibrant Dong Kingman watercolor.

The Duke owns several Kingmans, particular favorites.

Checquers sprawls upwards across four successive coastal plateaus, each higher plateau warmer than the last. All have their own theme, décor, lanai, pools, amusements, and concierge. This afternoon, it's 77 degrees down at the beach, 84 at the mansion, and a Kentucky-Fried 91 up at Top-Forty, Neddy's and Burtie's destination.

The Comet whirs ever higher past wind-sculpted sandstone boulders, patches of crimson October poison oak at their most virulent. Up this high, the sun-seared soil is like talcum.

Above the Comet's terminus at Top-Forty, bridle trails lead another 1000 feet up to the Coast Range summit. And for the catastrophically bored, a dangerous technical climb rises 600 feet straight up the rock face of Devil's Drumstick. Few indeed have stood on the Evil One's kneecap.

Neddy gazes up there now, wondering what on earth gets into people!

The Comet grinds on, acrid gusts of creosote sweltering up off the tram ties.

Neddy can pinpoint the fragrance—Proz's burnt peach pie.

She should never bake.

Or play tennis.

The Comet video monitor announces a Pari-Mutuel Paddleboard Tourney for Seniors, down the mountain at Olde Poope Decke ... "Be There—And Be Square!"

The "Weather-Beat 24-Cast" video crawl reads, "Chance of

evening coastal marine layer: 90%."

Fog tonight.

Crud!

Approaching the cranium-poaching terminus of Top-Forty, Neddy scans the breathtaking marine panorama like an unpaid utility bill.

"It's so hot!"

"But perfect waves..." Burt nods. "Eight-foot glass walls—one after another."

Neddy knows, yes, yes.

Since his movingly exorbitant nuptials thirteen months ago, he's retreated to the Wave Pool again and again.

"It's so predictable, Burt—eight-foot perfect overhead after eight-foot perfect overhead … you could explode!"

Burtie grins darkly. "Oughta take up golf."

"Hey, fuck you!"

That's more like it.

The Comet's electric motor *Rrrrzzzzz-es* to a halt—end of the line.

Thousands of feet above the sea, they hear powerful, crashing overhead surf! Neddy can't suppress an admiring gleam.

The perfect Trestles wave—steep, fast shoulders to either side.

They'll slide across scrolling translucence

streak through to daylight...

Banzai!

"Burt."

"Yeah?"

"What time is it."

CHAPTER 4

Paw

PEEVY PALMTRY HAS a problem.

Twelve years ago at Cañon Perdido Proper School, it was the same problem.

"Men…" she says, but hasn't the strength to go on.

Proz, sipping a Perrier and soda through a straw, sits next to Peevy, her slender legs arranged on the chaise longue like twin stalks of white asparagus.

She's lost Neddy for the nonce. It's part of their arrangement. He claims urgent business at the Duck Pond, and she adjourns to County Pool for something tall, cold and diet.

The vast free-form County Pool stretches off beyond the horizon. It earned its name by running seditiously from Santa Lola County deep into Carmelita County. In the Forties, it was known as the "Jeane Pool," which sounds too cute for the Duke by half, but an explanation exists. It was actually the "Norma Jeane Pool," named after an early pal of the Duke's back when Norma Jeane still used her birthname—Norma Jeane Baker.

Correct.

La Monroe.

But the Duke, unwilling to appear fastidious, or God forbid, "controlling," has allowed the great pool's association with lovely Marilyn to fade. Today, its early name is known only to a squad of ink-stained wretches, all competing to finish the first definitive Checquers monograph and land a shot on the Carson Show.

On the pool behind Proz's elegant shoulder, a palm tree-bedecked floating isle drifts nearer, and alas, farther. Tenor Rusty Arms, with orchestra, delivers "I'll Never Smile Again" direct from the torchy Forties.

Proz's slender pinky on the armrest notes the beat absently, tapping like the limb of a praying mantis.

Meanwhile, high up on the ten-meter board, observed by women of average I.Q., is Santa Lola's 140-pound heavyweight, Seferino Cordero. Olive-bronze, mortally serious, his black cormorant hair slicked down on his shrunken head, he executes perfect high-arching straight-toed one-and-a-half pike, after perfect high-arching straight-toed one-and-a-half pike.

Following each, he bursts to the surface, foam billowing up around him like uncorked bubbly.

Pulling his hairless frame up onto the deck, he adjusts his black codpiece.

Checks the house.

Scales the ten-meter board, all his female observers pondering the same three imponderables, to execute ... a perfect high-arching straight-toed one-and-a-half pike.

"What do you think of Gerald Thermos?" says Peevy, one eye on the ten-meter board.

"I don't know..." Proz says.

"Yes, you do."

Proz awaits the next pitch.

But Peevy takes something off the ball.

"He was looking at me."

"I know," Proz nods. "I like Gary Larry better."

"You don't like Gerald?" pouts Peevy.

"Well, you know what they say—hung like a State Fair zucchini."

"Proz ... ssser ... peeena!" giggles Peevy, on full boil.

But her grin darkens.

"They do?"

Proz smiles, standing her ground.

"Oh, I don't believe that," says Peeve, "he's too nice."

"Come on," says Proz. "How would you like a State Fair zucchini poking around down there?"

Peevy knows the correct answer.

"I get so discouraged," she moves on. "Isn't there anyone in this drippy paradise just meant for me?"

"You'll find him, just you wait."

"I've waited, twelve goddamn years—and here I sit! All I meet are halfwit surfers in rusty Dodge pickups ... wall-eyed beach-volleyball newts with an overbite ... Calexico busboys in heat!"

"I know, I know."

"You don't know!"

Peevy has puzzled over it long and hard—men aren't like in the movies.

"Why can't I just once get the bartender?"

Because, truth be told, Peevy is plain as a lead sinker. Mousy face, four feet-eleven, body like a stuffed laundry bag. It doesn't help that she devours fashion magazines like popcorn. Against all logic, she wears the latest anorexic six-footer fashions. For two years, she's crammed outsized high-fashion shoulder pads under her sweaters.

She looks like a defensive tackle in Peewee Football.

Her eye ponders Seferino Cordero.

Proz ponders too—

But not Seferino Cordero. Something is very wrong, she knows, without knowing what! It's like the burn you get way deep down inside after eating a jalapeño ... the furnace glow won't go away ... won't go away ... then hours later, when it finally does—it burns!

It's Neddy, of course.

They don't talk—won't talk!

But honestly, does anyone?

Is anyone really happy!

Not Neddy.

He couldn't be.

Could he?

Is Daddy?

Probably ... in some way she'll never understand.

There's so much more to him, far more than just "being happy."

She should call A.A.—they're supposed to help people.

"Your man will turn up, Peevy," she says, at last. "You wait."

Peevy snorts.

"He'll have zits on his back. He'll work at Lupo's Drive-In. He'll reek of onion rings and industrial cleanser."

"Peevy..." says Proz.

"He'll have herpes, and a girl in Oxnard that keeps giving it back to him."

"No, he won't."

"He will!"

"Will what...."

It's a male voice behind Proz—a deep rich *duh-rreeeeammy* voice!

Proz turns.

Peevy's already seen him. Her eyes are flashing all around the night sky like the searchlights at a Sammy Salvo Furniture Warehouse Midnight Blow-Out!

"Hi. I'm Eddie Coggins."

"Coggins?" says Proz.

"Whatever you say," says Peevy.

He smiles—but now Peevy squeals!

"Two-Paw!"

"Two-Paw," nods Eddie Coggins.

He paws the ground—and not sheepishly.

A little modest, thinks Proz, liking it.

A little lickable, thinks Peevy, moistening her lips.

There was talk of Two-Paw Coggins coming today—but it was too much to expect ... even at the Duke's!

To say merely that Two-Paw, or just Paw, is the star pitcher of the recently crowned World-Champion L.A. Dodgers, is to say, Jesus Christ was a journeyman carpenter.

After one season in the majors, Paw Coggins is a clanging yowling twelve-alarm scandal! He and the Dodgers, to the fiscal annoyance of Dodger management, swept last week's World Series with Baltimore in four straight games. In truth, of course, the victims' identity was all but irrelevant—nobody had a chance!

For the first time since open flame, the Series was wrapped up in the third week of October ... and two of the four Dodger wins were Paw's. He's entirely too much of a good thing! Debate over him rages to all hours in dugouts, clubhouses, cocktail lounges, bars, boîtes, tavernas, cantinas, bodegas, after-hours clubs, bottomless bars and the Commissioner's Office.

The game's never seen his like, and the reason is simple. He pitches from both sides! Removing his unique symmetrical Rawlings glove—it has a thumb on either end—to rub down the ball, as pitchers do, Paw takes his signal from the catcher.

But until he puts his glove on one hand (or the other), places one big toe (or the other) on one end of the rubber (or the other), the batter, sad bastard, has no clue where the ball is coming from.

By then, it's far too late to lean in clear-minded and "see" the ball.

To date, no switch-hitters have countered by changing batter's boxes. Well, one All-Star tried. He's playing remedial ball now in Cuernavaca!

Worst of all, Coggins delivers the full inventory of pitches from both sides ... 91-mph fastballs (89 mph on the righty side), splitters, curves, sliders, slurves, 74-mph change-ups (with excellent disguise) and a nigh uncatchable knuckler.

In April, "the Coggins fracas" was just gathering steam when a conservative political pundit and baseball fool, foraging for fodder in a slow news week, swooped to Coggins' defense. Batters have always switch-hit, he declared—why not pitchers!

Here's why not.

No batter in the United States, Canada, Mexico, the Caribbean, Japan, Korea, Taiwan, South America, Australia, or anyplace with a roof has a voodoo's prayer of hitting Paw! He pitched six no-hitters—three of them perfect games. His ERA was 0.48. Of the handful of runs he allowed, most resulted from mishaps with his uncatchable knuckler.

Unlike most aces, he has no regular catcher. Three are platooned. All are in counseling.

And being a National Leaguer, he batted sixth in the order—needless to say, from both sides. He hit for a .263 average, with six home runs.

By early June, the breezes out of *Sports Illustrated* were blowing sour—Paw must be stopped! Anti-Paw sentiment swept every National League city—except, of course, L.A. (The Santa Monica Green Party, following their lights, came out "anti.") In response to this widespread anti-Paw sentiment, a spontaneous pro-Paw reaction rose across the land—and thanks to Paw's tall, dark and glandsome looks, 72-percent of pro-Paws were women who'd never voluntarily watched an inning of ball in their life.

Even Vin Scully, unflappable voice of the Dodgers, flapped.

Robert Redford has a Coggins "project" in pre-production, and for once, he concedes he isn't right for the lead.

Coggins could run for President.

The Commissioner prays he will.

*****

Peevy considers the dark-eyed man standing above her.

Even in the permissive Eighties, her thoughts may not be characterized....

Toweling off after his swim, Paw is six-packed, tall, slender, limber, merciless. A mat of tightly curled black fur adorns his chest like a Roman breastplate.

And his brief jet-black swimsuit hurts his cause not at all.

"So pleased you've come," Proz offers.

"And I bet you can!" blurts Peevy, crashing around the universe out of control.

Two-Paw's smile is undimmed.

Hmmph, nods Proz—insensitive.

Gorgeous, but not her glass of Chablis ... not that she's looking!

Still, he does have a certain *Idunnowutchamuhcallit....*

"Congratulations on the Series," says Peevy, carefully omitting "World" to sound network.

Since childhood, Peevy has despised baseball and all its works, yet she can recite every 1984 World Series statistic. Coggins gave up just four hits in two nine-inning outings and—

But wait ... a pitcher winning two World Series games of four in just five days—preposterous!

Not at all, states Dodgers' pitching-mechanics coach Jack Bump.

Using both arms, and just as significantly, both legs, says Bump, each side of Paw works only half as hard. He regains full strength after each outing in a tick over half the time....

"Wanna see?" says Paw.

He presents his right hand to Peevy and Proz, smiling like a million. The huge diamonds in the Big Daddy World Championship gold ring glitter like shattered mirror.

"Oooooooo…" giggles Peevy.

The precise context of her giggle is illegal in five Southern states. Paw winks.

"I just don't know where to wear it … on the left?"

He pauses holding the runner on first.

"Or the right."

"The right looks perfect," blurts Peevy, completely missing this high-insider.

But Proz grins.

"Wear it on your best side."

"*Touché!*" he bows.

She's struck the heart of it … is his southpaw side better, or is it his righty?

Like all else about Paw, opinion is split right down the middle.

"So," gleams Proz, "... which is it?"

The million-dollar smile.

"All depends, hun. Some days it's the left—some days the right."

"I'd take both!" Peevy barks, licking her lips.

Proz flashes her friend a furious smile.

"But you're not drinking," she says, "… is it Eddie?"

"Paw."

"Paw?"

"Paw."

"Paw…" Proz assents, at last. "What will you take?"

"What are you having?"

"Oh, nothing."

"Good—I'll have one."

"You don't even drink!" croaks Peevy.

"Makes me sleepy. I hate missing anything. Let's find me a tall cold nothing."

He turns to locate a waiter.

Immediately, Proserpina's eye slides below the equator.

Remarkable.

But no, no, she's keeping things in perspective. He's a ball-player, albeit an immortal one. He has no interest in the finer things, probably thinks John Cage is a basketball player.

He should've been!

But her smile re-focuses. That is the most divine black bathing suit she's seen since Cary Grant visited Checquers when she was a dangerously curious ten-year old.

She can admit it. He's upsetting.

And so is the nude image streaking across her mind!

She sizes him up once and for all. Not enough culture to grow yogurt ... but a great heater from both sides.

Whatever a "heater" is.

"I never much cared for baseball," she says.

"Why should you," he smiles. "It's just a game."

Oh, she thinks.

Oh, my.

CHAPTER 5

Kahuna

THE DUKE IS AN El Greco, tall, gaunt, angular, long of limb, vaguely haunted.

He's the kind of imposing personage you instinctively defer to—then feel grateful for having done so.

His nearly seventy years on "the planet" bespeak abiding calm. Whether it's a Havana *claro* with a torn wrapper, or a Senate Subcommittee examining his position in Salvadoran currency, he will manage.

Monty ... we're on a first-name basis by now ... dearly adores his Top-Forty Wave Pool. Eleven or twelve surfers—no crowding—are riding its towering, thunderous liquid sculpture ... when now and then, one will fling himself off his board just to be pummeled in filtered crystal-clear spring water. Chlorine-free and 82 Kauai degrees, it's pure as the champagne in Proz's wedding slipper.

Purer, Neddy smirks.

Other mid-Eighties wave pools exist in Canadian malls and Japanese theme parks, but designed by liability lawyers, their waves roll but don't break. The Duke's massive oceanic ground swells *crash!* And the pool's programmable bottom contours can replicate famous surf breaks at Windansea in La Jolla, Trestles in San Clemente, Rincon below Santa Lola, and the powerful shifting peak at Santa Cruz's Steamer Lane.

The "set of the day"—about four o'clock—delivers ten-foot walls, demanding the riders' best. As always, raw instinct is the heart of wave riding.

The Wave Pool's small dirt parking lot, just beyond the surf and Top-Forty's white-sand beach, is furnished with a yellow '49 Buick ragtop, a beige '42 Dodge Woodie, and a maroon '39 Plymouth Roadster (with the optional dual spotlights and bumper overrides). The cars are available for drives around Top-Forty's system of dirt roads, leading to panoramic views of Santa Lola and the Santa Lola Channel.

To the Duke, the cars are vital.

They allow his guests to wander free, "doing what surfers do."

The parking lot's picturesque fourteen-foot long swayback wooden gate was salvaged from San Onofre that black day old San Onofre Surf Club closed forever—literally to become a nuclear powerplant. The gate, the surf, the old cars and palm trees all evoke San Onofre's big waves back in the Golden Forties and Fifties. At day's end, Monty would host huge, gracious luaus for his surfing friends from Newport, La Jolla and Old Portuguese Bend.

Then one day, bronze-chested and beaming, the Big Kahuna—Monty, none other—glided inshore, hiked his ten-foot balsa under his arm and met beautiful Constance Cleaver on the beach. Visiting from Rhode Island—the "real" Newport, she said sassily—Constance asked him where he found his courage on the big waves.

He didn't know what to answer.

On and on it went—for decades....

Up at the Wave Pool these days, when sun-bleached afternoon settles over Monty's spirit, and the roar of crashing surf meets his ear in just the right way ... for moments, he glimpses it all again—

But no.

No, no....

In those brilliant days, there was Constance ... always Constance.

*****

"Adore the pants," smiles Twitty Conway, despising them.

Peevy Palmtry smiles right back, with no hint of misgiving, bless her heart.

Rising to her full four feet-eleven, she models her wares in stubby twirls. Straight out of September's *W*, the pants are lime-green, with a crisscrossed, tightly bound yellow-harness motif at the waist, looking for all the world as if it may burst any instant! Adding license to chic, scalloped cutouts down the outsides of the legs from hip to ankle imply a saucy "commando" absence of linens.

At a distance, she looks like she's been set upon by Dobermans.

"Very nice," smiles Twitty, switching topics, "... so, who was the hunk you and Proz were keeping all to yourselves at the pool?"

"I was doing nothing of the sort!" Proz snaps. "You mean, you're not a baseball bimbo this year like everyone else?"

Twitty Conway laughs. "I know who he is—and he's gorgeous! Peevy, how did you let him get away?"

"He wasn't with *me!*"

Peevy draws sharply on her Tequila Mockingbird ... Checquers' National Drink, her first of many. It's going to be a long party.

"Don't look at *me!*"

In Peevy's sanctum sanctorum, she's been with no tan hunks ... ever! Dreamy Paw Coggins was with legally married, pointlessly discontent Proz, who has a husband ... not unmarried, un-tall me!

Proz needs a Paw Coggins like a year of cramps!

The ladies are seated at a linen-covered table on the South Polo Green—faced away from play.

They've seen it!

Each wears a glam, wide-brimmed, white-with-navy-blue-band sunhat—all except coolly indestructible Lissa Montenero. Auburn-haired and bareheaded in blazing sun, Lissa is exquisite, ethereal, the envy even of herself.

In addition to Proz and Misses Palmtry, Conway and Montenero, their circle has been widened to admit May Wight and Leslie Wong of The Smart Set, Pasadena Chapter.

All wait, crissakes ... for something to happen!

At this lapse in conversation, all turn to Lissa.

Five feet-eleven, long, lean, lithe, forever smiling out of context, she is bright-eyed and serene ... Audrey Hepburn as the Faerie Queene.

"I met him last March at a party in L.A.," she confesses, glancing across her shoulder at events on horseback.

But Peevy is appalled.

"You met him and didn't tell us!"

"It was March—before baseball season—nothing to tell."

"There is if he looks like that!"

Peevy is struggling to untangle herself from the thatch of black fur on Paw's bronze chest—can't work herself free!

And isn't it just like Lissa—off at some miraculous party in Pacific Palisades or Palm Springs or La Jolla, dreamboats floating free like lotus blossoms on a pond! If you're rich enough, the entire global population is 2000, and you know them all!

"He's stupendous!" Twitty gushes now.

Which is news. The last time Twitty "gushed" was the Checquers evening Sean Connery winked, "... charmed, Miss Twitty."

"Well, come on, Lissa!" urges May Wight.

"What's he like!" demands Leslie Wong.

"Tall," Lissa says.

"We know that!" Twitty growls.

"You asked me what he's like."

Peevy is panting.

"Tall…" Lissa nods again, below room temperature.

"Come awwwn!"

Twitty wants it all in five bloodstained modifiers.

"He's wunnn-derful," Peevy blurts, off her leash, "… sweet and friendly and gracious and sensitive—with the dreamiest voice you ever stuck your tongue in!"

Leslie Wong giggles.

May Wight stands pat. She's making someone, a future pick to be named in the draft, a good wife.

But Twitty Conway's attention comes to rest on elegant Lissa.

What's this?

Annoyance in those dark-green Cleopatra eyes?

"Come now, Lissa," she purrs. "Did he fail to fall head over C-cups for you!"

The indestructible brow arches.

Maintains a Mona Lissa smile.

"Tall…."

*****

"Well, well…" the stentorian basso pronounces.

Neddy and Burtie turn.

Duke Monty steps out onto white-sand beach from the interior of Top-Forty's legendary Uli Haoli Bar.

The Uli Haoli is weathered barnwood and corrugated rust—the definitive expression of knockdown back-island tropical decay.

The Duke's sun-crinkly grin takes them both in.

"Look what the cat caught."

Neddy would've enjoyed a simple, h'llo.

"Hey, Duke!" Burtie bubbles just the same. "How's tricks?"

Always amusing, this Burtie, is the Duke's view. The world needs more like him.

"Grand to see you, Balfour, how's your chess game?"

Burtie's smile never dims.

"That's cold, Duke."

His first-round elimination by the twelve-year-old with zits in the Platinum Coast Chess Tournament was early this morning … years ago!

The great man grins.

"The surf was bigger an hour ago…."

It's the oldest canard in surfing—the waves were always bigger before you *losers* showed up!

But the Duke's waves are as big as he chooses to make them….

Neddy smiles back stubbornly—flying the flag.

"We only came up for the sun-poisoning," Balfour explains.
"Splendid."

The Duke turns to Neddy ... here it comes.

"Where's Proz?"

"County Pool, Duke."

"Couldn't entice her up?"

"She's with Peevy."

The Duke ponders its niceties. "Fine afternoon, no?"

Non sequitur after non sequitur is Burtie's thought.

"Well, the bar's open," says the Duke. "Kick back or hang ten."

With a summary click of the tongue, he's sidling off down the beach again in that swivel-ass, dog-tracking John Wayne ramble.

His tall frame bends low under the palm fronds at the next beach lean-to.

Neddy's head shakes.

"Nothing he says follows from anything else. It's like talking to a moron."

"Bloody brilliant moron!" Burtie laughs. "He's always playing."

"He doesn't like me."

"I doubt that, Ned. He likes everybody about the same."

Neddy says nothing—it's just too filthy.

Burtie nods.

"Gotta get over that, Bluto, it shows."

Exactly what Neddy doesn't want to hear....

They step into the Rag Shack, another instance of corrugated rust and knockdown back-island decay.

But the Shack is stocked to the rafters with new or newly laundered (the cooler choice) swim suits, in all varieties ... ball-buster East Coast Jansens nobody wears to sun-bleached, loosie-goosie surfer "baggers"—the baggier and more sun-ravaged the better.

Burt snickers, undressing.

"He's too much. Everything's a contest to him."

It puts the burr under Neddy's saddle.

"He's just ornery."

"Pays no attention at all..." Burtie beams. "Says exactly what he likes—no wonder he's loaded! Guys like that ... he knows what he's doing every second. Wouldn't you enjoy haggling with someone if you already knew you were making him nuts?"

"Disgusting."

"Just a game."

Ned pulls on a pair of righteous faded-yellow baggies.

Burtie's rolling up his clothes.

"Hey, Ned—don't want to know what time it is?"

Now Burtie's grin narrows to a squint.
"Bet you could beat him at golf."
"Fuck you, Burtie."
"Attaboy!"

CHAPTER 6

The Whole Damn Gibraltar

NEDDY GLANCES AT his watch.

"The son of a bitch!"

They've bellyboarded forty-five minutes at Top-Forty, and it hasn't moved. What's he got to do!

"Three fifty-five," Burtram Balfour volunteers, unasked.

They're sprawled across the white sand.

Wave after glorious Top-Forty wave lines up behind them ... peaks ... curls ... crashes!

Burtie peers up at the sky. "Listen, old sod, old buttcrack—"

"Burtie ... WHAT!"

"I'm the only one understands you."

Burtie speaks over the roar of the surf ... "Lissa's here today."

"Keep your voice down!" Neddy growls, turning heads on the beach.

He drops to a mutter.

"... she is?"

"Neddy, Neddy. Can't fool Uncle Burt."

"Just shut up!"

At that, Neddy comes to his feet as if for the National Anthem.

He stomps off to the Uli Haoli. He'll get a Mount Gay and tonic and take a moment—or decade—collecting his thoughts.

But all too soon, the cursed compadre is tracing his footsteps.

He orders Burtie a Dos Equis.

Burtie arrives and nods the bottle back.

... gone as last week's *TV Guide*.

Burtie releases a gaseous *Forrrrrr-rruppp!*

No matter.

Neddy's thoughts are far away ... in Gardenia Gazebo.

He's worked it all out.

He'll rendezvous with his jungle flower ... his Venus ... several Comet stops below the great house, overlooking the sea but bloody little else.

Gardenia Gazebo is a hidden grotto of gardenias, brambles, and by Checquers standards, utter neglect. Located near the Comet's disused Kentonia Concourse, the only other tramside attraction is the old Belle Époque orchestra shell, "Band In Boston," scene of nationwide radio hook-ups in the Fifties, featuring Stan Kenton and June Christy at their apogee. The Duke never missed a show.

But Neddy knows he has to be careful.

Burtie is on to him.

His nuclear secret could spread now like Hong Kong Clap.

But not to worry—he's shown the cunning of the Lombardos. The note he left in the deluxe lady's black Jaguar sedan is carefully unclear, craftily unsigned. He requires absolute security. No paparazzi.

He'll fade into the bush just as all hell is breaking free up at the mansion—and united, at last, with his jungle flower—

He'll importune, flatter, startle, stroke, cajole, flummox, and if the sledding be good—

God knows, he's not without his attractions....

And he's read all the "good" parts of D.H. Lawrence.

Passion is his destiny!

Ah, Sorceress...

Goddess on earth!

He hasn't been so abso-tively, posi-lutely *Bozo!* since Robin Wood in Fifth Grade....

Exquisite Lissa ... forest flower—

She's nothing like the rest!

She's taller....

*****

Beneath lolling palm fronds, the Duke practices Santa Lola *realpolitik*.

He's in conference with City Councilmen Al Carbon, Dale Varp, and Marvin Mudhutt.

They practice their statecraft, while judiciously draining their drinks. Now, one by one, Varp, then Mudhutt, and last, the Duke, take thoughtful strolls back to the Uli Haoli Bar to recharge.

Al Carbon, cleverly arriving at this "far-reaching discussion" with a cocktail in each hand, remains in situ admiring the surf—

When in he slides, gliding, gliding, his mode of propulsion all but undetectable, Larsen E. "Ken" Stukud.

("*Stoo*-kid" now you ask.)

Ken is Santa Lola's premier used-car "skater," that singular operative his sales associates would joyously stab in the eye. As if by levitation, though it is definitely not his "up" ... again he achieves the dealership front door just as another doe-eyed prospect blunders in!

Stukud nods to Al Carbon....

Smiles broadly.

He has flat eyes, flat feet, flattop haircut, a flat brown double-knit jacket over a green, red, blue, pink, vermilion and dayglo-orange rayon shirt. Yellow Bermuda shorts dangle above skinny, white, hairless legs. At their base, orange socks are bunched up above rubber-soled brown oxfords worth the price of a taco.

One oxford is at ten o'clock.

The other at two.

Ken is from Fresno, but that isn't stopping him.

He proffers the glad hand to Al Carbon...

"Howdy-hi ... Ken Stukud."

Al Carbon smiles dangerously.

"Stupid?"

"... Stukud."

"Ah."

"I'm down at Lowe & Stukud Used Cars—Camino Carne, corner Sabado Bingo."

Marvin Mudhutt arrives just now from the Uli Haoli.

He eyes Ken with interest.

"You say ... Stupid Used Cars?"

"Stukud," Ken enunciates.

"Ah."

Stukud's teeth smile in all directions.

"Some gathering, huh."

"Monty does it up brown," says Al Carbon—alluding subliminally to the motor merchant's rubber-soled oxfords. "Why haven't we met—is it Ken? That dealership's been down there quite some time, *verdad?*"

Ken nods, spiffed at Councilman Carbon's Spanish-y lingo. Real Native Santa Lola.

"My uncle had it before."

"Mm..." puts in Mudhutt. "Mort Coover?"

Stukud's smile blazes.

"Never caught him, did they..." notes Carbon.

"A mystery to us all," Stukud says equably, giving a thought to the set of his briefs.

Dale Varp returns now from the bar.

Up for reelection in two weeks, he's a blur of hearty handclasps.

"Don't believe we've met ... I'm Varp, City Council."

"Howdy-hi—Ken Stukud."

"Stupid?"

"Stukud."

"Oh."

"Ken runs Lowe & Stukud," Carbon informs Varp. "Used cars down on Camino Carne,"

"Corner Sabado Bingo."

"That's fine, then," Carbon nods. "Never caught Mortie, did they."

"What's that?" inquires the Duke, just arriving.

Stukud smiles like a '53 Buick.

"Swell to acquire your acquaintance, Mr. Duke."

The Duke smiles grandly.

"Quite a shirt."

Stukud smiles right back—he knows flattery.

It's Dale Varp's round: "Ken here runs Stukud Used Cars."

The Duke nods. "Stupid Used Cars?"

"Thassit!"

Ken thrusts out a hand, closing the deal.

"Good to meet you, Stupid," says the Duke.

"Likewise, I'm sure."

"Amusing yourself?"

"Yessiree-Jack. Like I says, one slick party yuh gotcherself."

"Yes," smiles the Duke. "Surf's good today."

Stukud turns to the Wave Pool ... *but the surf's good every day!*

"I get it," he blurts, trusting his instincts, which are impressive. "Couldn't be better, right?"

"Could be if I want," the Duke says, "... just turn the dial to Waimea."

Whatever that means.

Stukud's smile glows like Kilauea at night. The Duke's a nut-case. Meets 'em every day.

Just then, two surfers amble in, boards under their arms.

They greet the Duke.

"How be dee waves, bruddah?" the great man says in fluent pidgin.

"Bosssss," enthuses the blond.

"Splendid. Like you to meet Ken Stupid."

The surfers laugh.

But Stukud, a regular guy, shoves out the happy hand.

"Ken sells used cars in town," says the Duke.

"Stupid Used Cars," beams Ken. "Camino Carne, corner Sabado Bingo ... c'mon in, have a look!"

They shake.

Moments shimmer.

What he wouldn't give to have these fat-walleted blondies knee-paddle onto his lot!

*****

Presently, the City Council wanders off down Top-Forty Beach.

They'll caucus with a group of absentee ballots farther along the beach wearing unmistakably pointed hats.

Now it's just the Duke and Ken.

Hey, this is great!

The Duke's head tips towards the waves.

"Bet you could use a few of these hoe-daddies for customers."

Ken beams ... this guy is good!

"Could happen," the Duke nods, "... you keep on plugging."

"Oh I dunno," says Stukud—knowing very well.

He takes a pull of rum and Coke, his admiration for the great man like nuclear fusion.

Talent like that, you could sell a Nash!

"Say, Duke," he says ... in five minutes they're already buddies, a knack of his, "I been meaning to ask."

"What's that?"

"Well, you know, I mean ... how the hell do you get away with it!"

"Get away?"

"The Wave Pool, like. The car races and flying the ultra-lights—all of it!"

"Hilarious, no?"

Stukud is on to him ... the off-balance replies and all. World-class technique—but there's nothing new under the sun.

"What I mean is, Duke, aren't you afraid somebody'll break their ass and just sue the living shit outta you?"

The Duke smiles at Ken.

"Someone could very well, as you say, sue the living shit out of me."

"Yeah..." Ken nods. "So what about it?"

The Duke emits the deep-throated chuckle of infinite wealth.

"I have the best-heeled attorney and the biggest-shouldered Security in Santa Lola County, and the world. I never use them unless someone behaves badly. People know that, so they don't behave badly."

"Yebbut—"

"No buts."

Stukud knows the deal.

Vance Crankenfuss, the Duke's chief counsel, has practiced law before the full range of legal forums.

And in Doug the Thug, Monty has a soldier who for two and a half decades practiced the art of unfriendly persuasion around the corner from Tillary St., Borough of Brooklyn. Retiring to Checquers and taking time to learn The California Way, Doug is the kindliest, most polite Hun on the Left Coast. Off-duty, he's a perfect gentleman, in spite of the accent and deep pockmarks—which have their professional purpose. Doug does what he can "... in a town where millionaire broads go to church with no panties."

"Got it, boss," nods Stukud. "But it still sounds, y'know ... risky."

"Then, let me explain it so you understand—but this doesn't go beyond we two."

"'Course not."

"No!"

The Duke's voice is hard as Krupp Steel.

"Not beyond us!"

"Okay! Okay!" says Ken.

This grampa's unb'lievable....

The Duke nods.

"I have nothing to lose, Ken—nothing—want to know why?"

"I'm all ears."

It's winsome candor. Some ears are large—Ken's are steakhouse portobellos.

And he wants to know why so bad, he's forgotten his bunion.

"Because, Ken ... I'm too rich."

Ken Stukud's laugh is hearty.

"There's no such a thang!"

"I can buy any statement, align any settlement, underwrite any maneuver, back any legislation, satisfy any judgment ... check?"

"Check!"

"I said this is between we two—quote me if you will, but I advise against it."

"No fuckin' way!"

"With the right money, Ken, you can finesse things more ways than ordering Chinese. It's why friends—and some who aren't—come up here and make shitting hyenas of themselves! They race 427 Cobras at the Raceway, fly around in Kajun Peppercorn ultra-lights, take a good chance of getting their ass in a sling ... because they know I take excellent care of them no matter what! Up here, life is free, nothing to lose! They don't have a piece of the rock—they've got the whole damn Gibraltar!"

The Duke's smile is beatific.

"The law, Ken, is just for people who can't afford something better."

Stukud is in awe ... not least, because in the last few minutes the Duke has made serial use of Ken's first name.

It's money in the bank!

He's so blinded, he fails to note the approach of two young Porsche Carrera prospects.

"Ah, here they are," grins Duke Monty. "The Moondoggies."

It has a subtle bite.

Ken Stukud would enjoy knowing why.

"Ken, meet Neddy, the son-in-law, and Burtram Balfour, his particular pal. Boys meet Ken Stupid."

Burtie grins warily.

Neddy smiles, maintaining a firm hand.

"Howdy-hi," says Stukud. "A pleasure!"

"Ken's in used cars..." the Duke says.

"Camino Carne, corner Sabado Bingo," Ken proposes. "C'mon in, have a look—we got what you want!"

After this candid exchange with the Duke, Ken is in a greater rush to Make It Big than at any time since brunch....

CHAPTER 7

Blackened Redfish, Two Orders

HOW TO COME to terms with Checquers....

Conjure the Peninsula Hotel, the incomparable Hong Kong original at its serene colonial finest, and you have the better part of the thing.

Like the Peninsula, Checquers is refined, effortless, graceful. The expectation of luxury is its own reward ... to wish is to greet satisfaction. A feeling like warm sun on the shoulders, the sensation is both exciting and tremulous with repose. In these surroundings, time assumes the rhythm of the heartbeat at rest. Like the Peninsula of old, Checquers creates peace—abiding confidence in one's own well-being.

What sets Checquers apart from even the Peninsula is its relationship with its guests. Unlike commercial patrons at the Peninsula, all at Checquers are welcome invitees. The distinction, and the cordial feeling of goodwill arising from it, are measureless.

As re the Duke's famed "Great Parties," the plain truth is, these may or may not reflect objective reality.

Today's celebration, for example, arises from a splendidly blown telephone call. On the afternoon in question a few weeks back, the Duke placed the instrument to his ear to hear his daughter's distinctive smoky voice—yet no hint of adoring "Daddy Dear." In the interest of good reporting, the day in question was foggy and drear, doubtless contributing to Proz's dour affect. But there could be no mistaking her gist. She was miserable and it was all Neddy's fault.

The Duke eyed his shoe, needing no further assistance on the point. But Proz backpedaled immediately. It wasn't really Neddy's fault ... "the doofus." Her marriage, she supposed, was "the inevitable clash of souls."

She moved precipitously on, the Duke pondering his oxblood right wingtip.

Her life was meaningless—

Not like "the old days."

No big parties.

No fun guests.

No cakes or door prizes—

She needed a cat....

So that was how it stood, the Duke nodded—missing entirely the possibly cardinal feline complaint.

No matter. The Duke saw his way forward.

He must declare a party!

Immediately, Checquers' hospitality professionals were put on emergency footing.

Orders were placed for excesses of fresh salmon from Alaska, over-shipments of papaya and mango from Mazatlan, surpluses of tree-ripened peaches from Georgia, redundancies of Carolina beefsteak tomatoes, herds of living Kennebunkport lobsters, a tractor-trailer of well-hung Wichita prime beef ... stampeding party-wards by "earliest possible."

And packed expressly for the Great Party by Kosmo-Freeze at Alameda Rubirosa, corner Sabado Bingo (formerly Custard's Last Stand, formerly Foster's Freeze), were three-dozen No. 11 tubs of purportedly sugar-free Kosmic Karamel yogurt—Proz's fave!

Last and most overabundant, in addition to the beers and wines of all regions, a carload of fig brandy and rose champagne was committed from the Duke's Montgomery Cristo Vineyards ("Monty Cristo"—it tickles the boy in him) in Oregon's Willamette Valley.

The spirits arrived with greetings from Master Vintner Brother Vinnie, blessing the Duke, his guests and livestock, and appending a "righteous" recipe for jalapeño, *maiz*, and tequila *soupe fraiche*.

The media were alerted.

Multitudes were summoned.

"Thursday Great Party To Be SPECTACULOUS!" said the headline created by event-hardened *Santa Lola Times-Press* columnist/beat reporter *Jeannee!*

No, she thought—

"SPLENDACIOUS!"

Used that in May.

"STUPENDIFEROUS SOIREE SET!"

That's got it....

Jeannee! beamed triumphant.

Widely acclaimed in Santa Lola for her singlehanded Team

Coverage of Society, Lawn Care, and Commercial Fisheries, *Jeannee!* is known on the street as Ms. Jordan Glanz—no exclamation point.

Four-feet-ten in steno pad and heels, her primary attributes: menacing overbite, aspirations to Junior League, suspected non-swimmer.

Having specified a strong string of sizzling sibilances ... *Jeannee!* knew her work here was done.

Sending her Roget's plodding square-rumped back to the barn, she punished her dry scalp with a thumbtack.

Nodded to the portrait of Wallis Simpson and "Eddie."

And strode into the shank of the Santa Lola midday.

*****

Neddy, Neddy, Neddy, his life is a wasteland.

He hates Gardenia Gazebo.

Hates gardenias!

And the word "Gazebo" ... there isn't enough hate to go around!

He laid the note right on the front seat of Lissa's black Jaguar XJ6 sedan, cool as a cat burglar—

She couldn't miss it!

And she said, "yes," two weeks ago on tedious Billie Boggs' tedious 99-foot tedious yacht.

... it couldn't be 100 feet!

He asked her, would he see her at the Duke's party, and she said, yes, she'd "see" him. Buh-loody "Yes!"

Any Eighth-Grader reading a dirty paperback knows what it means when a beautiful woman says, "yes," to a leading question like that!

So....

Where in blast!

Waiting deep in the Gazebo shrubbery, he has time to think ... perchance to brood.

These are the times that try Neddy's soul—early evening. Something's always going wrong now! Long ago, he gave up meditating on the cliff at sunset like the City College idiots. They looked so cool doing it, but when he tried, his brain zoomed all around like a horsefly ... get the cleaning ... scratch his nose ... buy anchovie paste.

Meditation was bad for him and—

Where IS SHE!

He peers out from behind a bush, low and sneaky.

Nada.

Zip.

Squat.

Things are getting started up at the house...

He hasn't got all night!

There!

What was that!

A sort of rustling—then *sssssssppp!*

Like a newspaper in the bushes by the Gazebo—

Rsss-ssss. PPP-ttttt!

Sssssssss-sPPP.

Somebody's there!

No wonder she hasn't shown herself.

They must have absolute privacy ... and she's protecting him—the darling delicacy with the sleek calves.

She sensed danger and vanished to avoid discovery by this, this—

... *rssss-lll-*ing, paper-racketing swine beyond the shrubs!

What kind of malicious mothergrabbing Hottentot—

Shhht!

Ssss-ssPPPP....

Enough!

Neddy rises to his full, admired six-feet-one.

Strides one forthright step forward.

Thinks better of it, and brushes a shrub noisily.

Good, it hears him....

Rssss-ssspp!

And isn't afraid.

Hmm....

Bugger it! Neddy stalks out past the final shrub, ready to throttle—

He sees a cut-stone bench...

Rather a nice cut-stone bench, overlooking the sea.

The low sun is yoke yellow but—

... what style of organism is this?

It turns.

Looks up frankly and smiles, h'llo!

It has a small, pitch-black face, with white teeth that shine like Caesar's Palace at midnight. In the dipping sun, its anthracite smile positively gleams!

"Lovely place to sit," it offers, "won't you join me?"

"I, well ... no, " says Ned—the supple mind deserting him. "Thanks but—"

The smiling face nods.

"What are you reading there?" inquires Neddy.

The diminutive blackness beams with disarming warmth.

Holds up a heavily *rrsssssll-*ed copy of *National Review.*

"Why? Do you read this?"

"No," says Ned. "What is it?"

"Ahh, not political—very clever of you. Sometimes I think it is best."

"And you?"

"It's not what you think," says the compact little man.

"I don't think anything!"

The fellow giggles, taking him now at his word.

They pause to admire the glow of late afternoon.

"Do you teach at City College?" asks Neddy.

"No," says the halogen smile.

"From San Francisco, then...."

"Not at all, why?"

"No reason," says Ned.

"I don't follow."

He smiles with engaging sweetness—for the downtrodden, misjudged, ill-treated wee fellow he undoubtedly is.

"Well ... you *are* reading."

"Ah. Yes," smiles the fellow, "... reading." He nods out to sea. "A lovely place this Santa Lola—and in ways, so very out of the world."

Confusing little bugger.

But his hand comes out now. They shake hands where he lives.

"Keita Mammady Fallo," he says.

"What?" says Ned.

"Keita Mammady Fallo."

"You're talking nonsense."

"Keita ... Mam-mady ... Fallo. It is my name."

Neddy smiles.

"I am not American."

"Hah!" nods Ned. "Couldn't tell it from here."

But Neddy was beginning to suspect something off-brand ... the pipey voice and all.

"I am from Pretoria."

"Yes? Canadian?"

Keita Mammady Fallo peruses the declining light, the sun now drooping well and truly into the drink: "South Africa, don't you see."

"Not British Columbia?"

"No. And your name?"

"Neddy Lombardo. Santa Lola, don't you see."

"Rather."

"Say listen, Kittie—"

"*Kay*-ta," Fallo says—pushy sort.

"Kay-ta ... how long have you been sitting here? I have a reason for asking."

"I'm certain you do."

43

"I mean to say, did you hear anything?"
Neddy is playing this deftly.
"See anything?"
Less deftly.
"Any person?"
Down to brass tacks. "A woman?"
"Ah-*haaah*-haaah-haaah!"
Keita Mammady Fallo displays countless pearlescent incisors.
Shakes the wee head—he has seen no one.
Neddy is sure now.
The dear wisp has been here to "see" him, but espying Keaton Mammary Philo, she stole off!
Caring nothing for her own deepest needs, thinking only of his good name ... she lit out like a cockroach across a hot griddle!
Leggy goddess—she is his!
He takes the visitor's hand now—shaking it like throttling a badger. "Oh, my!"
Neddy beams happily. "Enjoy your *Time Magazine*, Mr. Felon!"
"Fallo, don't you see."
"I'm sure we'll be seeing each other later ... if the lights are on."
WHOOOOOPS!
But no harm, Neddy decides—they're buddies.
His new friend laughs, "If the lights are on ... yes, yes, silly fellow."
Neddy nods.
Winks.
Good bloke this.
The internationally connected Neddy steals back now into the bush.
Fascinating, these foreign nippers. We can learn much from them.
Rissssle-ssssssppp! he hears behind him.
Of course.
Filmo's *Newsweek*.

*****

Windows in a casino ... Crap!
The Bigg Casino stained glass windows are playing hell with Snake's mood....
So it's getting dark outside—like he gives a damn!
For Snake, the baccarat lasted only a while, he doesn't know how long. What he really needed was stud poker.
And he told Ski Kobalefffsky, get lost, go play some blackjack, crissakes. Nothing poisons stud like a lot of slack-ass jabber about the

weather.

Sure enough, the minute Ski is gone Snake's game comes alive.

He's right where he needs to be. Knows the deck ... where it's going. Not the *Why,* a'course—you never know the *Why,* it's the whole point!

But where the hell is this dipped-in-gold Montenegro bitch?

Monte ... *nero!*

Whatever.

She'll show, or they'll hunt her ass down.

She's probably outside....

Where it's getting dark—BIG DEAL!

*****

Keeping a weather eye out for rhino, Neddy navigates farther into the bush.

He's deep in Gardenia Gazebo, stealing away from his natty wee pal, Keemo Mammary Fido, or however he styles himself. Neddy craves now the less kempt parts of the Gazebo, bereft of unsolicited freelancers.

But not halfway into the Green Hell, he hears a ... trounce!

Banging!

SLAM-*CRRRASHHHING!*

"Shee-*YYTTTTT!*"

... a lady's voice.

Can it be?

The slam-crashing draws nigh.

Is it....

The Yeti?

Suddenly, right before him, tramping down the front rank of shrubs flat as a crop circle...

Is the *zaftig,* earthy blonde Brunnhilde universally regarded as Ms. Twitty Conway!

"But—but—but," he claims, like a small Johnson outboard.

"Neddy!" she gasps interestedly.

Or is she just winded?

Nope—

has her breath.

... but she's "glowing," as they say.

Wipes a glistening cobweb from her reddened neck.

Swipes at her hair as if styling it in one mighty ... thwack!

"Deeear-est!" she declares, closing on him...

A lady wrassler circling, circling, setting up the initial armlock.

To his alarm, she's never looked healthier.

"Do you realize," she says, "the hell I went through getting down

45

here!"

"But Twitty, what are you..." he says, buying time—
A second will do.
"You could've taken the path...."
She stops circling.
"Neddy?"
"Twitty?"
She stands upright.
Matter of fact.
"Got yer note."
Be sly now—the fox, Ned thinks.
No time for swandiving into the soup!
"Your note!" she insists.
"... that *you* left on the seat of my Jaguar!"
A line of cold sweat breaks across his lip. "Twitty, I've no idea
what you—"
"Hell you don't!"
She extends a meaty arm.
Shakes a scrap of white paper before his nose.
He lunges, but she snatches it back as if from a naughty kitten.
Now it's he, circling, circling ... cursing internally the syphilitic
surfeit of black Jaguars.
He's stepped in it now!
"Come, Twitty—let me see. I don't know what you're talking
about!"
"Don't know, my ass! Are you telling me you didn't leave this note
in my car!"
He shakes his neck, persuaded his head will follow.
"Swear to Christmas, Twitty."
Moved momentarily by his reference to the blessed feast of giving
and receiving, he smiles.
No dice.
Twitty's eye boils.
He cocks his head at the curio again—innocently getting a better
look.
"No you don't!" she glares.
But his darling never got the missive...
It's why she didn't show!
He steeplechases to the next hurdle—
She is his!
"All right, Twitty—what's the tune?"
"Tune? I don't have any tune!"
In spite of all, he's smiling like a pelican.

Twitty holds up the note.

"You're saying this isn't yours!"

"Is it signed?"

Twitty stands her ground.

"If it's not yours, what in hell are you doing down here!"

He beams.

"Talking with my companion, Mammary Felafel, from Victoria, Africa. You'll find him just there."

Neddy points in the pertinent direction.

"Why?"

"Horse apples. I'm showing this to Proz—she'll know your handwriting!"

And his ass is blackened redfish....

But it's nothing to him—

He's won the pearl of great price!

"Lordie, Twits, so suspicious! Go ahead, show it to the Duke himself! Print it in the *Times-Press* with a recipe for Mushrooms Manfredini! And while we're talking, Twitty," he says thunderstruck at his own wit, "… why are you down here?"

No reply.

"You have some good reason for coming all this way through the shrubbery."

Make that two orders of blackened redfish....

His is a position of substance—

She's guilty as Milhouse!

She can't show the thingie to Proz without exposing herself as a backstabbing slut—or however Proz chooses to paint it.

"Come along, Twits," he croons, recalling a line he either did or didn't hear on the London stage, "… shan't we go back up to the house?"

Even if she tells, even if the fan is well and truly shit-hit—

The Dark-Eyed Queen is his!

Lava-flows of pleasure surge in his heart, or quite nearby.

"Come, Twits—let's!"

He offers the red-necked lass a guiding palm.

She takes it like fish-and-chips in *The World News*.

But life is an imperfect repast.

Even now his beloved bides her time up in the great manse...

Husbanding her affections.

Fashioning her fantasies.

Dreaming fondly of the brilliant future they two will share.

She'd be a damn fool not to!

CHAPTER 8

Evensong

"BEG YOUR PARDON?"

"Whatzzzat?"

"Thought you said something."

"No."

It doesn't stop Doug the Thug.

Indeed, it's exactly what he planned.

He smiles downwards upon the sun-reddened man standing at the

bar.

"My mistake. I'm Doug."

He gets back an off-center smile ... "Ski Kobalefffski."

"I know," he says.

"Yuh-do?"

"They call me Doug the Thug."

Ski's eye flickers ... "I know."

"So what brings you here, Ski?"

"What brings *anyone* here!"

Doug sips his drink. Nods.

"But what brings *you* here? You're not invited."

Ski thinks fast ... comes up with nothing.

Doug moves on.

"Where you from?"

"All around," Ski says.

"No, originally. Do I hear Tillary St.?"

Ski chuckles ... about as uncomfortably as chuckling gets. "You don't sound like the Mayor of Santa Lola yerself."

"Sheepshead Bay," Doug says. "So where—Ft. Hamilton?"

"Do I look like Ft. Hamilton?"

"The Point?"

Ski beams. (His low-beams.) "You're good, gotta say it."

"You'd be wrong if you dit-n't."

Doug looks ahead.

"What's the deal with you two? You think we let everyone win at blackjack all day?"

Ski couldn't ever remember feeling like this ... except one or three times in a squad car.

"Well?" Doug says. "Do you?"

Ski thinks fast again ... comes up with nothing.

Doug nods. "So what's the play? Come on, one professional to another. You are a professional—we know."

"What play? What the hell are you talking about, anyway? And why Doug the Thug?"

"It's just a name—because of Brooklyn and what I did there."

"And what was that?"

"And what I do here."

They look at each other.

Ski Kobalefffsky isn't difficult to pick out. He wears a blue-and-white flowered Hawaiian shirt, black jeans, a Dodgers cap that's been deep-sea fishing more often than not. He's dirty-blonde, average size, looks able to take care of himself, that's about it.

Doug the Thug is even easier to find, the only man at the bar, or in the county, who's bigger, stronger, and mayhaps scarier, than Battle, the Duke's USC defensive tackle/mahogany mountain chief barman. Debate rages over whether Doug or Battle would win in a war, if no weapons were allowed. With weapons, no contest ... Doug.

At Checquers professional functions—to Doug, every Checquers function is professional—he wears a massively big-and-tall black worsted suit, a black silk shirt buttoned up to the collar, no tie, black Italian shoes. A thick black porn-star mustache tapers bushily around the edges. Minus the mustache, he'd be a tenor-sax player in an experimental L.A. jazz big band. Experimental L.A. jazz big bands don't last, but Doug lasts. With the mustache ... he's the Thug.

"Truth is," Doug says, "I might've guessed Red Hook, and I might not. I had help, a guy in San Pedro that knows you."

"In Pee-dro ... whozzat?"

"He told me—The Point. I wanted to see what you'd say when I asked."

"Who? What guy?"

"Nobody. He knows you. Now I know you. I know about Snake down at blackjack, too. He and I haven't had the pleasure yet, but I'd say he likes winning a little too much, wouldn't you? But that's another story. You guys come here assuming a little too much—"

"Now wait just a damn minute, pal—"

Doug's massive paw comes to rest on Ski's blue-and-white-flowered Hawaiian shoulder.

A little squeeze and a minutely lower note in Doug's mouth-of-the-cave voice serve to moderate the weather.

"Stay calm, now, Ski—everything's fine and it's going to stay fine. We're all going to wind up real calm ... it's what I do."

"I don't even know what you're talking about."

"Just don't get to thinking something big's gonna happen, Ski—it's not."

A moment passes.

"Not gonna—trust me."

Doug puts his glass on the bar, half-empty, and walks away.

*****

The day is softening.

Mauve shadows pad across flawless lawns. Bright light melds to old gold.

Up at Top-Forty, the Duke strolls the white sands of his Wave Pool one last time, finely alone. Events are to be hosted, curiosities celebrated, but before leaving, he'll experience it once more in sweet melancholy ... the adieu to sun and surf.

"Hey, Duke, c'mon in!" the surfer chorus barks.

He smiles.

Waves.

"Wish I could," he says, for too many reasons.

He makes his way to the Comet, at last, and steps aboard for the long, leisurely cruise down the mountain.

Meanwhile, far down below the great house at Kentonia Concourse, a stressed pair boards the upward-bound Comet. The lady removes a gardenia twig from her blonde tresses, wipes a wisp of hair from her reddened face.

At the same time, a diminutive coal-black presence turns in his seat, three rows ahead.

He smiles graciously. "Ah-hah..." says Keita Mammady Fallo. "This will be the lovely lady you awaited, Mr. Lombardo."

"No notion what you mean, Kato."

Twitty says nothing ... glaring past Neddy, past Keita Mammady Fallo, straight up to far, twinkling Aldebaran.

Fallo's smile is undiminished.

He turns forward again.

"… yes, yes, silly fellow."

Part Two

CHAPTER 9

Skag-yoo-wahh

All well and good, you say ... but _how!_

How _in hell_ did old Cyrus Rutt accumulate such riches in the first place!

And how _in hell_ did Montgomery Overdale Rutt, his son, multiply them virtually beyond mathematical expression!

Duke Monty's story, being more recent, is easier to tell.

On the fateful day in 1944 when his father, after tea, smiling to the end, passed into the Santa Lola sunset, Monty had already vastly improved the family position. Playing Alexander the Great to his father's Philip of Macedon, Montgomery Rutt applied withering sums in Sacramento, and a little later, in the coastal regions just south of scruffy, lawless Pueblo de Nuestra Señora la Reina de los Angeles de Porciúncula—the City of Angels. From there, his investments ranged into the Great Southwest. These were eclipsed by major acquisitions in Manhattan, the rival to the massive Fifth Avenue holdings of the House of Windsor, on and on.

Compounding these positions in the U.S., and more recently, across Asia and the world, Montgomery Rutt confirmed his place on an ever-shrinking list, finally numbering just one.

Owing as much to his courtly manner as to his devastating wealth, "long ago" (in California, thirty years will do nicely) Montgomery Rutt came to be "the Duke." It was as ineluctable as naming the nearest tall, treeless peak "Baldy."

Confirmedly a Westerner, the Duke still richly values the occasional "Hi, Monty," but for most, this is out of the question. Just as there is no joy in addressing W.C. Fields as Bill Duckenfield, or greeting Cary Grant as Archie Leach ... the Duke is the Duke.

Yet none of this explains how it all began.

Take a bit of Darjeeling, then, get comfortable and suspend your expectations.

*****

Everything began for young Cyrus Rutt when it was too late to turn back.

It was 1891, and he was approaching San Francisco by water. The times were, as ever, troubled. Beset by economic depression and massive unemployment, the "Gay Nineties" were anything but gay ... Cyrus Rutt could hear them with his well-attuned ear, thundering!

Born a year before Lee and Grant met at Appomattox Court House for a good deal more than tea, Rutt was raised on an upstate dirt farm near Elmira, New York, though to restless young Cyrus, what was "up" about it eluded him. When he could, he moved on, passing several restless years in his twenties in Ohio and Indiana.

Then one day in 1891, seized by a blinding impatience, he boarded the westbound train for Gomorrah by the Bay, "before it was too late." He didn't understand that dour admonition. He simply obeyed it.

At his first view of the Golden City, from the throbbing deck of a walking-beam Southern Pacific Oakland-San Francisco ferry, his belly spoke truth—if he were to succeed in this land of promise, he had much ground to make up.

But Cyrus Rutt possessed a talent in short supply in rowdy, randy San Francisco—he could listen. Like an owl. And one night in Belle Poivre's Golden Bustle on the Barbary Coast, minding his own damn business not at all, he heard loose talk at the next table—actually, very loose talk three tables up! A man with a swollen tongue, blotchy nostrils, and bloodshot rheumy eyes was booming, as boomers will, about his two years in the wilds of Alaska.

Cold, the boomer said, cold as a suffragette's saddle.

Cyrus Rutt rolled his eyes, prepared to listen-in elsewhere.

But the boomer's next utterance riveted him.

When the time came to return home, said the loud one, he found himself with insufficient funds to purchase transit. So in little more time than it took to briefly operate a pick and shovel, he scooped up enough gold nuggets from the creek beds near a grim little Indian village called "Skag-yoo-wahh" ... native for "unpleasant squaw yelling" ... to pay his First-Class passage south, plus all his gaming along the way.

The others at the table eyed their cards, drawing and discarding. They'd heard it all before. So had Cyrus.

Gold in Alaska ... it was like ghost stories. If there were anything to it, all the world would be up there, snarling and snapping at each other like bitch guard dogs.

Yebbut ... thought Cyrus Rutt.

It was the siren song of a million fool's errands.

But as fools go, Cyrus Rutt was wicked diligent. With counsel from an old Barbary Coast forty-niner, he learned all he could about the theory and practice of placer mining. In May, 1893, four years before the famed Great Klondike Rush, he boarded the steamer *Portland* at Schwabacher's Dock. Some days later, in early June, he stepped off onto the mudflats of ... its name was Skagway, and if there were objectionally loud native women about, he didn't hear them. He purchased saws, nails, mining goods, provisions, and two horses, and set out north like Sancho Panza.

Fortune smiled on Cyrus Rutt. White Pass, in the high St. Elias range, would later earn the name "Dead Horse Trail," thousands of Klondike Rush pack animals driven to their death in its snow and ice. But Cyrus Rutt was an upstate farm lad. He knew horses and the value of the seasons. Just as important, in 1893, long before the Stampede, he was not required to pack in a full year's provisions. In 1897, for cause, the Mounties made each Stampeder haul in two tons of supplies. The 100,000 Stampeders rushing north—30,000 actually made the goldfields—would overwhelm the tiny northern trading posts in a fortnight.

But in summer, 1893, Rutt found few people and little ice. White Pass proved it could blizzard in July, but he was in no rush. Resting his horses when they showed stress, he descended to heavily forested, bright-green Lake Bennett in high spirits. Years later, the Stampeders would raze the surrounding forests to the ground, building thousands upon thousands of boats, to drift down the Yukon River 400 miles to Dawson City and the goldfields. They'd pass through life-threatening rapids below Miles Canyon—but they had the advantage of Cyrus Rutt. In 1893, neither the goldfields nor Dawson City existed.

Having no clear destination and a profound distrust of water, Rutt began the long journey down the banks of the Yukon River. Along the way, he heard of small gold strikes far downriver, but he had no grand expectations, and the news encouraged none. Weeks later, far below a bleak little Indian fishing village at the confluence of the Yukon and Klondike rivers, he came to bustling Circle City. A spectacular $400,000 gold strike here by two Russian half-bloods had spawned a brand-new boomtown, boasting two theatres, eight honky-tonks, two-dozen saloons, a library, and a school.

Gold dust was in the air, and Cyrus Rutt knew how to buy a round of drinks. He settled in nicely.

Yet within a week, he learned Circle City's few paying claims were failing already—and he had a feeling. He'd heard something might be starting up back near Fortymile Creek—and he just had a feeling.

He traveled back upriver to Fortymile trading post, bought

provisions from Fortymile's Billy Kilgore, and rode to the mouth of the Klondike River, a tributary of the Yukon. Two Indians he'd met there when he first came through, Skookum Jim and Tagish Charlie, had been friendly.

He'd scout a creek or two there.

*****

In three weeks, Rutt was back at Fortymile Trading Post filing a claim.

It wasn't news. Many claims were filed that year, and nothing came of them. He bought winter provisions from Billy Kilgore at the trading post and rode back up the Klondike.

Seasons passed.

Rutt returned to Fortymile six or seven times in three years, each time staying just long enough to purchase provisions. When his small cash stake ran out, he began paying Kilgore in gold, swearing him to secrecy ... a load of good that would do! But he would try. The braggarts down in Circle City boasted deafeningly about their good fortune, but Cyrus Rutt was an upstate Yankee working alone. He would keep his own counsel. Using Kilgore as his bank, he traded small amounts of gold for his modest needs, promising Kilgore a huge reward—$100 in gold—for his silence.

But word would get out.

The world would come swooping in, jaws watering.

Billy Kilgore would do what he would do, Rutt knew. The rest was up to God.

The work was backbreaking. Rutt labored hard all fall and into winter for as long as the cold permitted, patiently melting permafrost, boring laboriously down to bedrock and pay dirt. But bringing out his diggings in brutal sub-zero weather, he had no way to assay his goods.

With spring and the return of running water, he could sluice for "color."

Yet now and then came magical moments. He'd finger out a nugget here. Another there. Deep in the ancient creek bed, he came upon bright strata—elegant horizontal bands rich with gold, deposited in neat layers like a cheese sandwich.

But evil times came, as well.

For weeks ... eternities ... the weather stayed at 55-below day and night. Blades of icy wind rent his humble log shelter. Wrapped in layer upon layer of clothing and fur wraps, he endured endless arctic night, praying desperately for hope. Black isolation tortured him, a fragile tissue of flesh locked in death's hard-frozen claw.

Midwinter madness howled all around, tolling the midnight of his eternal soul.

Then, as if to rescue him from himself ... the weather broke.

He was up and around...
Building fires, melting snow.
He'd make a small test—he must have hope!
Panning carefully, patiently, he prayed for ounces, a pound...
Respite from despair.
And he had his little wooden box of nuggets.
They came in all sizes—some as big as his thumb!
But then the wolf of winter raged anew.
Locked in cold-steel air, frozen in time ... nothing moved.
He sank into a terrible stillness—
it was safer not moving.
No...
Move!
His arm stirred, slowly hunting in numbing blackness.
Unsure it was his ... the glove crept slowly away.
Reached for the little wooden box.
In a dream
siren winds shrieking
his cracked fingers stirred the box
stirring ... stirring.
He heard it then...
The soft
Sugar-candy chatter...
Raw gold.
The glove came back to him slowly.
Tucked in.
He could pray again.
A few minutes, at least.

*****

He could not trust it—until it crashed over him like an ocean wave.
Spring!
His arms and legs were his allies again.
He felt joy in his muscles.
Their power!
If God is with him, now he'll take the measure of his labor.
Running water ... a miracle!
He can "clean up" his dirt.
Now he'll see!

*****

Cyrus Rutt endured three wintry descents into Arctic Death.

The tiny stream he was on, a western tributary of the Klondike, had no English name. He named it after home, Elmira Creek, for good reason. Numerous times, locked in winter's black fist, his father and brother had come to him. They talked to him and counseled him and gave him courage.

And he thanked them for coming.

His father had given him life...

Now he was teaching him to endure.

But after three black winters on Elmira Creek, he knew he would not survive a fourth—it was too much.

And he must survive.

He'd earned it!

In proof of this, well into the third spring, his dread vision of Billy Kilgore running along the Yukon River banks at Fortymile like a mad person, howling gold!-gold!-gold! ... never materialized. It was only a fantasy. A hoodoo of his black winter daze.

In a life rich with good contracts, his deal with Billy Kilgore proved the finest of all. The reason was simple, he decided. Billy was Canadian— his word was his bond.

Splendidly alone on Elmira Creek, Rutt spent his spare time in the summer practicing marksmanship with his two pistols and two lever-action Winchester carbines. He had a Model 1886 .45-70 and the old heavily used 1873 .44-40 he'd bought in Skagway "just to be safe." Alone in the wilderness, he calculated he would need twenty rifle rounds before reloading—nine in the '86 and eleven in the '73. And conveniently, his Colt .44 pistols used the same .44-40 cartridge as the '73.

He'd always been a better rifle shot than his older brother Franklin.

Now he improved himself with the revolvers.

In the spring of the third year—finally—visitors began coming in. They arrived mostly in pairs, as he knew they would, but he was not concerned. He had carefully salted away his goods. To all appearances, he was finding only modest amounts of color.

But the honeymoon was over, and it suited him. He had worked hard and long, and his strict secrecy was borne of scrupulosity, not cowardice. After three solitary, mortal Klondike winters, he had all the grit needed to set his jaw and raise a carbine to his shoulder.

But he'd rather not.

Humbly and gratefully, he accepted his labor's earnings. They were stupefying.

*****

In early June, 1896, Billy Kilgore brokered him four packhorses.

Cyrus paid in nuggets, but good to the end, Kilgore paid the seller in noncommittal Canadian currency.

And Kilgore swore he had not been the source of the Elmira Creek visitors. A Fortymile bar-side observer, Turkey Bill Everett, watching Rutt's comings and goings over the years, had put two and three together. Yet when Everett asked about Rutt, Kilgore said, he had denied any knowledge of a profitable strike.

No matter. Gossip becomes fact. Word was abroad. The only question now was how much gold had Rutt taken out?

And some wanted to know more than others.

He rode up the Yukon to the mouth of the Klondike with his new string of horses. In months, this same modest mud delta would become brawling, blasting Dawson City, the most cosmopolitan Canadian metropolis west of Winnipeg.

But not yet. It was still a sleepy, smoky little Indian fishing village. As Rutt passed through, he came upon his friend Skookum Jim, and Jim had news. A week earlier up at Rabbit Creek, a tributary on the Klondike's east bank, Jim said, he'd found three big nuggets.

"Yep," said Rutt, "it's here."

And two weeks earlier, Jim said, his partner, Tagish Charlie, dug into one of the multiple bands of gold in the creek bed Rutt called a "cheese sandwich."

Rutt nodded again.

Plenty more to be had.

But Jim's next news changed the mood.

"You know Turkey Bill?" he said.

"Turkey Bill..." Rutt repeated, at a loss.

"Turkey Bill Everett down at Fortymile?" Jim said.

"I don't."

"Big scar on his neck," Jim said. "Red hair."

Rutt didn't know many people at Fortymile by name, but the description hit home. "Turkey Bill—yes," he said. "He and two others rode in at my claim a couple of weeks back."

Skookum Jim nodded darkly.

"What about him?" Rutt said.

"He's bad."

"He certainly looks the part."

"Bad," Skookum said. "Me and Charlie were working the creek, and Turkey Bill and two others came in some weeks back. They started asking questions about how we were doing, and Charlie said, we were doing okay. But they wanted to know—did we find much gold? So Charlie ... you know Charlie ... he just smiled and said, have a look. He showed them a couple nuggets we found. They smiled back, real interested, and wanted to know if we found any more. A little, Charlie said. I already had a bad feeling—I wanted Charlie to shut up, but they kept on talking."

Rutt listened, his smile gone. "So, what happened?"

"He took them in and showed them—what did you call it ... the 'cheese sandwich?' They were grinning and nodding, you know—real interested about what Charlie showed them."

Rutt said nothing.

"That night, real late," Skookum Jim said, "they came back, and I knew we were in trouble. I don't know the other two by name, but it was Turkey Bill Everett and them—I'm sure as I can be. There was no moon and it was pitch black, but our dogs heard them and raised hell. We took cover and just waited."

"Yeah?"

"They couldn't see where we were ... it was kind of a stand-off."

"And?"

"With no moon, there was not much they could do. They couldn't shoot the dogs—they couldn't see them. They left. You got dogs?"

"I should," Rutt said, "... but I don't."

"I came down to the village, and Sergeant Guilfoyle was riding through," Jim said. "So I told him, and he just nodded like he already knew!"

"But you said it was dark—how do you know it was Everett?"

"You know. It's like Sergeant Guilfoyle. The Mounties just know!"

Rutt understood. In this country, if you don't "know," you're dead.

"Guilfoyle's a good man," Rutt said.

"He might as well be," Jim said. "If he isn't, nobody is. I see you got some horses. You planning to leave?"

"Thinking about it," Rutt said.

Jim didn't pursue it. It was the kind of information Turkey Bill valued.

Local intelligence exchanged, Rutt wished Skookum Jim well.

"Be careful," Jim said.

"Always," Rutt said with a mirthless smile.

He mounted up and was on his way.

Riding up the Klondike, it began to rain, a cold, murky, dispiriting rain, like the whole of the Yukon was crying. Cyrus Rutt rode slowly along, thinking and thinking. He knew better ... but there was nothing to do except think, listening to the rain pelt the brim of his hat. It was like fingers drumming on his forehead ... think what you're going to do, how you're going to do it ... what's the very best way to do it ... but there is no best way! He'd do things one at a time, one after another, and find out. He didn't know the answer. There wouldn't be any answer until he got to the end!

Meantime, all he could do was listen to the rain pelting his hat.

As long as he heard the rain ... pelting ... it was all right.

That was when he realized how desperate he was.

... hearing the rain.

He came to the mouth of Elmira Creek and turned upstream.

It seemed like riding into doom.

But he saw a rider up ahead.

The rider wore shiny black—a military rain slicker—and a Mountie hat.

Sergeant Guilfoyle!

He sat up in his saddle, heartened. There could be no other reason, Guilfoyle came up to see him!

The closer the Mountie came, the more buoyed Rutt felt—buoyed and grateful.

When they met, Rutt grinned. "What are you doing up here?"

"Nobody else around but you, Mr. Rutt."

"I hope not."

"I wanted to see that you were all right," Sergeant Guilfoyle said.

"Good of you, Sergeant."

"And I see you are."

"But I hear there's reason for concern," Rutt said. "I had a talk with Skookum."

Sergeant Guilfoyle leaned forward in his saddle. "Mr. Rutt, I wanted a word with you, but your string of horses answers my question. You're planning to head out, correct?"

"If I can."

The Mountie nodded. "Jim has a lot to say, Mr. Rutt."

"I've heard."

"I'd hate to have anything happen up here." The Mountie looked at Rutt's horses. "You're going to have your hands full handling all of these and defending yourself."

"I can take care of myself," Rutt said. "I have so far."

"You haven't been tested so far."

"I'm grateful, Sergeant. But I see no other way."

"No. But my duty is to keep the peace, and I think it may be under threat."

Rutt said nothing.

"I thought, when you're coming, I'd ride down with you to the river. How long before you're ready?"

"Two or three days, maybe. I'd be very grateful."

The Mountie nodded. "I'll be back in three days."

With that, he put his hand to his brim and continued down the creek.

Almost on cue, the rain stopped and the skies began to clear.

Back at his claim, Rutt spent two midnight-sun days in June, 1896 breaking camp and arranging his goods ... the humid air whining with mosquitoes and raw nerves. He was ready. As soon as Sergeant Guilfoyle came in, he'd load his weighty cargo on his horses and be off.

But that third morning, he heard rifle fire down Elmira Creek—several different guns firing repeatedly.

And he knew of only one "gang."

He grabbed his Remington .45-70 and rode towards the sound. Rounding a bend in the creek where it dropped down a brow, he saw gunsmoke in the trees on the left bank. Two men were pinned down on the right. One was Skookum Jim. The other was crumpled behind a tree in his scarlet tunic—Sergeant Guilfoyle!

Three riflemen crouched behind trees on the left.

Rutt took cover, worked the Remington's lever action and squeezed the trigger.

Gunfire coming in from a new position up the creek spooked the three.

Immediately, they backed away through the trees.

He heard it then in the distance ... horses moving off at a gallop.

Rutt rode down the creek. He saw by the way Jim bent over Guilfoyle that the Mountie was badly wounded.

When he dismounted, Jim looked up. "They got him first—before we knew they were there!"

The Sergeant was hit twice—in the arm, but far worse, in the gut.

Deep crimson spred across his tunic's bright scarlet.

His complexion glistened like moist porcelain, his skin pale beyond life.

His chest heaved...

heaved.

With a violent shudder then, his body clenched—

And he was gone.

"They were firing out of the trees," Jim explained—as if explaining could change it. "They got him on the second or third shot."

Rutt nodded. "You okay?"

"They wanted him."

"Could you see them?"

"I know who they are," Jim said. "Three of them, just like before."

"Bastards," Rutt said.

They tied the Sergeant onto his horse and rode slowly up to Rutt's claim. On the way, Jim recounted an incident down in the village. Sergeant Guilfoyle had confronted Turkey Bill Everett and the other two—Shaney Nichols and Mick Dixon—about the dark night raid at Jim's claim. He had his eye on them, Guilfoyle said ... if there was any trouble up at the claims, any trouble at all ... he was coming after them.

Rutt nodded.

The line was drawn in the sand.

Skookum helped load Rutt's cargo on the horses.

They rode out with Sergeant Guilfoyle and the string of horses, Rutt not looking back ... he'd seen it.

Down at the village, they drew a crowd. Guilfoyle's body was taken down off the horse and covered. The children all pushed and shoved, looking close—before their parents scolded them with swats and told them to get away.

The body would be sent down to Fortymile by boat. Skookum Jim would convey the story. Everyone liked Sergeant Guilfoyle.

But Cyrus Rutt wasted no time. Jim would confirm Rutt's positive role in events. And he had no idea if being in a hurry now was the right thing or not ... but he wanted to get going upriver immediately!

He wished Skookum Jim and Tagish Charlie well and headed out that afternoon on the long trip up to White Pass and Skagway. Early the following September, his cargo in securely pad-locked steamer trunks, he sailed out the fjord southbound from Skagway.

A garrulous good fellow in normal times, Cyrus Rutt richly valued companionship. On the trail, however, he was no more than courteous to those he met. The country was wild—and gold was gold.

Word of Skookum and Tagish's massive Klondike gold strike didn't reach the outside until months later, in spring, 1897. But when it did, their Rabbit Creek claim was instantly renamed "Bonanza Creek."

The Stampede was on!

*****

Yet there were rumors.

Something happened on Rutt's trip up the Yukon.

And decades later in modern Santa Lola, word is the Duke knows the story. Inevitably, of course, wild tales must rise up around a legendary clan like the Rutts. The Duke says only, "They were desperate days, when men did what men do"—changing the topic precipitously to the prospects for a lasting peace in the Mid-East.

Yet the mystery of Cyrus Rutt's homeward journey persists. This much is known.

In September, the patriarch—possibly unharmed—loaded his cargo on the Talya Inlet packet and steamed south to open water. But instead of voyaging to San Francisco ... "Ships sink," said Rutt, still distrusting water ... he disembarked at the nearest American port, Seattle, afflicted with "acute seasickness."

Curious.

The inside passage to Seattle is a reasonably placid fetch. Was this *mal de mer* a fabrication?

Or had he suffered complications resulting from a bullet wound to his left forearm, as one account has it, the result of a mad gunfight on the Upper Yukon? And was his strict seclusion in his cabin during the entire voyage south to Seattle a medical necessity?

Well...

Was it?

Nobody would care if Cyrus Rutt had not arrived in the Bay Area one of the richest men of the Bear Republic—and "the planet." Initially, he went to considerable lengths to conceal the extent of his wealth.

Arriving at the Southern Pacific Depot across the Bay in Oakland, his worldly goods, clothing, toiletries, and miscellany required but one modest valise. His otherworldly goods, however, were off-loaded from the mail car in eight impossibly weighty locked steamer trunks. Transferred to a heavy dray wagon, they and Rutt crossed San Francisco Bay aboard the Southern Pacific walking-beam ferry *San Leandro*—the same vessel from which he first glimpsed the Golden City five years before.

He stood hard by his goods the entire crossing ... we may imagine him remarking, "Ferries sink."

On dry land at last in San Francisco, Rutt was a changed man. A radish-nosed waterfront local inquired about the unwieldy pad-locked trunks, but Rutt was an open book. They were Alaskan granite samples bound for the Geology Dept. in Gov. Stanford's grand new sandstone university down the Peninsula in Palo Alto. Departing the ferry at the fast a-building site of what would soon be the fabulous new San Francisco Ferry Building, however, the trunks went nowhere near the Southern Pacific Depot on Howard St. They rode, instead, three short blocks up teeming Market St. to Hibernia Bank's side entrance, thence to Selby's Smelting Works ... never to be seen again.

The pertinent fact here is, Klondike gold was not confirmed until the arrival at Schwabacker's Dock of the stubby, rust-encrusted steamship *Excelsior* the following July, bearing cubic millions in ore! Immediately, the 1897 papers proclaimed Alaskan creeks lined with riches ... you couldn't wade three feet without barking your shin on a gold boulder!

Cyrus Rutt would neither confirm nor deny the claims—who was he to preclude another man's dream?

But pressed hard by the *San Francisco Bulletin's* most brutish and insufferable reporter, he conceded it was Yukon gold that had created him the Golden State's newest millionaire.

Billionaires had yet to be coined, but Rutt and John D. Rockefeller were working on it. Trillionaires would have to wait until young Duke

Monty hit his stride.

A paragon of diligence and moderation while he was in the north, few even knew of Cyrus Rutt's presence—just as he wished. When the extent of his success became the object of intense Yukon River conjecture, it was Rosie ... the "Wild Rose of Fortymile" ... who liberated the truth. Pulling Billy Kilgore into the trading post's back room one Thursday night, she swept the papers off his desk onto the dirt floor and lavished upon him her most precious private currency. He was Canadian—but he wasn't dead!

By then, Cyrus Rutt was sailing safely south to Seattle. Billy's word had held ... his hundred gold dollars justly earned.

The high drama of the 1897 Klondike Stampede has no proper place in Cyrus Rutt's story. However, the legend of Rutt's eight mighty steamer trunks clattering off the Oakland mail car in September, 1896 did nothing to calm 1897 hysteria. Five burly teamsters had growled and cursed half an hour, jimmying the cases around with irons, sliding them crashing down onto the dray wagon, spooking the horses.

It took Hibernia Bank some four weeks to properly arrange Rutt's accounts. Meantime, he was accorded lavish credit and all the cordial goodwill attaching thereto. His first financial move, miniscule when compared with what was to come, applied significant funds to a huge, and to his canny eye, hugely undervalued, property down the Bay. Near a sleepy Mexican mission hamlet named San Jose, he purchased several large evaporation ponds along the southern end of the vast bayside mudflats. Still retaining virtually endless cash reserves, the opulent Cyrus Rutt was now, following the patrician usage ... "in salt."

The Stampeders, in their tens of thousands, toiled like the damned, struggling up the steep 35-degree incline of Chilkoot Pass, cruel tonnages of Mountie-mandated provisions strapped to their backs. All the while, Cyrus Rutt relaxed in the bay window of his Mission Dolores mansion, smoking Latakia and Balkan in his favored Oom Paul briar, stroking his mustachios and reading the *San Francisco Examiner*. He'd had quite enough of the malignant mutt from the *Bulletin*.

CHAPTER 10

Least Of The Mohicans

IT IS THE GOLDEN HOUR.

Checquers is under full steam.

Bigg Casino is going great guns ... always.

Elsewhere beneath the mansion's magnificent Constance Room, in legendary Get-Down Lounge, a jam-packed real-estate seminar is underway. Its headliner is beaming, black-horn-rimmed Vernal R. Jerms Jr., his topic: "A Winning Loan Application — Saying Is Believing!"

At five-thirty, two rooms farther east in cavernous, glittering Snug Harbor Ballroom, an over-subscribed Ballroom Dancing Class investigates the Waltz, Foxtrot and Oxnard Pachanga. The class is conducted by richly sequined and heavily made-up, in both instances, "Marvin & Ursula." They've been imported from neighboring Tuna Vista, known locally as "T.V." Santa Lola's servant's quarters, T.V. is a bedroom community of gardeners, maids, handymen, porters, domos (major/minor), bouncers, bank-tellers, custodians/janitors, plumbers, firefighters, police and ballroom-dance instructors.

But in mid-afternoon, Marvin & Ursula proved entirely too popular. The Ballroom Dancing Class fully booked, a second session was hastily scheduled for seven-fifteen, illuminating the Big Apple, Jitterbug, and Surfer's Stomp. In the headlong frenzy to get into Marvin & Ursula's second sock-hop, there were instances of shoving, expletives, hurled fruit.

Scalpers appeared briefly.

Then Doug the Thug, in shiny-black narrow-lapel sharkskin suiting, appeared asking for a light.

Message received ... the price of admission to Marvin & Ursula will remain one ticket, costing not one penny.

It's Checquers!

Speculation returned to where it belongs, wagering on the number of states to be swept in two weeks by the Teflon moviestar Commander-In-Chief. He'd live in Santa Lola, if he were not elsewhere engaged.

In Checquers' hushed Brown Study now—observed by none—the All-Comers Greater Platinum Coast Chess Tournament is rising to a systolic climax. The contestants are a child of twelve, the same victor over sporting Burtie Balfour early this morning, and lavishly Adam's-appled notary public Phil Spitzberm. The boy, Stephan—not "Stevie!"—has been drinking ... two half-glasses of cunning Spitzberm's strong *dunkel* beer.

It's the cocktail hour, after all.

And Spitzberm's strategy is making inroads.

He scores two quickly defeated checks, before Stephan excuses himself to "spit up."

At the youth's return, pale and quivering, Spitzberm slams him with yet another miserable check—effortlessly defeated.

And now, in an armor-to-armor clash rivaling Zhukov at the Battle of Kursk, Stephan reverses positions in a series of lightning thrusts, checkmates Spitzberm—and makes it only halfway to the Brown Study wastebasket.

Little rodent ... thinks Spitzberm.

Next stop for the vanquished notary public, Vern Jerms' scintillating second seminar: "Rancho Paydirt — Zillions In Desert Real Estate!"

*****

Out on the grand rear terrace, Proz is in her glory, and why not?

Surrounded by Santa Lola's leading literary lights, her tray-table up and seatbelt securely fastened, she's prepared to be dazzled in their collective high beams. And it's wonderful she's here ... her presence lends matters what the diamond stickpin does to the little black dress.

On her right hand is excitable Peevy Palmtry, the two of them seated in upright, sensible deck chairs. Too much time on a chaise longue, they're told, causes bedsores. Honestly, Proz is skeptical—but like eating red meat, there may be something to it.

At the moment ... for the moment is everything ... she's fascinated to learn that being creative is painful—and surely it is. Gary Larry, City College Lecturer, footballist, regional poet—and indisputably creative—insists!

"Epistemologically, ontologically, hydroponically," he avows, "creativity is agonizing—I don't know why!"

Gary is special that way. He can admit when he's in the dark.

Speaking of which ... look around you now. The temporal riot of day, ablaze at glaring noon's prideful peak, retrenching in face-saving mid-afternoon, indecisive during dusk's mauve muddling about ... has tossed in the towel. It's pitch-black.

Splendid. Checquers' dim rear terrace is ideal for a Santa Lola Arts Round Table. (The table in use, ominously, is square.) Debate flourishes like summer lightning, skilled cocktail stewards in white waistcoats maneuvering through lethal bursts of literary discord like Messerschmitt Bf 109s diving through amassed Boeing B-17s—but ... is it a waltz?

Far off in the void, "Marvin & Ursula" wheel and whirl to frothy Strauss, imparting to things a piquant *Titanic* humor.

The Round Table topic at the moment is Illusion v. Reality. In the early going, Illusion pulls out a commanding lead. But unable to make Bingo ... momentum slams hard left to Existentialism v. Nihilism. The riders go to the whip, the betting vigorous and even!

"I cannot agree!" says novelist Julian Axel.

It is indisputable.

Wealthiest of the pack by seven lengths, and by his alligator pumps shall ye know him, Axel is a #1 N.Y. Times Swell-Seller. Goatee-ed, sallow, with something gone flimsy about the eyes, Julian Axel has written a yard and a half of paperback thrillers with swastikas on the cover. His latest, *The Syndrome Factor*, deposes the postwar schemings of Joseph Goebbels' third nephew, Phil. It will be finished Tuesday—three-fifteen sharp.

"Existentialism," he deposes dismissively, "is nothing more than Nihilism with a capital 'E.'"

"*Mais non!*" objects Jean-Yves D'Ilesdeaux.

From the Sorbonne via V.W. bus, D'Ilesdeaux writes "filmic" criticism for the *Times-Press*. Axel dubbed him "our Hitchcocksucker."

But Duane Snit, next around the table, and a struggling exponent of Abstract Expressionist family portraiture, is having none of it. "I consider this entire debate a prurient emission of methane."

"Come now, Duane...." It's Gary Larry, seated across from Snit. "You really must begin working again!"

Gary Larry (it's "Garrett Larold" on his driver's license, but that was too laid forward) is a City College regional poet. Six-feet-seven, or worse, in his school years he was an unusually offensive tackle for the C.I.F.-runner-up Santa Lola High football Golden Madres.

He made Prep All-State, and no wonder ... look at him!

Yet Gary Larry ... soon to be in paperback with *The Lost Verse of Bronco Nagurski* ... is unsettling. A sports hero who emerged from athletic glory with a career in campus politics, he is nonetheless riddled with self-doubt. He bites his lip making cafeteria decisions. Denies jingling telephones. Stonewalls ringing doorbells. A trader in miniature jade, at which he makes a sordid return, he's written a series of curiously familiar paeans to the Santa Lola sunset, among them, "Rosy-Fingered Dusk."

But now Gary—or Larry, if that's how you see things—receives a hearty attaboy.

"Gary's right, Duane," concurs Gerald Schmidt Thermos, "you've got to get back on the horse ... we'll all feel better."

Taller than a fireplug, Thermos is an avant-garde City College professor and composer. Crinkly tufts of down cling to his dome like chicken feathers to a bowling ball. His latest work, received noisily at school, is the Bridal Suite in E# Minor for Brass, Piccolo and Howitzer.

But Thermos' resumé is complex. Rumored to possess a State Fair zucchini-sized personal baton, at this moment, he's working on nothing more avant-garde than the thickish turn of Peevy's ankle.

"... mmm, Peeve?" he croons.

And Peevy is on to him—not disapprovingly.

"But why bother!" objects struggling Abstract Expressionist Snit. "What's the point—nobody understands the work!"

Ooooo, thinks Proz ... this is getting really good!

"I know, I know..." Gary Larry sympathizes. "But Thermos is right—as artists, we all must work!"

Thermos beams at Peevy....

"Art is our battering ram," Gary says, "... bashing down bourgeois barricades ... mashing middle-class mediocrity ... torpedoing TV-dinner hypocrisy!"

Proz drags on her empty straw ... *Sssspoooooorrrrch!*

She needs another Perrier and soda.

"Art scales the highest peaks," Gary Larry gallops ahead, "breathing the rarest air! I feel your pain, Duane, I do—but Confucius says, he who carves the Buddha does not believe in him."

"Amazing!" Julian Axel barks like a Jack Russell. "That's what my novel is about!"

"Oh ... do tell!" Proz gushes.

But Axel's elation collapses now like a fallen soufflé.

"Ahh, dear lady," he allows mournfully, "... I cannot discuss work in progress—it's just too painful."

"I'll say!"

Snit, of course.

"What's that!" Julian Axel snaps. "You will inform us, if you *ever* complete *anything!*"

Snit leans in—

"You mean, if I make two-quadrillion dollars on some pre-pubescent fairy-tale about Martin Bormann parking cars in Vegas!"

Immediately, Gary Larry rushes in ... the unwanted U.N.

Peacekeeper.

"Now, now..." he says, raising his two enormous All-State forepaws—either one of which would make a fine sombrero. "Why don't let's all calm right down and have a few drinks."

Numbing silence.

"What's this, then?"

... a new contestant clocking-in.

All turn.

In the dim glow, incomparable Paw Coggins beams handsomely. His instincts are keenly attuned ... he can detect imminent athleticism at a hundred paces.

"Who wants tuh know," says Duane Snit.

Paw chuckles. "It ain't Sandy Koufax...."

"Son of a bitch!" exclaims Thermos. "Paw!"

In truth, Thermos prefers the California Angels. They appeal to his feminine side.

"D'you guys realize..." he drools just the same. "This is only the greatest damn—"

"Oh, pleeeze!" groans Julian Axel, *N.Y. Times* Swell-Seller. "Not a Bushman in the Kalahari doesn't realize!"

Coggins approaches the square table. "And you are?"

"Julian Axel—the novelist." Axel studies Coggins' tanned visage for any sign of a voltage surge. Not a flicker. Neanderthal....

But a new hand shoots forward: "Duane Snit—the diplomat."

Coggins laughs.

He gets it.

They shake.

"And lookie here!" Thermos enthuses now, gazing past Coggins' sainted left paw, "Nature's fairest bosom!"

"I believe that is, 'blossom,'" offers Gary Larry.

Twitty Conway comes juddering in, direct from the Comet. But she looks as if she's been busting steers ... what's that about, ponders Thermos! Twitty hasn't broken a sweat since running behind the Sal Mineo funeral cortege on Highway 101!

In the same moment, approaching now from the mansion, is lovely Lissa Montenero. Cool as Carrara marble, now she waves—a Kodak Moment on the ski lift ... "So what are you all up to?"

Julian Axel's smile gleams like a high-desert lizard taking the noonday sun. "We've been having a liberal exchange of ideas."

Proz smiles blissfully. "There's no limit to what they'll think up!"

Axel eyes her.

Something more had been hoped for.

But Paw's eye is on beautiful Lissa.

And as if brushing a ladybug off his lapel, Twitty steps up to Thermos. "Gerald, where are you at dinner?"

Thermos is all smiles.

Twitty has the best Dagmars in the parking lot—and Checquers has welcomed them all ... Jane Russell, Norma Jeane, Jayne Mansfield, the mature Marlon Brando.

"Wall-lll-uhh, I-yuh..." Thermos replies in an expert collywobbly Jimmy Stewart, "... shorr, Twits ... luv to!"

She giggles. The snazz-o wink he returns commits to far more than there ever really was.

*****

Padding stealthily through shades of night, he eyes it.

The dim rear terrace glimmers afar like a charcoal briquette.

Noiselessly, like Chingachgook, he crosses vast lawns.

Takes cover in lavish shrubs.

Crouches behind grand statuary—of Garbo, Harlow, Harpo.

Drawing near, a coyote in the suburbs, his hunted eyes sear pinholes in night's black muslin. He sees them all.

The City College lunk.

The big-stink novelist.

Thermos and Snit.

And holy pudenda—Twitty ... the wife ... exquisite Lissa!

Lissa's dark hair is swept up, up and away, her cheekbones agleam like the chrome figurine on the Duke's 1929 Hispano-Suiza Dual-Cowl Phaeton. Those classic hood goddesses all had names. Lissa is "Breezy Victory."

He steals closer.

Stumbles on a low branch.

"Shit."

Instantly...

Doomsday squawks.

"Heyyyyy, Lombardo!"

"Halloooo, *Bonzo!*"

"Neddddy-pooooh...."

He shambles in ... a defeated black marlin boated on light tackle.

He's stricken suddenly with an overwhelming thirst—valium and tequila ... there's an idea!

He's met with a raspy male fugue:

"H'llo, old trout."

"Old cheese."

"Old goo."

The Three Horsewomen of the Apocalypse abide, each after her fashion. Lissa—grand gal—betrays no trace of forbidden amour. Twitty smolders with accusation. Proz radiates nothing at all.

Damned if he knows how to return it all with just one face!

Then it dawns—Proz hasn't seen the note! If she had, she'd be doing one-arm push-ups, shrieking like a ruptured boiler!

"Ladies…" he bows, no clue what to feign next.

Securing the note will mean working on Twitty for an hour. Maybe more.

He eyes Lissa … fret not, my sweet, we shall be delayed but an hour. Maybe more.

And she sees it—he sees her seeing it!

She is calm, serene, betraying no hint of the infernos raging below.

Speaking of which … his heartburn is back. He failed again to resist the Duke's Top-Forty pastrami tacos. Noshing them without agony, you have to be half Mexican, half Jewish, and half piranha.

But first things first—the note!

Belly afire in numerous compartments, flames licking at the firedoors abaft his molars, he studies the wife.

Hmm … she looks better than he remembers.

But she turns now. The ladies will adjourn to Checquers' No. Four Cargo Hold to dress for dinner.

Julian Axel offers her his hand. "Are you acquainted with Proust?"

"Yes…" she beams, "we met in La Jolla."

Neddy clicks his tongue. Close enough for California.

Lissa follows Proz, one pace astern, no glance, no sign.

The doyenne of dissembling….

And now he and Twits are alone. He'll face the project belly-to-belly. "Twitty," he smiles, letting his voice drop a steamy half tone, "where are you at dinner?"

She's heard this somewhere recently—

But, oh, yes … it was her.

Yet mindful of marital meltdowns, with all they threaten—and beckon—she won't put Neddy on the bus.

Still, she has so very much on her plate! She thinks of "Zuke," her pet name for Thermos … these rumors start somewhere!

She conjures it now—the deserted Tennis Pavilion & Paddock Club … soft moonglow flowing over "him," her mystery midnight parfait. He presses his male entreaties against her, she sinking into the settee, her naked back pressed down … grating on the scratchy goddamn—

No. She's remembered to spread a terrycloth bath sheet over the coarse vinyl and...

He's insistent—but she remains cool in his clutches.

Nonchalant.

Reaching for her Tequila Mockingbird ... make that a Blue Margarita ... she savors the moonlight, indulging elegant reluctance ... but then, ahhh ... conflicted surrender ... we mustn't, no, mustn't. No, no. Yes. Okay ... no ... ummm, yessss....

She's falling, ohhhh, glorious.

It gets rougher, ravenous-er, going-er and going-er

... really going!

O-wwoooooh, reallyreallllygoing ... he feels so CUTE!

... OHHHH-yesyes ... *HO-HO YOWEE! YOWEE! YOWEE!*

Neddy indulges Twitty's forbidden millisecond...

And she's back!

She nods, as if thumbing through so-so upholstery swatches.

"Honestly, Neddy, I'm not sure where I'm sitting."

She smiles.

"But I think that'd be wonderful!"

She bows. Smiles ... tah-tah.

Gliding into the manse now, riding wing-and-wing on a freshening westerly, her spinnaker is in full bloom.

It comes to her in a flash ... she's a damn rock star!

What a PARTY!

*****

"Hell, you don't!"

"Hell, I do!"

"If you don't, I'm calling Cannizaro!"

"Yeah, that'd be smart. Call Cannizaro why don'tcha!"

Snake Sneave snorts.

"Get Cannizaro on Checquers' phone records ... genius!"

"I'll do it, I swear," nods Ski Kobalefffsky, "unless you get off yer ass and quit playing poker. Help me get this thing on the road, or I'll call!"

"And what good are you—blabbing about the goddamn weather and the goddamn Dodgers ... and the *whooooo*-cares election! You're the one's supposed to find her! All we know is that Lance Fasterbinder—"

"Vance Crankenfuss."

"... he's got no more idea where she is than you! It's your job to find her—get off my back!"

"Okay, okay," Ski nods. "Calm down!"

He waits a beat. "So how much did you win?"

"Plenty!" Snake spits. "More almost than this whole job is worth."

"Bullshit."

"Not bullshit. Twenty-six large, last time I counted, and that's a while ago. I can't afford to quit, these guys're ducks! It's like some horrible nightmare," he grins ghoulishly. "Only I'm the monster!"

Ski studies his shoes. "I did thirty-four large in an hour at blackjack...."

"Yer ass."

Ski nods. "I won for an hour straight—no sign of a pit boss ... spookie."

Snake doesn't care. He's still enjoying the monster he became.

"But we gotta move, Snake—gotta find her. They'll be here any minute! You don't want him to find you sitting on yer ass playing poker, do yuh?"

"Relax, Sue Ann. You find her—that's your job! I'll be right here."

CHAPTER 11

Cave Dwellers

GLIDING UP BEHIND HIM, talons spread, the ducal grasp clasps Neddy's guilt-edged shoulder.

"The jig is *up!*"

Neddy achieves full lift-off!

Duke Monty winks at Battle, Checquers' master barman.

A well-muscled mountain of milk chocolate, Battle is Checquers' ex-star USC Trojan defensive tackle, and so-so Domestic Science major. He emits an operatic laugh now ... Paul Robeson as a steel-drivin' man—mixing multiple Tequila Mockingbirds.

But Neddy would object—hardly cricket mentioning "jigs" around Battle! This may not be just the moment, but Neddy will protest, if not now, in his lifetime.

"Some kinda whack-up you got goin' tonight, Duke!" Battle booms.

The Duke smiles, sunnily unaware of his near brush with the son-in-law's displeasure.

Events suit him down to his heels.

"Keep pumping, my man," he goads the Trojan on. Battle passes them two Kidney Punches, a Checquers specialty—three rums, four fruits.

"Son," says the Duke—on a tight timetable, "... I would have a word."

With no immediate exit strategy, Neddy bows.

They're in Checquers' Star Chamber—dark Tudor hardwood and gleaming marble flooring. The room is named after a storied Elizabethan sanctum where royal inquiries were conducted, judgments rendered, and heads handed down. By this hour of the Great Party, all exhibit the Checquers Gleam ... fish are jumpin' ... cotton's high ... nothin' goin' harm you.

City College avant-garde composer Gerald Schmidt Thermos has celebrated this delicate condition in "The Prodigal Grin," a Gigue for Bassoon, Spoons and Macaw.

Under the Duke's enfolding wing, Neddy is swept afield like a barn mouse. They skirt Ms. Monica Mott and Mrs. Lawrence Fischer. Rabbi Arnold Ziff, of Reformed Temple Bess Myerson, is explaining what Billy Graham has been yowling about all this time ... the news is good!

The next gathering stands five-deep around the same tall dark crud Neddy saw eyeing Lissa out on the rear terrace. He's performing some sort of crackpot calisthenics, flailing one arm out, rotating, and flailing the other arm out.

Tai Chi by Twyla Tharp?

"Duke, who the hell is—"

"Two-Paw Coggins?"

"Who?"

"Oh, my...."

The Duke's talons tighten, directing the lad deeper into the bush.

They pass a man in full South American military regalia ... than which no regalia is fuller nor more military. Generalissimo Virgilio Vicente Jaime Trujillo Batista Zapata de Basanova is detailing, by stadiumsful, the recently vanquished Maoist Shining Path insurgency and other wonders of his native land. Urging increased American aid for still fuller military regalia, he will undertake to crush all Marxists, terrorists, drug lords, and off-campus agitators.

Listening to the Generalissimo intently is City College sophomore Ahmed al Fakhr. Three months prior, needing a third car for his weekend slumming up in Santa Barbara, Ahmed was introduced to auto-sales professional Ken Stukud as "Mr. al Fakhr."

Ken, glowing like the Southern Pacifc Lark in the night, said, "Mind if I call yuh Al?"

"Yes..." said Ahmed.

But no harm, no foul. In twenty minutes, Ahmed, known to all City College as Motha, agreed to a price, signed the papers, and purveyed a check. Business concluded, Motha Fakhr drove off the lot in a three-year-old, four-owner, unrestartable—but gold—Aston Martin Lagonda Touring Sedan.

Of the many Saudi students at City College, Ahmed bears watching, though not for the reason one suspects. An avid devotee of film noir, at the slightest sign of disrespect anywhere in the Lower Forty-Eight, Ahmed restores order by quick-drawing the snub-nose .44 Magnum concealed in his black sharkskin suiting....

Finding a small clearing now, the Duke stops.

Turns.

It's the set piece before every confrontation, gunfight, or exchange of a five for five singles.

*****

Can't reach the li'l dickens!

Peevy grunts, arms akimbo, struggling to fasten her bitter last hook.

"Let me!" commands Lissa Montenero.

Peevy blanches.

She dislikes women whose clavicle meets her at the brow.

But the serene one secures the last anchor-embossed brass batten fastening the rear of Peevy's navy-blue, *W*-endorsed sailor suit. It's a rear-entry item, over-constructed, with darling vertical rows of brass buttons fore and aft, gold epaulets, and a standing gray collar like a sweet little smokestack.

She's a sawed-off Adm. Dewey.

"What a time we're having!" toots Twitty Conway into the full-length mirror across the room. The women are going at it hot and heavy in one of the several Ladies Dressing Chambers on Checquers' third landing.

Proz smiles back at Twitty, stroking her armpits with a wire brush. "Peevy," she says, "do I have a rash?"

"You do now."

But Twitty bubbles on.

"He should throw more of these. Remember in college—he'd have one every month!"

"Those were the days..." Proz sighs, in a mood. "But we were young—anything was possible."

Lissa Montenero turns. "You sound like Zelda at Juan-les-Pins."

"Zelda Lipschitz?" says Peevy.

"Fitzgerald."

Done with her!

But not to be intimidated, Peevy presses on. "Don't be sad, Proz, look at all you have—a loving father, freedom to do as you please, go where you please, buy all the clothes you like ... a husband."

Clunk.

In the ensuing silence, Peevy nods ... "Lissa, your seams are crooked."

"I know."

Witch!

Yet Proz knows Peevy's moody state.

"Darling," she says, "out on the terrace, I saw Gerald Thermos making eyes at you again."

Peevy snorts. "He makes eyes at road-kill."

"That's cold," says Twitty.

"They all do."

"Whoever 'they' are," says Lissa, brushing out her shimmering hair. Her dark-green eyes devour the image in the mirror.

"All he ever does is stare," Peevy shrugs.

"Maybe he just hasn't had the right opportunity," Proz proposes.

"Opportunity!"

Peevy tugs indignantly at her misaligned left epaulette—

There! Ready for Fleet Inspection.

"We all know the truth, don't we," she says.

And Proz hears it coming...

"I'm a runt," Peevy blurts, "are you blind!"

All claim 20/20 vision.

"Peevy, Peevy..." croons Proz.

"I'm standing in a hole!"

Peevy dissolves in hopeless sobs.

All three are at her side ... Twitty last by a Kleenex.

"There, now—"

"There, there—"

"There, there, there—"

She regains her composure.

"I feel so much better," she glugs unpleasantly, like swallowing chlorine in the pool. "All I need is dear friends like you..." she lies through her teeth—all of which sparkle like the star in Maurice Chevalier's eye.

"There, now..." they coo.

"There, there."

"There, um ... now, now."

Business suitably resolved...

It's Showtime!

Proz wears a safe skirt and sane blouse—Outfit No. Four, and counting. She twirls once like Loretta Young opening the show. "Yes?"

"Yesss..." all comply.

Twitty sets her canines. "Okay, ladies—over the top!"

With a harsh last glance at the mirrors, they step into the hall like dysfunctional geese, little Peevy first, next Twitty, taller Proz ... Lissa majestically last. In the hall's low light, she wears her mystery smile, gently aglow like a masthead light in harbor fog.

They're halfway down to the second landing, when—

A harried man in a barrage of warring plaids rushes upstairs.

Selects the smallest target.

"'Scuse—"

"'Scused," says Peevy.

"Where's the john?"

"You have the wrong person," says Twitty.

She nods behind her.

He smiles. "You'll be Proz."

"I seem to be..." she nods, concerned at his blinding color scheme. "Meet the Misses Peevy Palmtry, Twitty Conway, Lissa Montenero."

"Ken Stukud," he beams.

"Stupid?"

"No. Lowe & Stukud Used Cars."

Lissa laughs from her belly ... and blushes plum red.

Nice to know she can.

"Sabado Bingo, corner Camino Carne," Ken notes.

Peevy is radiant.

"... next time I need a stupid used car."

"Come on down! About the can...."

Not Cañon Perdido, they are agreed. Headmistress Pimblitzer confided, we shan't all be!

Proz nods up to the next landing. "Third door on the left. There's no sign—this isn't a hotel, you know, though I sometimes—"

"Oughta be! Duke'd make a bundle."

The silence of Giza....

*****

Ken Stukud bounds up to the next landing—he's put this off way too long.

Third door on the left.

But which left!

He shoves a third door open and—

Bloody-murder shrieeeeeeeks!

... ladies in panties and bras scurrying every-damn-where!

"Ooops..." he guffaws winsomely. "Sorry all."

He proffers a wink.

"Out!"

"What's done is done—"

"Get ... OUT!"

"Will I see you all at dinner...."

"*NOW?*"

He tries the "other" third door on the left—the one across the landing beyond the stairs.

Just as unmarked ... not his fault!

At last, a long satisfying splatter, before he can even smile.

Pheeeeewww.

Next amusement!

But he isn't done with this one...

She comes bowling down the main hall not quite antelopean—the volumetrically enticing Ms. Twitty Conway.

"Whassamatter..." he says. "Forget somethin' pricey?"

She blushes—or takes a first mincing step in that direction.

Meets his eye directly.

"I put something on too tight."

She dares him, and he looks.

Still looking.

He chuckles. "Your gloves?"

She grins. "If you say so."

"Say, Twitty—" He's been meaning to track her down, anyways—Bam Terwilliger, tennis pal of Archer Conway, Twitty's ol' man, tipped that Miz Conway needs wheels—and not just any damn wheels! Ken has the exactly-right pale-blue Saab convertible down on the lot ... low miles, four wheels ... make her a deal she can't bear!

"Glad we ran into each other," he serves. "Bam told me all about you."

"What about me...."

"How you're an outdoorsy, sporty number—likes the open air, and all."

The "sporty" has her checking for the exits.

But in Ken's defense, his mind never strays far from the creampuff pale-blue Saab ragtop ... though she surely is the Deluxe Trim Package.

Some Buick in her—but he's no Cadillac his ownself.

Wouldn't even hate himself afterwards.

He winks. "Where you sitting at dinner?"

She thinks of many things, of Thermos and Neddy and the Man in the Moon. She considers Neddy's note—but, oh, hell, she's in a party mood. Checquers does that. Neddy can't help making her betray her best friend ... nobody's fault.

She glimpses again the moonlit settee in the Tennis Center, terrycloth bath sheet laid out ... transistor radio low and dreamy....

"Ken, I think that would be smashing!" she says.

But lose the orange socks.

"Boss!" booms Ken.

It's one of the interior dialects ... means "okay."

She had a boyfriend from Modesto. Once.

Meanwhile, Ken settles on a price. 'Course, at this clambake Saab convertible prices could go waaaay craaaazy high!

At dinner, he anticipates a lively exchange on monthly payments.

*****

Neddy and the Duke stand toe-to-toe in the Bijou.

The great man meets Neddy's eye. "So what about it?"

"About what?"

The Duke traces the Bijou's elegant sculpted ceiling moldings. Checquers' acclaimed cinema and performance salon is sparsely populated at this hour. After the banquet, it'll be jammed with well-fed revelers.

And when Liza's in town ... it's "The Cabaret."

"I mean to say, son, how do things stand between you and Proz? Is she—"

Ned doesn't hold back. "The inevitable clash of souls, she likes to say."

"Yes—and you, what do you like to say?"

"Really, Duke, everything I try to do, I just catch a batch."

"Catch a batch...."

The Duke rolls it around on his tongue.

"I like that."

But he modulates. "I worry about her, you know."

"You and me both, Duke."

"Yes?"

"She's so excitable!"

He has to say something!

They're just about to get somewhere when, suddenly, the drive-in-movie-sized flat-screen TV on the Bijou wall goes: *PPPlink!*

A high-pitched electronic whine bores into Neddy's medulla oblongata.

The monster flat-screen TV is an engineering prototype vouchsafed the Duke decades before its release to the public. Widely thought to be Japanese, its world-famous manufacturer is quietly—undetectably—owned by one of the Duke's many offshore holding companies.

Santa Lola Channel Three Action News flickers onto the great screen now, featuring KooKie-Krazie-KorKie, KBUX-TV's beloved zany meteorologist. He gestures outlandishly at a featureless Santa Lola weather map—there will be no change. Today is like yesterday, like Tuesday, like May 14th. All that changes is KooKie-Krazie-KorKie's clown nose. It's purple in August, yellow in September.

Tonight, in the shank of autumn, it's a moody burnt umber.

Yet here comes KooKie—no clown nose—sauntering into the Bijou now!

No mystery. He records his weekly weather segments Monday

morning. He's done in time for a late lunch at Joe's Café, followed by his holistic Chiro-Eugenic Rejuvenation Seance at Santa Lola's Green Earth Life-Beauty Continuarium.

"Kook!" nods the Duke.

"Duke!" nods the Kook.

Splendid.

But twigging the Duke is busy, Kook moves on.

The Duke steps four paces ahead, intending Neddy to step four paces ahead.

Neddy knows it and steps three.

The great man turns. "We're very close, you know, Proz and I. That must be hard for you … that we're so close."

Ned savors the delicacy of injured affections—dabbing an experimental toe in this psychotherapeutic after-school mud puddle.

"Well?" invites the Duke.

"Sometimes she treats me like I'm only in it for the thirteen trillion."

"Oh, my!"

The Duke laughs.

Takes another run at it. "Oh … my!"

"I don't see what's so funny."

"My, my, lad, thirteen, you say … such a lugubrious number!"

The Duke's chuckle is fathoms down in his throat.

He takes a sip of Kidney Punch.

"You mustn't pay any attention to the cave-dwellers at *Fawkes!*"

He refers to the celebrated "World's 20 Richest" cover story in the recent issue of *Fawkes Magazine*, the breathlessly earnest white-shoes Wall Street financial journal.

"They get the order right—mostly," he says. "Beyond that, they're just bobbing for apples! We've made substantial improvements since thirteen trillion, oh, my, yes."

Neddy nods reflexively—the conscientious woodpecker plying his trade.

"Yes, yes," beams the Duke, "… I should say!"

Then, Burtie's right, thinks Ned—it's more … who knows how much!

And at least the old chanterelle has the decency to say so!

"You see what I'm saying don't you," the Duke nods. "Yes, I'm sure you do."

Neddy smiles reflexively—without a clue.

"You two are going to inherit far too much for it ever to be any kind of an issue … not of any sort!"

The Duke's smile warms.

Beneficent would be one of its characterizations.

"There's plenty of plenty, Ned. Nothing whatever for anyone to worry about. I want you both to relax and enjoy yourselves as you live out your young lives together. I hope you will give each other the very greatest pleasure humanly possible."

Humanly possibly.

Neddy sniffs around in it for clues.

"Remember, son, I was married thirty-four long years."

Neddy's still sniffing.

"I was a very lucky man—exceptionally lucky. I loved Constance deeply. But having said that, I know too well what 'humanly' means, if you take my point."

"Of course," Neddy nods, lying through his fedora.

He wishes he hadn't—but there was no halting it.

"I hope you two will take the very best care of each other, don't you see."

"Of course," Neddy nods, too automatically.

"Fine, then," the Duke nods, too automatically.

"If there is ever any way I can help, Neddy—anything at all—I hope you will not hesitate to let me know."

His eye narrows.

"No marriage is easy—not even the easiest."

Neddy is about to speak, but the Duke's hand comes up.

"I don't want you to feel you have to say anything, son."

"No, no…" Neddy says.

They nod, the confab at an end, both keenly aware it fell well short of the mark.

CHAPTER 12

Ripe

A GOOD DISTANCE FROM Neddy and the Duke in the Bijou ... due east at the approaches to the grand rear terrace, Twitty Conway, three suitors on ice ... is reeling a fourth to the gaff.

Keita Mammady Fallo, blissfully solo, smiles agreeably up at her. His *National Review* is open at the back cover. Only the Personals—his favorite—remain to be read.

"What's this, then?" accuses Twitty, speaking for Santa Lola, Tuna Vista, and the Greater Platinum Coast.

"Miss?"

"Why are you reading at this hour?"

She smiles gloriously.

"What is it you have there, anyway ... mmmmm?"

He holds up the magazine.

He's beginning to think it's banned.

But Twitty beams brightly. "Oh, I love humor magazines!"

"You are mistaken, Miss, it is—"

"No need to explain ... anything that is humorous—I love to laugh!"

She laughs musically—selling it.

"Yes..." Fallo nods. "But this is not a humor magazine."

"With a name like that—has to be!"

"No."

Sobered, she regards the traitorous journal anew.

And Fallo is matter-of-fact.

"It's very serious, actually—all except this." He points to an editorial column near the front. "Droll ... very piquant."

"Is it..." she frowns.

He assures her it is.

She's not certain she's enjoying this.

And he has a pipey singsong delivery—she will investigate further.

"You're not from around here."

"Pretoria," he says.

"Where?"

"South Africa."

"Oh, my God, I'm sorry!"

"Everyone is sooo sorry!"

He laughs quietly.

"We're hardly perfect, it is true, but you must be sorry for the tens of thousands in the lands to our north flocking to my country seeking employment. They are like the Mexicans flooding across your southern border for work."

"Mexicans? Here?"

He holds up the magazine. "You should read—it is all right here, and quite correct."

"Yes, but...."

She allows it to straggle lamely off into the bush.

... but Fallo follows its spoor.

"Apartheid? Yes, it is very wrong—completely!"

She nods sharply. "Very déclassé!"

He smiles and nods, as if recalling memories from childhood. "But it will pass. And there are other difficulties very nearly as bad—enormous crime ... terrible violence in the streets."

"You are amazing!" says Twitty Conway.

"Very ordinary, really."

"What's your name anyways?"

They introduce themselves...

And immediately find nothing to say.

But she likes this fetching, compact phenomenon.

Adorable.

"Listen, Mr. Fallo, would you be my guest at dinner?"

"I already am."

"No, no, no. I mean at the private dinner, the one with the Duke!"

"Oh, no, I do not think I must do that."

"Why not! Starts at eight. The Duke would love to meet you!"

"You are too kind."

"I won't take no for an answer!"

She won't.

"I leave you to your reading, then—but I'll see you at dinner!"

And she is off.

*****

Isn't It Romantic ... Rodgers and Hart with strings.

The lilting refrain *whhisssssss-es* round and round in Twitty's cranial ballroom.

Harp glissandos warm balmy tropic breezes in her head ... *daah-de-de-de-daah-dah....*

One dinner—four men!

Dah-de-de-de-daah-dah, dah-de-de-dee-yyyump-tee-ump-tah-DAAAAAH....

Four different, fascinating men—count 'em ... FOUR!

Pining.

Sighing.

Twitty stands on the peripheries of...

Yes, the Santa Lola Arts Round Table is at it again.

Ten-foot-tall Gary Larry has just read a free-verse manifesto, "Apache Quiche." Soft-pawed applause brings Twitty gently 'round.

But Duane Snit finishes the job ... "You mean, that's IT!"

"That's it," smiles Gary Larry, gratified.

"... quiche gives the Apache indigestion?"

The poet smiles. They've grasped its full irony.

"Proof positive," Snit nods. "Those who can, do—those who can't, teach!"

"Yes!" blurts Twitty, blissfully unawares. "City College is filled with that!"

But what does she care....

Fuddled, distracted, thoughts teeming, a-swirl in joyful abandon ... she flits off now, farther and farther along the terrace.

... drifting, drifting

... *isn't it romantic....*

The night ... cool ... entrancing ... a wet tongue on her neck—

Is it real?

Yessss!

Darkened trees, shadowy shrubs in the garden...

night spirits in a fantasy of—

but

... male footfalls

Coming fast!

She seeks cover.

... except the damn lights.

Crap!

"Twitty, dear!" she hears up ahead.

He's crashing along in heavy brogans, loud Madras blazer at full volume, black horn-rim glasses fronting coal-black pupils ... real-estate dreamboat Vern Jerms!

"But Vern," she protests, "aren't you supposed to be—"

He is!

This very minute, he's supposed to be delivering humor, enlightenment, and lovable larceny at the real-estate loan-application seminar!

He confides it to Twitty: "Keep the customer on the razor!"

He winks.

"... see what I mean?"

"But you have a whole damn lecture hall full of—"

"Exactly, my beauty."

He scans her frankly, top to bottom ... she'll do.

She knows....

daah-tee-tee-tee-daaaah-dmmmm....

He grins back—irresistibly.

"I'm only a smidge late, Twits—they eat it up, trust me. People hate lectures ... even lectures they love!"

"I certainly do."

Vern Jerms gleams like a gold tooth.

"You're special, Twits ... special. I'd hitch-hike to Guadalavista on a foggy night in a wetsuit and flippers just to barbecue you Saturday dinner ... I mean it, now, darlin'."

tee-yummmp....

"I hate real estate," she says, on a blind impulse.

"Nobody hates real estate."

"I do!"

"Who said we'd talk real estate?"

"What, then?"

"The moon!"

"Are parts of it for sale?"

"The stars!"

"Out of my price range."

"To a beautiful woman ... the stars are slaves."

Four men bagged, another begging crumbs!

"How's your wife, Vern."

"You're precious..." he beams, impervious.

"Okay, Mr. Horns. The Boy Scout Manual recommends a cold hip-bath."

"A beauty like you reading the Boy Scout Manual!"

She turns away sharply, headed for parts un-Vernal.

And she hears it now, broad-billed size-twelves hammering the flagstones in the opposite direction, headed to the seminar.

About time!

His public awaits, erasers in hand.

He's flown across her ceiling from time to time ... but she has four men already—Neddy and Zuke and Stupid and Hutu!

She strides the long curving terrace—indisputably ripe!

On a sudden impulse, she reaches into her bodice and digs out the scrap of notepaper from Neddy.

Silly boy. They all make mistakes.

And they aren't all tall, dark and flammable like Neddy.

But what about Proz....

What about her!

All the way back into Cañon Perdido Middle School, Proz's luck with boys stinks!

Twitty folds the note over and over until it's the size of a small, fat postage stamp.

Drops it behind a hedge.

There!

With the innate grace of the Conways, she glides into the the ducal castle of dreams now, bound for glory ... ripe, ready, a California Golden ... rich dessert for some lucky man.

Maybe two—it's the Eighties!

tee-yummp-tuh-daaah....

CHAPTER 13

Contact Sport

CANNIZARO AND PULPO look at each other.

It doesn't help—so they look away.

It helps.

Angus Cannizaro is four-feet-twenty—which isn't true at all, he's five-feet-eight. But he comes off shorter. It's something in his style. He's natty, dapper, well-tailored, 155 pounds—all the things he shouldn't be.

And everything he should be ... Pulpo is—big, glum, threatening, unpredictable. Pulpo has a church-key upper lip and pot-holed skin ... he's stubborn, impulsive, cruel, and just thick enough not to know it.

But with the two of them together, Angus Cannizaro, four-feet-twenty, is the most terrifying man you met all year. He can do *anything* to you ... or Pulpo will ... and never muss his tie.

But looks aren't everything. Take right now.

They're standing inside the entrance of Checquers' measureless Constance Room, no idea where to begin. They're like Ski and Snake when they first arrived, except Cannizaro and Pulpo haven't had the good fortune to stumble onto familiar turf in Bigg Casino. And standing in the palatial awe of the great Constance Room now trying to make sense of things ... Angus Cannizaro is getting angrier and angrier.

"Fix yer shirt!" he snaps, at Pulpo's pale-blue, rough-and-tumble chambray workshirt. "Where the hell you think you are—Rose Café!"

Pulpo tucks in. Cannizaro can get that way.

And Pulpo wishes it *was* Rose Café ... good chile verde, no phonies.

The boss keeps his cool there mostly.

"I know what," Pulpo says.

91

"What...."

"We could ask."

"Ask what!"

"This big-ass beer hall hasta have a public-address—we could page him!"

"Just shut up, Pulpo."

To Cannizaro's eye, Checquers' impossibly vast, high-ceilinged Constance Room is bigger than Union Station, and everyone looks like they're catching a train but they're late—except him and Pulpo.

They don't know what they're catching!

The Constance Room engulfing them honors the Duke's elegant late wife. It is the pattern of everything that makes Checquers supreme. During the day, Niagaras of light cascade through its leaded windows high along the north, west, and south walls. The cathedralic ceiling hovers impossibly high, its massive, dark ceiling timbers decorated in simple, glowing Moorish floral motifs of orange, bright red, yellow and royal blue. Underfoot, an immense inland sea of elegant cranberry tile stretches off endlessly, two-thirds of it covered by a stupendous scarlet, gold, beige and black oriental. Hand-stitched together onsite from eight huge sections, it is famously the largest Persian on "the planet."

The sheer volume of the great space, definitively more than a "room," separates naturally into lesser and grander spheres of focus. Furnished with an enormous array of cheerful floral settees and Chesterfields arranged in smaller, then larger, conversation pits, the room reflects the late Constance's gracious welcoming spirit.

Two inviting fieldstone fireplaces hold forth in the cool of evening, or whenever the outside temperature conspires to fall below 60 degrees. The first fireplace, in the center of the north wall, is small and cozy, ideal for Assam tea, crumpets with preserves, and a good book. But the other fireplace—in a different area code down at the far south end—is cavernous, a gaping great Elizabethan hearth nine-feet high and to the manor born.

A handful of yards farther west beyond the great hearth's joyous conflagration, comfy burgundy-leather recliners welcome all to enjoy cabernet, Kobe steak tartare, and the consummate glory of the Santa Lola sunset ... the envy of the entire non-Communist world.

The Constance Room is graced throughout with priceless art, including three immense medieval tapestries, six El Grecos, seven Rembrandts, and countless other instances representing the genius of Rubens, Holbein and a constantly revolving cast of medieval and Renaissance masters. A similarly ever-changing galaxy of Impressionists rotates through the central region of the Constance Room, while far to the east, in the atmospheric quarter known as "Café Bleecker," a dozen stark, hugely impactful works of New York Expressionism make their bravely uncompromising statements.

Sculpture by Rodin, Calder, Giacometti, Brancusi and Henry Moore are scattered throughout, interspersed with pieces of art glass and smaller objets d'art. And just inside the main entrance, in the place of honor, is a stunning collection of wedding vases, jars, and platters in black and beige from San Ildefonso and Santa Maria Pueblos. Hand-formed and fired one hour—and 400 years—north of Santa Fe, many of these exquisite devices were created by the immortal Maria herself, a personal friend and favorite of Constance.

Also near the main entrance is a splashy, measurelessly exuberant twelve-foot-high, multi-tiered Alhambra fountain. In gleaming indigo-and-white tile, this playful waterfall brightens all the space nearby with its joyously clattering music.

But when suggestible young Proz lingers too long within earshot, she needs to pee.

The great miracle of the Constance Room is the blissful harmony of its many contrasting eras, schools, and moods. An important, widely read interior-décor monograph has been written on the Constance Room's sublime spiritual accord.

But Checquers' recognition of the arts doesn't end with the Constance Room. A priceless Matisse Retrospective is currently on display in Checquers' 790,000-volume Library and the immense adjoining Conservatory. This exhibit arrived at Checquers after weeks at the Met in New York, one of many peerless displays cycling through the mansion—the world's premier museums anxious to repay the Duke's ongoing, vital, and bounteous largesse.

The Matisses themselves view their stay at Checquers as welcome respite, before the raucous hordes begin filing past in Rio de Janeiro....

Amid the Constance Room crowds, all hurrying to and fro, Pulpo sees Cannizaro is out of ideas ... and they really could ask.

"I just thought—" he begins.

"Don't think, Pulpo ... don't think!"

Pulpo knows exactly what he's going to say back—

But doesn't. The boss is on edge—tonight is big.

But he knows exactly what he would say, and on another night, he'd say it!

Instead, he listens to the splashy waters of the big-ass tile fountain, wondering, is there maybe a john somewhere near?

*****

"*PEE-VEE!*" Proz commands.

But immediately her voice melts, going all lambie-pie.

"... what was it you said, dearest?"

"My hair!" Peevy blurts. "I look like a rat!"

"No, Peeve, I—"

"I need a hotter dryer—or maybe a flamethrower!"

... if she could just get her hair LUXURIANT! She sees him clear as a windy day in Carmel, her bartender pleasure-boy ... five-feet-nine in running shoes, with the darling-est little turned-up nose, and abs like corn-on-the-cob....

But Proz's head shakes insistently.

"No, Peevy, you said something about husbands!"

"... come, Peevy," Lissa implores now.

"Oh, crap," Twitty barges in, "what she said was—"

"No, no ... wait!" Peevy giggles—the center of the whole, entire universe! "I said, even if he is one ... never call your husband a liar."

Lissa glimmers. "No, that wasn't quite it."

She's not even married, thinks Peevy—what does she know ... porcelain Watusi!

The ladies are seated in Checquers' brilliant, crowded Third Living Room. (There is no First or Second Living Room, a puzzlement the key to which died with dead-as-a-doornail Cyrus Rutt.) They sit now studying husbands' heads, necks, and buttocks, looking for liars.

The candidates circulate freely before them, members of The Two Hundred—invitees to Duke Monty's celebrated private banquet. In Checquers' distant east wing, the hoi polloi will dine at their leisure in the rowdy, good-natured Hunt Room. They will have a better time of it, some say—but not Neddy. On being rich or poor, he knows rich is better ... at least, less labor-intensive.

"Come, now, Peevy," beautiful Lissa insists, "tell us again."

Peevy eyes Lissa's auburn, LUXURIANT hank.

Oh, hell....

"I saw it on The Late Late Show," she begins, "I can't remember the exact movie ... yes I can, *Wife vs. Secretary*. Clark Gable is married to Myrna Loy, and he's on the verge of cheating with his secretary. She's Jean Harlow, and we all know what that means—but believe it or don't ... he's not!"

Peevy snorts dismissively like a diesel mechanic spitting chaw.

"Anyways, Myrna Loy gets an eyeful of Harlow and suspects the worst—in fact, knows it! And right at the end, after she's falsely accused Gable of cheating, he's talking to Harlow, and says—"

Peevy pokes-in her cheeks with her forefingers, indicating the signature Gable dimples....

"He says, 'There's an old Chinese proverb, my dear—If you want to keep a man honest, never call him a liar.'"

Lissa Montenero's smile is like sunrise over Diamond Head.

Peevy nods. "Like I said ... never call a man a liar, even if he is."

"Well..." Lissa begins, her eye on the far horizon.

But she'll let it slide.

"And I never would," says Proz, a woman acquainted with grief.

They stare at her like a nude butler.

"Neddy has his ways..." she says.

"But he's really very simple."

"The simplest!" blurts Peevy.

Peevy's been doing a lot of blurting today.

"Now, wait just a damn minute!" Twitty objects, rising to the defense of a gender that is her fondest admirer. "You speak of Neddy, and men, in general, like scummy pond life!"

Proz grins. "I never said, scummy."

Peevy giggles.

"Oh, come awwwn," Twitty bays, "don't you ever want to just—"

All wait.

"... slide under the first one you see?"

"TWITTY CONWAY!" Peevy blurts.

"I wouldn't put it quite that way..." Lissa allows. "But then, just how would I put it?"

Proz, a Monarchist, will hold her peace.

"Look," Twitty nods, "who are the hypocrites here?"

Peevy's completely forgotten her hair, "You're saying ... us!"

"Peevy, you've been waiting months for someone to dust you off!"

"Don't be crude," Proz giggles.

"Well," Lissa smiles, "who wouldn't—"

She laughs from her belly. "... enjoy a nice dusting off!"

Even Proz laughs now.

"Listen," Proz says now, eyeing each of them, one by one, "... I'm married."

Good, so far.

"With a husband who either is or isn't—"

... yes?

"A liar."

She nods—all in.

"But I take my vows extremely seriously."

"As surely you must!" says Peevy, foursquare for home and hearth.

"If Neddy is—well ... you know—"

They know.

"Must I be a shameless slut to get even?"

Behind Proz's shoulder, his back to her, but not his ears ... Chester Halimony nods, as if to Clive O.E.M. Monogram's mindless blather. But

95

he's not hearing a word—he hangs on Proz's every syllable.

Monogram, too, jabbers on and on, listening to Proz over his own palaver.

"Cheating is no joke!" Proz avows.

Halimony leans hard to port, nearly pouring dark rum down Proz's sweet back.

"Nonsense," Twitty snaps. "I say we do as men do!"

Lissa smirks. "You mean, snore afterwards?"

All laugh—inluding Halimony.

(Monogram is not amused.)

But seeing Halimony laugh—and suspecting the worst—Peevy shoots him a withering glare.

Immediately, he engages Monogram on the upside of AT&T common, Monogram nodding, nodding—his own glare meeting Peevy.

She sees she was mistaken.

"They're always saying it," Proz says, "Don't get mad—get even!"

"Disgraceful!" says Peevy, not failing to admire its felicitous elements.

The women hear quiet rustling.

Turn.

Halimony has leaned in entirely too far.

He's on one knee, wiping dark rum and tonic from his Gucci loafer with his cocktail napkin ... the only conceivable utility for the idiotic scrap.

He looks up.

Smiles.

All smile back.

"Near term..." he says, "I'm bearish on General Motors."

"Not at all!" booms Clive....

"So getting even..." Peevy says now, "how do I go about it!"

The li'l dickens!

The women erupt in peals of forbidden laughter....

It's Monogram on a knee, daubing scotch off his oxblood oxford.

"Seriously!" Peevy snaps, paying him no mind.

"Don't worry, Peeve..." Lissa says, "you'll find a way."

The moment collapses of its own weight—each woman alone again with her destiny.

Now they hear Monogram, chortling heartily.

Halimony is laughing, too—

Confirming everything.

Clive Monogram hasn't said anything funny since Pre-K!

But immediately, all hear it—klonggg-klonggg-klonggg ... the Grand Refectory mission bell to dinner.

Twitty eyes Proz.

What is she to do!

Neddy is handsome, swarthy, wound tight as a snapped towel.

And Twitty is nigh thirty, staring down the dark, deep, barren void.

Obediently, she migrates along the main hall with her bosom companions. She'll make the best of things. Tonight, she has a pride of suitors competing for her favor—and why not?

Striding into the Grand Refectory, heart a-tingle, she's alive with excitement, curiosity, ambition, vindication, joy, bravado ... and cold, cold feet.

*****

Farther along the main hall, an exchange occurs.

"Hi, I'm Paw Coggins."

"Really."

"The pitcher."

"Of all the Paw Coggins' ... that one!"

Lissa Montenero deals a smile—the most that can be said for it.

"I know it's the oldest line there is..." he says.

"Then, why use it?"

"But haven't we met? You look vaguely familiar."

"That's vaguely flattering."

"Then, I'm not just dreaming?"

She laughs. "Did you really say that!"

"I thought it was vaguely flattering."

"Where's your entourage tonight?"

"No idea what you mean."

"The bimbos in Marina Del Rey."

He proffers an unashamed laugh.

"In Marina Del Rey, probably. I gave them the night off. Want to join?"

"I think not."

"Do they bother you?"

"Should they?"

His deep laugh thunders. "Like poison!"

Not a bad laugh, she can admit.

"On the level," he says. "Where did we meet?"

"Last spring at Rancho Palos Verdes. Justin Case's party."

"Which one—he's had several."

"And you preserved my memory through all those many crowded parties."

He smiles winsomely.

Receives a dime in change.

"Am I bothering you?" he says.

"As I say, we've met."

His unfailing smile fails. "You never told me your name."

"You never asked."

"I'm asking."

She tells him, and he offers his right paw.

"Next time I'll do better."

With the slightest of bows, he withdraws.

*****

The Santa Lola Arts Round Table, taking time to clean and oil its weapons, reconvenes on the rear terrace.

And Gary Larry, "feeling" City College Lecturer, footballist, and regional poet, is pleased to announce a blessed event.

"I just wrote it at the bar."

"Ooooo..." enthuses Celia Oddthorpe.

She loves anything fresh-caught.

A unisex Curate at the Cathedral Church of St. Biff In The Trees, Celia wears a white clerical collar with her black fleece L.L. Bean smock.

"Very excellent," affirms musical hepster Gerald Schmidt Thermos.

A sidelong glance is the most novelist Julian Axel will invest.

All eyes turn now to Abstract Expressionistic family-portraitist Duane Snit. But at this point in the drinking...

They turn away again.

Gary Larry is pleased. "I'll just read the first six pages."

my volkswagen heart

> flat-opposing
> boxer four,
> a-clatter in
> motive despair,
> tetraethyl
> soul sparking foul,
> oh misfiring
> heart, my stalwart
> symphony of
> cacaphony.

> bald and tireless
> I ply my bias—

"Nah-nah-nah," growls Snit, *"... awwwright!"*

He's had enough.

Gary Larry, inured to illegal chop-blocks, horse-collar tackles, and iniquitous officiating, stoically returns the idyll to his backpack. It's new, after all, it may need a re-read. [Blank-verse enthusiasts will find the complete text in *Oil Changes*: Larry, Gary, Santa Lola Vocational University Press, 1984.]

A matter of substance now coming to mind, Golden Madres No. 78 excuses himself to the men's.

The ensuing silence lasts long enough to need a haircut.

Finally, Gerald Schmidt Thermos opens with a dime: "I, too, have been working—"

Immediately interrupted by Duane Snit, "You sound like D'Islesdeaux ... I, too, *'ave bee-een wohhrrr-keeeeng....*"

"Oh, Duane, do fuck off," chortles Thermos agreeably.

"Oooks!" he nods now, with a bow to Curate Oddthorpe. "Pardon my French."

Celia Oddthorpe smiles. She's heard the word.

In Hong Kong, it was.

"I'm working on an avant-garde marching band," Thermos proceeds, rekindling the flame.

"Oh, my!" Celia Oddthorpe smiles.

She loves a parade.

"One hundred pieces," boasts Thermos, "... seventy drummers, six nude majorettes, and five pyrotechnicians on rhythm firecracker."

"You said, one hundred..." Julian Axel says. "That's eighty-one."

Axel is good with numbers—does his own taxes.

"There is the surprise!" Thermos booms. "The rest is an all-male goose-stepping nude Bugle Corps!"

"Ohhh!" approves Celia—Episcopalian and unafraid.

"Imagine," Thermos gushes, "all marching up Avenida Murrieta!"

"Amazing..." concedes Duane Snit—a broken man.

"And firecrackers!" Celia Oddthorpe beams. "Gol-leee!"

Thermos is elated. He'll give this some thought. Like the Rockettes the key is to find nineteen well-matched men ... unless, for the ladies, variety is the spice of life! He'll ask Peevy at dinner.

"But what would the frog *theeenk?*" Snit puts in nastily. "He *ees* never around when you ... *neeed heeem.*"

"He went home, Duane. Hates the sight of you," Julian Axel says. "Can't really blame him."

Duane Snit sets down his Tequila Mockingbird.

"Listen, Tennessee ... if you ever get up out of that goddamn chair,

I'll sit you right down again in a fucking great hurry!"

Hong Kong ... Celia Oddthorpe is certain.

A mahjongg tournament.

But this time Julian Axel—the better for his bourbon—comes resolutely to his feet.

Ditto Duane Snit!

And with no outsized football lunk onsite to direct traffic—

Lay on, Macduff!

Fists fly, shattering chairs, tables, cocktail napkins, thin air.

The carnage is squalid.

An agonizing groan escapes Duane Snit. Attempting a wanton head-butt, he missed Julian Axel, and hit an oaken post.

He slumps precipitously...

But Julian Axel is on him like a tick.

They strain.

Grunt.

Tumble illogically like loaded dice.

... and Gary Larry is taking suspiciously long in the men's.

Snarling Snit and battling Axel struggle apart, punishing "the Ecology."

Snuffling,

scowling,

sprawling,

they Indian-wrestle brutishly across the flagstones like red-faced lobsters—

When in he rushes ... Golden Madres' No. 78 Gary Larry—not an hour too soon!

Moving with uncommon frisk, he towers over the holocaust.

Seeing neither player holds any cards, his derrick-like left arm prizes Duane Snit's neck briskly—raising him straight up in the air!

Fists felicitously free,

Duane Snit swings wildly at Julian Axel's passing head...

Smashing to pieces an elegant Mission-style lamp fixture.

(Replaced by dinner—it's Checquers.)

Ducking Snit's failed blow, Julian Axel crashes into an end table...

Reducing it to kindling.

(Replacement end tables are on back order.)

Sprawling haplessly rearwards like a crab...

Julian Axel smashes his funny bone on the flagstone—

"AAAAAaaa*yyyaaa*-cckkk!"

Grimacing in agony, he holds his forearm away from him like a spoiled bratwurst.

Gary Larry sets Duane Snit down on his flailing knees—

and in a consummate fury, Julian Axel lunges.

He would pull the pestilent painter's pate from its pus-engorged trunk!

Skillfully, Gary Larry belays an Axel right cross—

Just as Duane Snit, winding up massively behind Gary Larry's back as if to hurl the grandfather's clock down the front hall…

Thrusts his fist up to the elbow in Julian Axel's undefended belly.

"*VV-vvvoooouuusssshhhh!*" Julian Axel replies—

Liberating breath first ingested during the Carter Years.

Staggering out to the rail now…

Axel bends over headfirst to decant an excellent rarebit, taken with a so-so pinot blanc on July 4th….

Gary Larry stands back, taking stock.

Both combatants reel now in self-inflicted calamity.

Julian Axel pants between retches

… coughs

… spits

… *glutches.*

Duane Snit, meanwhile, inventories instruments of mortal force mistakenly left in his Datsun pickup—one claw hammer, in particular.

Julian Axel gasps, his lungs straining to include whole quadrants of the hemisphere.

His short-circuited funny bone clatters in his skull like cable-car bells in distress … *crannggggk*-kuh-*clang, crannggggg-crannggggg.*

Emetic electrical surges **beeeezzzzz** up and down his spine.

He seeks, in vain, a graceful way to display a final quart of clam chowder.

Meantime, "feeling" Gary Larry turns to Celia Oddthorpe.

"I'm sorry."

"Fucking all right," she says.

She's a rock.

"Fucking fine," she affirms. "Art is a contact sport."

Deeply grateful, Gary Larry feels something untoward towards her.

"Glll-*llecccchh* … hoooo-*ettttttch* … *ptt-pttt-ptttt*," says Julian Axel…

At last … the banana-cream pie!

"SSSS-ssss-ssss-ssss…" sniggers Duane Snit.

Measured in liters, he is the clear victor.

Yet Julian Axel will cease vomiting.

It will be a long, barren month before Duane Snit entrusts his macerated knuckles to the attention of even an infant's grasp.

All the while, Gerald Schmidt Thermos obsesses, his best course, on the boffo marching band. He sees it all in brilliant Panavision, leaping breasts, satiny insteps … and plenty to keep the ladies on tippy-toes!

In deepening quiet, he is the last to come around.

He beams at Celia Oddthorpe now, eyes bright.

Gary Larry addresses Duane Snit: "... all right?"

"Piss off."

It's a yes.

"Julian?"

"*GLECCH*-ghh ... gleccc-*gghh*, ptt-*PPPtttt*."

"Gerald?" inquires Celia.

"Oh, yessss..." croons the bandmaster, capturing the dreamy balladic tones of the very early Sinatra. "... all two hundred!"

His marching plans have fructified nicely.

Curate Oddthorpe, for her part, soars on wings of blind instinct.

"When proud stallions meet on the mount," she declaims, "... it is their destiny to clonk horns."

"That would be rams..." it is proposed.

"I said rams..." Celia Oddthorpe snaps. "Of course!"

CHAPTER 14

The Lone Granger

EARS BACK, TAIL HIGH, Neddy clatters down the hall, late, as usual!

He pumps his arms as best he can, while tying his tie. But like others of his best efforts, the tie winds up far over to the left, skewing away from dead center like a gob of lard spattering across a hot griddle.

Ahead, he smells the great Checquers banquet—as do the dead in Reno—but he's still a time zone away!

And it isn't only the rich aroma that smites his mental nostril, flaring out now like a mallard's tail plane coming in on final approach. What strikes him most is the cosmic smugness of The Two Hundred—We Incomparables! The hubbub up ahead, table after table of it in the Grand Refectory, serves to convince all present that they are as rare and inviolable as fed-and-bedded wild boar!

The thought rattles around in his brainpan now like—

Good Christ—cufflinks...

forgot cufflinks!

... youuuu *TU*-mescent, flaming *CAR*-buncle!

We will go no farther—Neddy has his own unique way of lighting into himself, and he's at his offensive best when he's late for the Duke—which, it seems, is always!

Yet the sobering truth, though Neddy doesn't twig it, is the Duke is not waiting for him.

Hasn't given him a thought!

Anticipating the pleasures of his grand banquet, just ahead, the Duke strolls the Grand Refectory like the Archbishop in the arboretum, resplendent, congenial, nodding to his flock, here, there, and over there.

They nod in return, even bow—or close enough for California.

At Neddy's eventual arrival, the patriarch will receive him with good grace, seasoned with a grain of salt ... the fountainhead, after all, of early Rutt plenitude.

Stated plain, the Duke views Neddy's lateness no more gravely than he would a tardy Checquers tradesman. Tardy tradesmen at Checquers are rare, of course, and almost never a focus of the Duke—though he can conjure the sensation. To Duke Monty, Neddy is a solipsism, unconventional, by instinct, unpredictable in the extreme. He sees the lad as sublimely self-defined and not a little enviable.

He is what he is.

On which point, it's taken a long decade or three for the Duke's singular Monty-isms ... "He is what he is," "It is what it is," and others ... to take hold. But by 1984, they've long been central to Monty's world, and he takes deep spiritual consolation in them. They declare things to be exactly as they are, especially, things he finds difficult to grasp or be resigned to. They calm even the most truculent realities, rendering them negotiable and reasonably free of self-serving and evasion.

It was early on, during the troubled Sixties, that the Duke's business associates first began noticing his affirmations. Initially, they seemed mere eccentricities, the tics of a great man. But they were the Duke's tics, they must be taken into account. And as they were ever present, inevitably, the inner circle gradually adopted them. In time, they migrated outward, a winsome instance of the "trickle-down" metrics preached by the Duke's good friend, the Teflon moviestar Commander-In-Chief. The president gleaned these affirmations while dining high atop the Duke's magnificent Campanile. A regular visitor, amid the turbulence of national and Cold War politics, the president takes time at Checquers to review his innermost thoughts while gazing out upon the azure reassurance of the eternal sea.

Yet only gradually did the Duke's affirmations radiate outwards into society at large. After all, on first hearing ... "It is what it is" sounds almost simpleminded—an autistic mumble to be dismissed out of hand. Applied to a baffling decision or risk-filled negotiation of the kind the Duke and the Commander-In-Chief face all too often, however, this declaration affords startling rewards. It supplants anxiety with plain thinking and sturdy commitment to the facts. If unpredictable results loom, the mantra provides valuable leverage ... the outcome will and must be faced.

And the truth of the affirmations is hard earned. The Duke used them in his worldly affairs for years, but then he suddenly and traumatically lost his wife. He learned it then, at depth; life is not necessarily what it "must" be ... it is what it is.

Over time, these pragmatic, humbling "blunt instruments" of the Duke's gradually became the fashion in Santa Lola, and people saw their power. After all, the profound value of firmly accepting consequence is a core strength. On the other hand, there was resistance farther afield. It didn't help that the first benefactors of these affirmations were the old-line Santa Lola financials. In the Ostentatious Eighties, when nothing is quite costly enough, quite gaudy enough ... the garish prosperity of the vast nouveau class declined to take its marching orders from Santa Lola's ancien régime. They were born rich—they didn't know how to "par-*tay!*"

Yet phone call by phone call, fusion Thai lunch after fusion Thai lunch, the affirmations spred abroad. In time, they reached Hollywood— and by then, the trail back to Santa Lola had gone cold. Just as well. Hollywood resents outside counsel. But when the Duke's slogans made it to the late-night talk shows, they were a sensation. "It is what it is," says Johnny Carson, and suddenly, it applies to Des Moines refinances, Secaucus divorces, Biloxi washing-machine warranties.

All the while, up among the tall eucalypti on the Platinum Coast ... if it's good enough for the Duke, it's good enough for all.

The Duke's view of Neddy's punctuality, as distinct from his view of the occasional tardy architect ... tardy architects, the Duke came to know, are very often the right ones ... is singular. Gliding now from tongue-wagging youth to something considerably less certain, Neddy deeply intrigues Duke Monty. Against all odds, and with no real training—which is to say, doing it right, the Duke will argue—Neddy has arranged to be seen by his peers as "their better."

Of course, carrying the skeleton key to Checquers doesn't hurt.

Yet Duke Monty's assessment of his son-in-law is unchanged. Well done, he will say.

The Duke knew Neddy's father, Big Patsy, well—rather too well, in retrospect, but what's done is done. And the truth is, Big Patsy could claim no rightful place under the Santa Lola sun—a fact Patsy simply refused to notice. It was his finest quality. The Duke can't help smiling at the memory of Big Patsy. He had a personality like live ammunition. He was limitlessly entertaining, scaldingly funny, an entirely satisfactory son of a whore— literally, the story goes, but we don't choose our parents.

He was a thoroughly good-natured scoundrel, which is infinitely preferable to a lemon-faced moralist. In another town, he would've been mayor.

No—chief of police.

But a father? He tried. Everyone tries. He did the best he could, but it wasn't good enough. People forget that about Neddy, and they can't.

To the Duke, Neddy's mercurial nature is like a wirehaired terrier, striking, amusing, unimprovable. On the negative side, he could always become "the more so." Civil behavior, after all, is only voluntary, and without it, all else fails. But reduced to fundamentals, the Duke finds

Neddy, as Commander Whitehead liked to blather, "curiously refreshing."

(Whenever Commander Eddie came to Checquers, he invariably claimed the Bentley wouldn't start, just cause to stay over for Chef Rodant's nonpareil Eggs Benedict.)

In the Duke's eye, Neddy shows irrepressible spirit, and now and then, something finer. The lad hasn't found his legs yet—in lapdog Santa Lola, there's little hope of that. But during their recent heart-to-heart about his and Proz's marriage, Neddy held his eye on the ceiling, the floor, the complexion of his lime slice ... yet said nothing altogether impossible. He was the essence of restraint—no small achievement for a wirehair.

*****

Cannizaro sees someone now who isn't late for a train.

He's wearing white gloves, a good sign.

He stands inside the front door of the Constance Room next to a waist-high, shiny-black ceramic crock with some ugly design all over it—a stupid big snake shaped like a lightning bolt!

Cannizaro nods to Pulpo to keep up and be quiet.

"'Scuse, pal ... where's everyone going?" he says. "What's the big rush? We're trying to find some friends of ours—any idea how we can do that? Seems like everyone in the whole world is here tonight, and they're all in a terrible hurry!"

"Yes, sir," smiles the man with white gloves, "everyone who is anyone."

He nods politely.

"It is the dinner hour, sir, people are going to the two dining venues."

"Dining venues...."

"There is the Hunt Room, sir, where many will dine, and the Grand Refectory, where the Duke's personal guests are welcomed to a private seating. Do you have any idea where your friends might be?"

"The Duke's, definitely."

"Of course."

The man smiles.

"It is limited to invited guests. You think your friends will be there?"

"I'm sure of it."

"And you have an invitation?"

"Damn right. Where's the Grand Reflectory?"

"Yes, sir ... through that door, past the Jackson Pollocks."

He gestures to three enormous cataclysmic paintings like huge hanging licorice-and-cream pizzas.

"Down the hall—along to the right."

Cannizaro eyes the paintings.

"Enough to kill yer appetite."

"Very likely, sir."

"Well, you've been more than a guy," says Cannizaro, flashing a twenty.

"Oh, that won't be necessary, thank you, sir—straight along the hall. Follow your nose, you can't miss it."

"Past the paint-ball fight..." Angus smirks.

Pulpo snickers.

They set off across the enormous Constance Room, swept along in the throng.

"This is gonna take some doing," Pulpo says, "... no invitation, and all."

"These dim bulbs, you watch. Just keep your chute shut."

Pulpo nods, "Like a French safe."

*****

Clack-clack-clack-clack!-ing down the south hall comes tardy Neddy.

Past the empty Green Room...

Through deserted echoing Alabaster Alcove...

Finally, crissakes ... panting, panting ... the Grand buh-leeeeding Refectory!

In rosy tumult, the 199 diners shuffle aggressively for position at five double-bowling-alley-long banquet tables. Countless feints and last-minute thrusts forge a mob-rule seating, satisfying the many, cosmically defeating the few.

But arranged seating is intolerable: Don't Connecti-cate California!

In the contagion of high spirits, none take note of Neddy's clacking in the hall—except Duke Monty. He turns, smiling broadly, the lad's brogans crashing through the entrance.

Monty watches the young runabout cut throttle...

Come down off plane...

Nudge the dock.

Splendid.

Neddy scans the grand prospect with wirehaired frisk, wiping his neck with his handkerchief like a Louisiana sharecropper.

Ah, but to the multitudes regarding him now, he is irresistible! Every female grasping the concept will flutter a lash his way. An immediate celebratory crowing elevates the general hubbub—if not directly attributable to Neddy, it can find no other proximate cause.

And why not! He's perfect, dark, gleaming, his black hair slicked back by the Jet Stream ... his tie knot in Peru. What is it about the Exorbitantly Rich ... every little thing—how they dress, devil may care, inexplicably, haphazardly ... spot on!

The Duke admires Neddy quite as much. After their recent *tête à tête* re Proz, the lad is far richer than he once thought.

"More money." The most lascivious two words in the tongue.

Ned, the Duke reflects, has every reason to be zany ... slapdash.

And he's worn a tie—no mistaking his good intent.

He's the second-richest man in the room. He can be as late as he damn well pleases! He lost his father early ... it's always "early" ... and he's on his own. Allowances must be made.

Now to pick out what it is that weighs on him so.

*****

"Neddy, meet Eddie Boyle," proposes Clive O.E.M. Monogram ... "The Dumb Shit."

They're on station, at the far end of the second of the Grand Refectory's five endless tables.

Neddy shakes Eddie Boyle's hand.

Bestows the cordial grin.

Eddie Boyle nods back.

Eddie has a blond Sundance Kid mustache, just like everybody else in the Eighties. But unlike everybody else in the Eighties, he's had his since LBJ, when it was risky business.

And the whole truth is, Neddy mistrusts Eddies. "Ed" is another matter—a blunt instrument you can deal with. But Eddies give him the willies ... and Willies are a whole new item.

"Eddie's down at Pearl's Landing," informs Clive.

"Yes?" nods Neddy promisingly.

The fauna of Pearl's Landing down in the harbor are accorded singular standing in Santa Lola. As in every coastal port, harbor, inlet, and tidepool, commercial fishermen are special, no one quite knows why. And no one knows where this special standing is meant to lead. It makes conversation with them unusual. One tenured forehead at City College asserts that, concerned as they are with sustenance, they are the sea's "men of the soil." Surely, there's something to this—but what! One reason Santa Lola commercial fishermen, in particular, are men of the soil is, they rarely leave the harbor. They pass the warm, sunny days walking the docks, drinking Oly, and defaming absent friends for living off their waitress girlfriends or syphilitic trust funds. An instance of the former, "Slow Eddie" Boyle, or just "Slow Boyle," is a charter member of the Santa Lola Fishermen's Grange. As such, tonight he is the Great Party's "Designated

Fisherman." Just one will suffice. His presence demonstrates that Santa Lola is winsomely democratic (small "d"), vertically inclusive, and wholesomely in touch with its roots.

Bidding Eddie a polite nod, the formalities served, Ned rotates now a brisk one-eighty degrees, and like a Spaniel off its leash, he's down the second table to dead center—ditto The Dumb Shit.

Slow Eddie is left rolling and pitching in their wake. For stability, he clutches his Tequila Mockingbird. To Eddie, the ancient mariner's dictum applies—red sky at dinner ... sailor take umbrage! He doesn't like Neddy. Monogram is irrelevant, let us count the ways ... but Neddy!

Smartass.

... treats people like they're some kinda drunk commercial fisherman!

Rolling beam to beam, Eddie rotates his own one-eighty degrees.

Complexion like boiled lobster, with sentiments to match, he says nothin' tuh no one—has his code—and stomps the fuck out!

Way back dead center at table two ... Neddy has his code, too. He follows Clive O.E.M. Monogram's porcine eye. It's all over Proz's ass like feathers on a goose!

As we watch Neddy, little is known of his exact thoughts. They may fall short of a possessive fury, and they may not. Whichever it is, Neddy is indisputably "the hubby" ... and he likes to keep his hand in.

*****

In a galaxy farther and farther away ... the Hunt Room & Grille grazes deep and long.

Despite its societal shortcomings, immediately apparent to the Two Hundred in the Grand Refectory, hundreds in the Hunt Room enjoy the devil's own good time—the less said the better.

All the while, the Duke's triangle-tip steaks, immortalized decades ago on the beach at old San Onofre, hiss and spit on three jog-around barbecue pits by a railroad siding east-nor'east of the Grand Refectory. Cloudy billows of smoky account rise up from the pits, waft across open country, float over crew-cut turf, barge in through the open Grand Refectory windows, bearing a wanton scent.

And despite his gracious smile throughout, this wayward breeze pains the Duke. He never actually leaves his body, yet in spirit, he will ghost out the gaping windows, steal across the sculpted gardens, through the deep hedges ... migrating to his flaming pits.

The sensuous searing bouquet calls out to his most primitive self.

By ironbound custom, however, Monty's mortal presence remains in the Refectory ... his dear late wife kept a seemly manor. The gracious host is present for his honored guests, she said, not fooling about with the help at some hobo culinary inferno.

East and West may meet, fall in love, joyfully wed and be fecund, but ne'er shall the twain be confused, one with the other....

No, these many years along, the Duke faithfully abides by Constance's stern rubric. He will ignore the siren call of his "Killer Steak" ... massive slabs of triangle-tip, infused with fresh garlic, diluted liquid hickory smoke, low-sodium soy, and Pico Pica hot sauce ... flamed and scorched in hellfires to the earliest threshold of medium-rare ... their juices rich as full-blooded claret. They are ambrosia—sign and symbol of Santa Lola Fine Living. Killer Steak's recipe has been freely shared, courtesy the *Times-Press* and tireless *Jeannee!* Ideally experienced at the Duke's own estate, it is a birthright of Platinum Coast Living. Killer Steak separates forever this beloved isle from municipalities, principalities, monarchies, Workers' Paradises and Sun Cities, eking out their mean existences on "the planet."

The Duke will not set foot outdoors.

He will not indulge his holy culinary conflagration.

The staff is well trained.

They broil with the Duke's Private Joy.

And Constance, watching from her celestial Newport, sees Monty evidence no sign of unease ... nodding, smiling, chatting with his subjects ... suffering with tireless good grace.

Part Three

CHAPTER 15

Buckingpork Palace

And so it begins.

Deep-tanned waiters stream into the Grand Refectory in black Hugo Boss suits and hot-purple shirts with Nehru collars. Swirling around the ends of the five long tables, they eddy into the aisles, the Two Hundred prepared to be done in.

The Grand Refectory is both splendid and splendidly informal, in the gracious Spanish-Californian way. An inviting glow abides, hovering in the soft evanescence of candlelight. The dark wood banquet tables stretch off to incredulity, softly agleam, their elegant surfaces styled to seem agreeably rough-hewn ... though nothing in the Refectory is in the least "rough." The place settings are bright scarlet-and-yellow linen, adorned with hefty monogrammed sterling silver Checquers cutlery. Oversized dinnerware, in bold primary colors, promises festive fare in gala abundance.

At the far west end of the Refectory, another enormous multi-tiered Alhambra fountain, this one in green-and-white tile, holds forth. Its joyful waters chatter cheerfully—and Proz mindfully sits well out of earshot, at the center of the great second table. By the by, if you are under 40—in Santa Lola, it is encouraged—this second table is the place to be. The "Younger Set" ... tip of the hat to the eponymous *Times-Press* bi-weekly supplement by gyring *Jeannee!* ... radiates outwards from here, the fair Proserpina at its red-hot center.

During Santa Lola's countless months of summer, a broad outdoor terrace, beyond the Refectory's leaded glass doors to the west, invests dining with tantalizing drama, evening's light waning ... waning, to the last spoonful of dessert. And beyond the terrace is Lady Constance's elegant "La Ventana"—broad lawns, ornamental gardens, and peerless monumental French and American sculpture. Far in the distance at twilight, the violet glow of the Channel Islands and velveteen sea assume ever-deepening mauve ... bowing, at last, to gloaming's descending cloak.

But tonight's autumnal curfew dictates a different course. The Grand Refectory will rely upon its own amusements—they are generous. "Los Huevos Rancheros," the Duke's avant-garde Mariachis, from 35 miles south in Oxnard, serenade the banquet with warmth and charm. Passionately Mexican in heart and harmonies, they render soulful song in romantic voicings of trumpet, guitar, accordion, and guitarrón.

"Acid Mariachi," Neddy cracks, and the Duke concedes the point.

The Refectory's court jesters are the Duke's four Technicolor macaws. Each is over forty and has seen it all. Housed in a massive 14-foot-tall mahogany-and-brass abode near the main entrance, they are favorites of the Duke, who feeds them daily when he is in residence. (Nearing 70 now, he is onsite most days.) The macaws provide a running commentary on events until promptly at ten. A black-velvet canopy then descends around their aerie, and a bronze plaque cautions against disturbing them.

Like seniors everywhere, they value courtesy.

"*Squawwwwk!*" remarks "Hoover" now—a red one. The others are "Milhouse" (the other red one), "Bonzo" (bright blue) and "Jimmuh" (yellow). Hoover's squawk, loud enough to sit you straight up in your chair, incites the throng to party-down!

And why ever not! The culinary universe beckons. Presuming the ingredients are at hand, and sufficient warning is tendered, Master Chef Rodant enjoys satisfying special requests. But honoring long Checquers custom, the vast majority will order the "Duke's Double"—whole Maine lobster and Killer Steak. An alternate menu is provided for Democrats.

Dining in the Refectory is on a Roman scale. The only heathen element absent is a vomitorium.

In Protestant Santa Lola ... never!

Speaking of hurling one's haddock, a degree of gossip persists along these lines re beloved Proz. She lumberjacks down her full portion of Triangle-Tip and Maine lobster, with plenty of Downeast boiled potatoes and butter, yet remains wicked thin!

And candidly, at Checquers the topic of purging is not new. Norma Jeane—lovely Marilyn—maintained her famed curves while bolting Checquers dinners like a trash-compactor. Questioned on this, her bombshell bluntness served her well ... "A girl's entitled to take her comfort!" Case closed.

Like her mother before her, Proz is blessed with a demon metabolism—never shows an ounce. The one time purging was broached (by nervy Peevy, of course), Proz's riposte reflected a stalwart never-complain-never-explain view of boundaries, personal privacy, and the right of everyone to just shut up.

In fact, her stinging reply to Peevy ultimately rose to the level of Federal policy! For as Peevy and Proz spoke in the Grand Refectory Ladies Salon, Maura Bund, wife of one of the Joint Chiefs of Staff, was completing her affairs in a nearby stall ... and it didn't hurt that Maura B. readily identified Proz's charismatic smoky contralto, as unmistakable as Satchmo's yaaazzz-baaay-bih!

But hearing Proz's sharp reply to Peevy, it was to Maura Bund as if Providence had swooped down to rescue the Army, Navy, Air Force, Marines and Coast Guard! Reconstructing herself hastily, Maura rushed back to the Refectory front table and tugged Hubby-Dear's sleeve. Adm. Morris Lemuel Bund and the Joint Chiefs had struggled endlessly with the Gordian knot of sexual orientation in the military, but now Maura told Morrie she had a complete armed-services sexual-orientation policy—in just four words!

Having dined and drank well, Hubby-Dear said he would be pleased to hear it. Maura repeated Proz's biting rebuke to Peevy on the intensely personal matter of purging ... "Don't ask—don't tell."

These things all start someplace.

*****

Sun-darkened servers stream in. Tributaries of white and red vintages flow. Tidal surges of German Kulmbacher Monkshof, Czech Pilsner Urquell, English Bass Ale, and Irish Guinness Stout gush ... all fresh on tap after crossing the pond on Duke Monty's climate-controlled Boeing 747 flagship freighter, "Checquered Career."

But of all tippling goods, the Duke takes greatest pride in his own 1971 "Monty" Cristo Homecraft Zinfandel. A 100-percent varietal of "architectonic proportions" ... *Jeannee!* hip-deep in her Roget's ... it was pronounced "world's greatest zinfandel" by Banlieue Vineyards' winemaster and kingmaker Ivan Tchelistcheff himself!

Fresh-shucked Wellfleets, Apalachicolas and Atchafalayas on the half-shell are dispensed in their *milliards.* Avocado nachos, Olvera St. taquitos, garlic-roasted artichokes, and other preludial fineries arrive ... hot to the touch! Each server has a ten-client theatre of operations, and every table has two free agents, "people persons" to expedite and "relieve concerns." Less apparent, these free agents are also certified EMTs ... because you never know!

The dinner service conveys gracious calm ... yet everything is here already!

It's Checquers.

Neddy is still slightly overheated from his recent steeplechase—

though to the ladies, his perspiration conveys an indefinable "something."

Opposite him at the second table, he ponders Murderer's Row ... Rear Adm. Peevy, the diminutive, bituminous Canadian literary git Mr. Marmody Whatssis, Twitty (of the *bluddy note*), and Clive Monogram, Timeless Dumb Shit. Clive is seated next to some jerk with bent teeth, a flat-top, and a mad shirting of orange, green, purple, brown and day-glo pink!

Farther down is lovely Lissa with—what's this ... a pickup-truck thief!

And one seat farther, defensible in every regard, is bosom pal Burtram Balfour, talking to everyone at once.

Neddy beams to all, showing none of his cards.

The only thing going right for him just now is his wife—she's off at the head table, babbling with three out-of-town nonentities he doesn't know ... doesn't want to know!

But directly across the table, The Dumb Shit is craning his idiot neck right around backwards like an ostrich in a wrestling pin hold. He's trying to ogle Proz, but it's an impossible gawk. She's 180-degrees behind!

And conveniently in the next seat beyond Proz's vacant chair is Chester Halimony, the master racer up at Santa Lola Invitational Raceway.

"Chester," Neddy nods presently, "how did Clive do up at the Raceway today?"

Monogram is motionless, neck twisted backwards like a rope of modeling clay. Up at the track, he spun out thrice, damaged a priceless Porsche Speedster, and finished dead last in the two races he managed to complete.

"You'll have to ask Clive," Halimony defers.

The rope of clay shows signs now of unwinding.

"I hear," Neddy begins, "... he had some trouble up there this morning."

"Trouble?" says Halimony.

"And this afternoon!"

"Yes?"

"Yes!" says Monogram—unwinding madly now like a rubber-band propeller. "Yes ... I had some trouble, Neddy—*yes!* And where were you all day, hiding in a culvert?"

"I was, Clive. I hate seeing a grown man cry."

The D.S. no longer craning his neck at Proz, Neddy grabs the Pico Pica bottle, splashes hot sauce on his guacamole and stirs it in.

Chef Rodant shouldn't let his guacamole beaters pander to gringo tastes ... Guacamole should hurt!

He takes a moment now to glance "on high." The Duke sits dead center at the first table, amused by anyone who is amused by him—a large class. He beams high and low, surrounded by billionaires, millionaires, well-to-do, Beverly Hills financial firemen, a real Santa Lola fireman (Bobby Ming), UCLA Economics and Political Science Ph.D.s, Cathedral Church of St. Biff's own Bishop Spike (with wife Maude), Assemblywoman Wanda Vindik, Messrs. Varp, Carbon and Mudhutt ... all of them punctuated by wives, dates, hobbies and enemies—sweet, sour and bitter.

Turning back again, Neddy takes the opportunity to smile at Twitty.

She smiles back, as if lunging into a juicy ripe Carolina peach.

"Enjoying yourself?" he inquires.

She leers back, peach nectar gushing down her chin, well, figuratively.

"And how!"

If he'd gotten here a moment or two sooner, instead of hounding about in the halls like an autistic Weimaraner, he could've weaseled right in next to her and gotten the damn note!

And flaming hell—here comes Proz!

Neddy rises just the same ... suave, polished, one foot in the grave.

Yet he's momentarily dazzled by his own formality.

This is indisputably "a moment." He could just as well be the Duke of Kent at Ascot.

Kent-ie does prefer hot guacamole!

With dignity, even a certain flair, Neddy draws back Proz's chair.

Waits....

Waits!

Against all that is in him, at just the right tick...

He slides the chair under her tucker—naught amiss here.

Good lad.

And she smiles all around like the Duchess of—

No, she doesn't!

She doesn't smile like the Duchess of Marlborough or the Douchebag of Denver!

Vehemently to the contrary, they smile "like her!"

She is Prosperpina Rutt-Lombardo of Checquers—it's bloody well enough!

Let them do whatever they do in Buckingpork Palace...

This is his wife!

Queen of the entire Buh-leeding Planet!

CHAPTER 16

Calling Mr. Toastmaster

AGAINST HER BETTER INSTINCTS—they are formidable—Lissa Montenero is spellbound.

Eight seatings nearer the Grand Refectory's green-and-white-tile Alhambra fountain than Neddy and Proz, rough-and-tumble Ski Kobalefffsky goes on and on. He has stories to tell about growing up in Brooklyn that make Lissa wonder ... at this point no more than that.

But it fascinates her to hear what he says about Red Hook—that unimaginable place. She tries to think of it like San Pedro, the tough little Los Angeles fishing port over the mountain from her elegant home in Rancho Palos Verdes. San Pedro is full of Serbs and Croats and Bosnians, all bombing each other's meeting halls on alternate weeknights.

But no, no, no, says Ski ... "Peedro" is nothing like The Point, trust him.

She can't go that distance. She hardly knows him.

Yet the things he talks about make her question—not for the first time—what she's missed in life. She's glad she missed them too, no argument—the roughness, the living by your wits and wondering, minute to minute, what will happen next.

She wouldn't want any part of it.

The thought makes her shiver.

She shivers right now!

It makes Ski smile.

But it's fascinating—like some awful James Dean movie, all scarred and scared.

But she loves listening while he talks about it.

And Ski loves telling her. It doesn't hurt that he's surprised right out of his socks she's listening so close. Who'd have thought—a gorgeous rich babe like this?

Crazy!

So he goes right on telling her all about it, the Point, and the things that happened. How he used to survive, just sort of. But the more he talks, the more beautiful she gets, just more and more. Her eyes glow like the beam of light in a glass of red wine. He doesn't even like wine ... but he could learn to. He doesn't know where he's been all his life—why he hasn't gotten around a delicious babe like this before!

Where he's been, they don't make delicious babes like this ... this Lissa with the green eyes.

Out to lunch, that's what.

He's been out to lunch his whole damn life, and suddenly here she is!

He doesn't know what to think, how he got here.

Even why she let him sit here with her!

He ought to be out in the Hunt Room on the back deck, eating burgers and barbecue and drinking draft Oly with the jerks, where he belongs!

She's a nut, being nice to him, with the terrible things he's here to do!

Crazy!

She doesn't know about it, 'course—

But she will. No getting out of it.

When he looks in her eyes and sees how she's listening to him so close, this beautiful, holdable babe, just waiting to be talked into a backseat—

By him!

Jesus.

He keeps talking, and nobody breaks in—

She won't let them!

It's a dream, but somebody else's dream.

Doesn't she know!

'Course she knows.

She's just playing him.

She's too smart by a mile.

She knows more about what's what than any ten people he ever met. All he knows is how to beat people out of what's theirs—

But she knows how to live ... just to be quiet and like it! She's not like him—she knows better.

... what's she up to!

But she just keeps asking him, tell her more.

—about Johnny Cigs and Ziggie The Nose, and the day all the hall lockers caught fire.

She wants to know why we did it—what did we think we'd get out of it?

Nothing.

Payback.

Things guys do!

... it's The Point.

She wants to know if we ever felt bad....

No.

We didn't get caught.

Everyone was pissed...

a good day.

But he loves her eyes.

Deep shining pools

… it's nuts.

He's never seen anything like her up close. She's better than the movies—just as beautiful, except he can make her talk back anytime he wants!

But Snake....

Jesus.

What's going to happen to this popsickle when Snake gets going— Starting right after dinner!

*****

He's down at the far end of the very last table by the men's...

Edwin E. Mulverthud.

"Special Ed."

He earned his name the old-fashioned way.

He's an idiot.

Early in the banquet, even before the taquitos, he asks his server, no hint of unease—for ketchup.

"Catsup," he says.

With this primitive unguent, he will improve the Duke's lordly, mesquite-broiled, three-and-a-half-inch-thick—but in Ed's case alone, well-done!—slab of triangle-tip Killer Steak.

Correct...

Special Ed's from the Midwest.

The Shelbyville Mulverthuds...

Those ones.

Farther along this last and least-honored table—but dead center—

120

Mr. Justin Magnus rises now from his chair.

Still rising ... he rubs his blood-red proboscis.

It resembles a County Fair plum tomato, by this hour far the worse for Checquers single malt.

Accomplishing the vertical, Justin Magnus steadies himself, no mere turn of phrase in tonight's rough seas.

Immediately, there is concern all around—over far more than Justin Magnus' equilibrium. A Known Toastmaster, he is prepared to tender something of a salutary and embarrassing nature to our honored host, Montgomery Overdale Rutt.

Justin Magnus steadies himself.

His last public gesture, in his cups at Holy Eucharist two Sundays ago, was to trip at the St. Biff's Communion rail, swan-dive into the Celebrant's chalice, and disperse its blessed contents like victory champagne, staining Bishop Spike's finest white-satin stole beyond commercial salvation ... but in seconds an EMT appeared.

It's Checquers.

Magnus, of course, was unharmed....

The sacrament resumed in due time—without the nettled Bishop Spike.

But tonight, Magnus' past missteps are behind him. He stands the Refectory's pitching foredeck now, clang-clang-clang-ing his crystal water goblet with a soupspoon like the despairing last fire brigade in Olde Chicago.

Seeing him, seasoned Checquers diners lean into their Wellfleets with a will ... nothing good can come of this.

Magnus now brings down the butt of his Killer Steak cleaver massively on the groaning board in three deafening Thonks!

Well-meaning innocents begin clanging their own water goblets in concert.

... and those with hearing loss peer out, at last, seeking to know what is the disturbance.

The disturbance is Justin Magnus.

"I think we *allll*..." he decries with full volume, the Refectory at a dead halt.

But he depresses the clutch.

He will start anew.

"I know *allll* of us here in this great and noble and incomparable edifice—"

He turns the mental page, curious to know what will follow.

"—in which we find ourselves on this stupendous evening ... and if any of us *can* find ourselves in this colossus, you're a better man than I!"

Chuckles from those divining wit.

Special Ed barks like a harbor seal!

"We find ourselves once again…" Magnus declaims, "in the company of the best of the very best—I mean, each and every one of us, one to another … you and me! We are summoned by the *immensely* immeasurable generosity and *ostentatious* graciosity of our inestimable host … I speak of his *magniloquence*, the Duke!"

He doesn't need to start the ovation…

But does anyway.

Applause and cheering take on a suspicious life of their own—all except for Special Ed … the "catsup" tendered him is Heinz.

The Shelbyville Mulverthuds are Hunt's people.

"I have had…" Justin Magnus resumes, "the *gran-di-ose* honor—"

He pauses—savoring it.

"… to enjoy, on occasions past, our host's gracious hospitability at many another—"

"Put a sock in it!"

(… second table, vicinity of young Lombardo.)

"I wish I *could* put a sock in it," booms Magnus … skipping not a beat, give him that. "But my gratitude … and I may say, all of ours … cannot be muffled by a sock, nor even a whole foot!"

Wary smirks.

Tittering sibilances.

"I mean to say—" he booms.

"What *do* you mean to say?"

(… Lombardo—yes. Crimson grins all around.)

"On behalf of this *grandiloquent* gathering … participants, guests, dear friends … on the auspicious capital happenstance of…."

The deck pitches—Magnus righting himself forcefully.

"On behalf of my family, and of all the families of all so graciously assembled here in this *splendacious* Grand Refectory … participants, guests and friends—we *allll* have … been welcomed to this auspicious … both worthy and unworthy—"

Good Christ … he's lost the thread!

"—likely and unlikely … invited to this great pile this *loquacious* evening, good sirs…."

He's reeling himself in for all he's worth!

"—and so, and so…."

"… may we just rise, one and all, big and small—"

"Short and tall…."

(… young Lombardo!)

"To salute the grandest … noblest … *richest*—"

Ooooks!

"benefactor of all mankind … including all *womankind* … ladies, women, girls, and equal persons of all sorts and sizes everyplace...."

He rocks backwards to bellow:

"... The Duke!"

"*THE DUKE!*" brays the Refectory, surging to its feet.

... ruffling the macaws.

All drink deep—

And the deck pitches violently, Magnus sprawling backwards into his chair—

Of course ... unharmed.

The Duke comes to his feet now, his hands rising after some moments, quelling the celebration.

Following a suitable spell of hoots and cheers, all take their seats.

"I am obliged to say something."

He pauses a-twinkle.

"... just as surely as good Justin Magnus was not—"

A groundswell of breathless inhales...

Release in tsunamis of pent-up hilarity!

It subsides only very gradually.

The Duke nods to Magnus.

"Seriously, I thank Justin for his kindness ... *splendaciously* rendered!"

A second round of laughter—less spontaneous, but just as needful.

Magnus is motionless in his chair, staring at his shoe.

"It's a delight to welcome you all tonight," the Duke says, his basso profundo carrying to the farthest corners of the great space.

"But our purpose this evening is to celebrate my dear daughter, Proz—the pride and joy of an old man's heart."

A great ooooooo*WWWwwwaaahhhhhh*... rises up from every female breast.

"Bless her dear heart," the Duke beams, "... Proz picked up the telelphone one day and—"

"Ohhh ... *Daddee!*" she scolds, accepting adoring smiles from all quarters.

"No, no, my darling—let me finish," he smiles, looking at the floor momentarily. "Proz said she was unhappy. We never have any big gatherings like we used to, she said, no big celebrations! Well, I'm no fool. The time had come..." he booms, "*TO DECLARE A PARTY!*"

Hosannas and wild table thumping.

The heavy Checquers sterling silverware jingles like sleighbells!

His hands rise again—open palms reining all in.

"Every one of us has days like Proz was having ... but unfortunately, we don't all have the means to do something about them! Justin Magnus is quite correct, though it makes people squirm—we are not all rich."

No sound.

"We can't all do zany foolish things just for our own pleasure—it can change everything!"

He nods reflectively.

"But there are times, too, when it changes nothing. We lose our health. We lose those we love. Some of us lose the path altogether, and only the love of those closest us can bring us back. Life is what it is. But many of us, like my good friend Justin here, do their very best. Justin, I am so grateful for your kindness to me."

Eyes closed, at last, Magnus is like the Buddha. In the morning, he will have no recollection of the Grand Refectory.

"So then...."

The Duke raises his Monty Cristo Homecraft Zinfandel.

"I wish you all a wonderful evening! I hope you will find in it one sweet memory to last you all your days! To my beloved Proz, then—and to you all—a hale and hearty ... Cheers!"

"*CHEERS!*" the Refectory roars, surging to its feet.

Only gradually ... the hallelujahs wind down.

Promptly, Los Huevos strike up a *latino* favorite of the Duke and his Constance, the enchanting "*Con Tigo En La Distancia.*" Its charm flows gently out into the great space, bearing gentle witness that love's beauty is as fragile as it is precious ... as fleeting as it is timeless.

CHAPTER 17

Belgium Somewhere

DOUG THE THUG wears his best Tillary St. smile.

"Take a load off. Have a seat."

Cannizaro looks at Pulpo—nothing doing.

Pulpo obeys, continues standing.

"Getcha some coffee?" says Doug.

Cannizaro makes no move.

"How do you take it, light? Sugar?"

Doug nods to Crusty Yamaguchi. "Have Service send some down."

They're in a small maintenance room beneath the Casino.

No one is sitting, not yet, at least. It's still early in the first round.

Next to Yamaguchi is Santa Lola County Sheriff Mickey Bunt, County Deputy Maynard, and Security Red Deputy "Don't-Call-Me-Dog" Dodd. Through the wall, they hear the moan of the machinery responsible for heating and filtering the water at this end of Checquers' enormous County Pool ... once the Jeane Pool but nobody cares. What, precisely, is "maintained" in this maintenance room is unclear. It is stark—bare concrete floor, old wooden chairs, pale-green Fifties foam-and-plywood couch ... a roughed-up old desk from the Hoover years.

But three phones.

The heavy door they came through swung shut convincingly. At that, Pulpo looked at Cannizaro, but Cannizaro was busy not looking back. Cannizaro had done everything he thought necessary to get them seamlessly into the Grand Refectory. They stood out like Zulus.

"No coffee," Cannizaro says with an edge, not sitting.

"Tea?" Doug's eye glints. "Don't suppose so."

He looks at Pulpo.

"Nope."

"Sit down," Doug says. "Make yourself comfortable."

It's code everybody understands. It isn't about sitting down.

"We gotta talk, Angus, we all know that."

Doug looks at them, one then the other.

His tone changes.

"I said sit."

Cannizaro sits.

So Pulpo sits.

One point for a takedown.

Cannizaro and Pulpo make the best of things on the uncomfortable pale-green foam-and-plywood Fifties couch.

"What are we doing here?" Cannizaro says. "If you don't want us in your snotty dinner, we'll leave, we don't want any trouble."

Doug the Thug smiles.

"Course not, Angus. Your pal Kobalefffsky—that's who you're looking for...."

"What of it?"

"What does he want?"

Cannizaro doesn't answer

"And your other friend—where is he?"

"No idea what you mean."

"Marlon Sneave. Snake. The L.A.P.D. knows what I mean. Black Ford Torino. They came in at two-twenty—want the license number? We know where Ski is."

Doug bears down. "And we know where Miss Montenero is."

"You know just about everything about everything!"

"Yep."

Cannizaro is about to say something, but he thinks better of it.

"Last we saw..." Doug says, "Snake was right there." He points to a spot at the far corner of the ceiling—straight up through the floor. "The Casino. Had a good day, too—won a bundle. No idea where he is?"

Cannizaro shrugs. "It's how he got his name."

"And you, Pulpo?"

"Like *he* said."

Pulpo looks at Sheriff Bunt.

"I'd take that coffee."

Cannizaro gives him a look.

"Black," says Pulpo. "Sugar."

Deputy Dog checks again, but Cannizaro's head shakes, no.

Ten minutes go by, it seems.

"You two will leave just as soon as we find your friend Snake,

Angus."

Doug loves saying Cannizaro's name.

"All four of you leave together. This could get to be a long night."

"You can't hold us!" Cannizaro protests.

"Why—you gonna call the Sheriff?"

Doug smiles to Sheriff Mickey Bunt. Back to Cannizaro.

"You think you're in Pee-dro, Angus? Explain it to him, Crusty."

The Japanese-American enforcer, hands clasped behind his back military-style, watches—mostly Pulpo. Cannizaro is Doug's to watch.

Then Crusty crosses the room to Doug, says something in his ear. Doug shakes his head.

Crusty tries again, and Doug nods.

"Sheriff," Crusty says, "... back in a few."

"We'll be right here." Bunt pats his service revolver like on TV.

The instruments of persuasion concealed in Doug's hulking big-and-tall black suiting are left to the imagination.

Crusty climbs the steel steps to the maintenance-room door. His bearing inspires confidence—one more disappointment for Cannizaro.

The heavy door opens.

Slams shut.

"If we don't find Snake soon," Doug says, "this room's gonna get smaller and smaller. Let's try one more time, Angus."

*****

Twitty Conway nods at "Kenny."

(It went from "Ken" to "Kenny" during the artichokes.)

"I adore Saab convertibles," she says, "... they're so intellectual!"

"That's it!"

She's doing his work for him! It's going so swell, he gets greedy.

"Talk about intellectual!" he says. "It was owned its first two pampered years by the wife of an English Prof. out at the University—a poet!"

"Wow! Who?"

Twitty did a guest shot out at the U. the first quarter of her junior year—but she didn't like the food, and especially the people.

Ken Stukud has no safe reply re the poet, and so cuts bait.

"He's gone now—went to Brigham Young."

"Ah," says Twitty.

"She said she didn't want her darling Saab going to a place like Idaho."

"Brigham Young is in Utah."

"Even worse! Deserves to stay right here in Santa Lola ... find it a good home, she said."

All the while, City College Modernist Gerald Thermos nods, smiles, as if listening to a tape loop of middlebrow Mozart. He dislikes automobiles and all their works. The smile is his marker, should conversation turn to composing, coeds, or discount fireworks.

"I'm definitely interested," Twitty beams.

"You don't find Saabs a little dumpy?" Neddy says.

"They're Swedish!"

"Beautiful powder-blue, too," croons Stukud. "Just like your eyes."

"Ohh!" she laughs, taking it right where it's aimed.

What the hell, thinks Neddy, the note'll be fine. She doesn't look like she's up to setting off any grenades under his ass.

"Kenny..." she purrs now out of the blue, "ever been up to the hot springs?"

"Heard of it."

"What've you heard?"

"It's like a hot-tub in heaven ... a dream you can drink during!"

She beams. "Like to go up?"

"We all would!" puts in Gerald Thermos, speaking for Santa Lola, Tuna Vista, and the more reputable precincts of Santa Barbara.

"Why don't we!" says Twits.

Kenny grins. "Is it true what they say?"

"Yep."

"Not even skivvies?"

"Nope."

He laughs waaay out loud.

"Okay!"

"You'll see," says Twit.

"Bet your life I'll see!"

She laughs for exactly the right reason.

*****

Which nettles Proz no end.

Sure, she'll go up to the hot springs, she loves it! But she loves it like she loves a hot-stone massage four times a week ... while the damn newcomers are all mooing and moaning like dairy cows at milking time.

You'd think they never saw a curly black hair before!

Maybe she and Neddy could sneak up before the crowd....

Silly.

He's not interested.

She wishes he were.

But she can be so willful.

... so can he!

Stop it—she's talking about her now!

She's let this go way too far. She convinced herself he's too much trouble—which he is. But so is everyone! They have too much, expect too much, get too angry too often too easily!

She's let it go far too long with Neddy, and now they're in real trouble—everyone knows! She sees Peevy watching her. And Twitty. And Chester Halimony ... especially Chester Halimony.

Don't they have anything else to think about!

No.

And she and Neddy pretend they don't care—but she cares!

Maybe he doesn't....

(Wouldn't that be something!)

She stops a moment to think seriously ... is it her fault?

A lot of it is his fault! She knows what he's up to. He thinks he's being clever, but it's simple arithmetic. Not caring about her means he cares about someone else, she knows him *that* well! She doesn't need to know who it is ... but she knows, anyway. And maybe she's given him reason to think it's okay! He thinks she's sweet on Clive! Clive's a dear and means well—but he's fun like a night in the woods without a flashlight!

And Neddy acts as if she and Clive are really up to something. It's insulting. Clive Monogram! He lives with mother! Collects comic books! She'd rather do it with a taxi driver.

Or Montenero's thug pirate!

The way things are going tonight, she doesn't feel like her Daddy's daughter—to whom things are due! These Great Parties used to be magic, but tonight she feels nothing! She's like poor Peevy ... and Whoever-Is-In-Charge-Up-There, please help Peevy find her way!

Tonight is all wrong. This is supposed to be like the old parties ... a celebration of whatever turns up. There was always some huge surprise. Something that really changed you! Those parties were always—

She stops in mid-thought, the ceremonial pound-and-a-half Maine lobster set down before her ... red-orange, steaming-hot, divine.

Neddy gives her a hooded smile. It's her favorite thing on "the planet." She rations herself lobster like she rations herself *Casablanca* ... never wants the thrill to fade! She hasn't had a lobster since ... forever.

She looks at Neddy.

Nods all is well.

It has to be.

But it isn't! Tonight she won't eat her lobster—won't tear into its hard carapace like a starved cat, reducing it to shattered shards, digging out every tiny speck of sweet, rosy-white flesh from its weensiest nooks and crannies ... she will not!

Well, she won't eat the claws...

Won't eat the body...

She'll eat the tail—she must!

It would be selfish and ungrateful, wasting this beautiful offering.

But the rest ... no claws, not tonight.

"All right, dear?" Neddy asks, presuming her reply.

"Who's that man Lissa's talking to?"

"No idea. Why?"

"You keep looking his way. Does he owe you money?"

Her voice lowers to a grumble.

"... or are you looking at Lissa—and don't say you've no idea."

"Why are you starting with the tail?"

"Don't change the subject."

"You save the tail for last."

"Stop it, Neddy."

Her voice is down around her ankles.

"You're after her—I know it."

She breaks the lobster's back, separating the tail from the body with a sharp twist like a voodoo priest snapping a live chicken's head away from its body.

Her eyes meet him directly.

"I'm doing things differently tonight, darling—right down to the lobster. Sound interesting?"

"I don't know what you mean."

"About Lissa? Of course, you do."

In a trice, he's on the ropes ... and he knows it.

How does she do that!

She's into his head like a bullet!

He fires a furious glare past Lissa ... past the pickup-truck thief ... to Burtie!

But Burtie's a pal.

He wouldn't tell.

"Love to know what you're thinking," she says.

She opens the split underside of the stiff lobster-tail shell. Pries it open like an alligator jaw. It makes a stubborn, plastic *craaakkk!*

She slips out the succulent Chateaubriand of pearlescent six-pack-ab tail meat, drawing it free as gracefully as slipping her size five out of a satin pump.

She holds out the gleaming alabaster lunk—match that!

Setting it on her plate now, she sucks her fingertips, one by one by one, indulging each little *pluup!* between her lips.

"I don't know where you get all this about Lissa Montenero," Neddy says, using Lissa's surname as if she were continents away ... over in

Belgium someplace. "But she's making an ass of herself with Tugboat Billy—nobody knows who he is!"

"Vance Crankenfuss Esq. knows," Proz says. "A San Pedro fisherman or something."

"Or something."

"I don't know. A fisherman."

He nods. "I had him pegged for a fisherman."

Her eyes gleam.

"Right, Neddy—you're Bond ... James Bond."

*****

Twitty Conway has "Kenny" pinned.

He's betting his socks he'll get laid at the hot springs—and she's betting his socks ... still day-glo orange ... she'll get the Saab for a grilled-cheese on rye.

Yet there's also intriguing, tidy Keita Mammady Fallo, so courtly, so polite. And she can admit to a certain physio-ethnic point of curiosity.

His luck may just be starting.

But Proz and Neddy ... she's been watching them—not staring, mind. But she's missed not a flared nostril. When Proz starts muttering under her breath like that, something's waaay up! They keep looking at Lissa and the thug, then snarling back and forth like teenagers trying to get to second base.

Who's the thug, anyway—a lumberjack? A mobster dressed up like a deckhand? Does it even matter!

Twitty knows just one thing, Ms. Proz is on her game tonight—and when she's on her game, she is her father's daughter. Neddy, dear, you best watch your not-unattractive ass!

It occurs to her to wonder if she can relocate the note.

It might prove useful.

Or not.

Who knows?

Could she even find it again in the dark?

Crap, what a party!

CHAPTER 18

Behind The Matisse

"GOTTA GO NOW...."

The Duke's grin is wider than a mile. "Those three words always came to mind talking to Big Patsy."

They've cleared away the main course now. A mood of fond reminiscence settles over the elders at the first table, dessert orders discreetly being taken.

The Duke's eye is kindly.

"Every time we were together, even when we were having a splendid time, you could almost hear it—'Gotta go now.' He was very funny, Patsy Lombardo. He could make you laugh whenever he wanted, and he knew it. He could put you in your place, too. But he always had this look—a sidelong sort of, 'Gotta go.'"

The Duke laughs deep in his belly.

The table, the part within earshot, hangs on every word.

In the far corner of the Refectory, meanwhile, on a small riser, her short straight hair gleaming like black satin, sultry, world-weary jazz singer Anita Rangoon sets the mood with Harold Arlen's haunting "Ill Wind."

"Big Patsy was one of my favorite people," the Duke nods. "We had our differences, certainly, but it's surprising what good friends you can be with people whose ends contradict your own. People are two different things—their motives, and who they really are. If you are overwhelmed by a person's motives, you may never see who he is—you feel too threatened. But my father always said, wait until you get to know him—or her—over dinner, it can make for fascinating friendships. And Big Patsy was the most

132

fascinating! What people don't understand about a man like him is, in the end, he was just a businessman. I don't mean, he was cynical—that commerce is on the wrong side of ethics and good intentions. And as things worked out, he wasn't, either, but in the beginning, nobody knew that. It's like nobody knew in the beginning that both Johnson and Nixon would go belly up. Some things you don't see coming.

"But Patsy ... when he first moved here, I had him and Monica over for dinner, just as my father would advise. Patsy wasn't any happier about it than I was, but it's something I'd learned to do—and he was accustomed to having a 'sit-down.'"

The Duke's eye sparkles.

"Well, we're sitting up in the Campanile, when I first noticed it ... he's telling me how he liked my Campanile, how it was very Italian in its way ... but all the while, his eyes are saying, gotta go now. It tickled me. Despite my misgivings, I liked it. It was human, and I trusted him for it. I hadn't forgotten who he was and what people in Santa Lola were saying about how it would be if he moved here. Bad things were definitely possible. But I started to relax with him. It was as if we could keep 'business,' whatever that came to mean, out of things and enjoy dinner together. It didn't solve any problems, but it was the beginning of something useful. Like all businessmen, he was looking for solutions—and maybe I could help.

"It was Monica, Neddy's late mother, who began to relax first. She was very intuitive—the brightest penny in the roll. She told Patsy to tell a story about Perth Amboy when they were growing up. It was about a kid getting caught stealing hubcaps in Metuchen and Woodbridge and selling them in Perth Amboy—and the kid happened to be the high-school Vice Principal's son!

"Well, the minute Patsy began telling the story, he lit up. He loved nothing more than a good yarn about everything going to hell. The cops caught the kid with a trunk-full of hubcaps, impounded his '33 Ford, and notified the father. To preserve the father's good name, Perth Amboy Justice was administered. In two days, the kid was tried, sentenced and emerged with a clean record on a train to Quantico, the newest Jersey recruit in the U. S. Marines! Big Patsy's eyes shined like diamonds—that's how it was where he came from!

"I asked him if he was ever in the Marines, but he said, 'Hell, no, I never got caught!'"

The table rumbles with laughter.

"But surely there was more to it," suggests Maybourne Dunne, a millionaire-in-waiting. "He wasn't brought into the fold as easily as all that!"

The Duke smiles.

"It's a mistake to assume too much based on a man's public

persona, Maybourne. Patsy was very bright, he just didn't express it like a Stanford man would."

Maybourne Dunne's M.B.A. was from Palo Alto.

"His motives," the Duke continues, "weren't as low as we would have them be. If he could get by without kneecapping someone, good ... do you see? He was more than ready to turn a corner when he moved from New Jersey out west—and more especially, when he moved from Beverly Hills up to Santa Lola. He didn't want to be the Public Enemy—he called it 'the old way.' You have to remember, Italians in America had a rough road. They had to be tough, and keeping a little of that around had its uses.

"I liked him fine. He could talk and talk and make you laugh—but he could listen, too. And he could change when the time was right. He came a very long way. But I'm sure Neddy was brought up by a very different Big Patsy than the one I knew in Santa Lola. A lot of eggs got broken making that omelet."

*****

Suddenly, Lissa is gone.

Twitty doesn't notice, at first.

She asks Peevy, did Lissa go to the Ladies?

If so, who with? You don't go alone—what's the point!

Dunno, Peevy says.

Twitty looks up and down the table.

No one is missing. Just Lissa.

Unless she got the runs.

... but Lissa doesn't get the runs!

Then, why?

Peevy says she saw Lissa talking to one of the special waiters—the ones that look like they have nothing to do. And the goon sitting with Lissa looked pissed. Lissa smiled to him like she'd be right back, Peevy says—but then he looked even more pissed!

"The loo..." says Twitty. "Shall we?"

"Coming," Peevy says.

"Me, too..." Proz nods.

"Me, too," Neddy very nearly says, but catches himself.

Slipping his chair back now, he follows at a discreet interval.

*****

Five minutes earlier, Crusty Yamaguchi, Nisei Chief of Security Red, was in no doubt.

Military-press khaki shirts and olive-drab uniform tunics must not invade the Grand Refectory at dinner—he mustn't upset the party. Unless absolutely necessary, he would wait in the shadows at the Refectory entrance. But seeing Miss Montenero with the one man he must protect her against—he had to act!

He summoned the table captain, a kid named Drape he knew only from Checquers full-staff meetings. No matter. Drape was paid to say, yes.

Yamaguchi ordered him to inform Miss Montenero she had a phone call—a family emergency. Drape went into the Refectory, and Yamaguchi watched. Drape, Miss Montenero and Ski Kobalefffsky ping-pong-ed it back and forth, back and forth. If push came to shove, Yamaguchi would have to go in and break the tie ... but no, here she came out with Drape.

Her beautiful face was a mask of confusion and distress.

"What's it about?" she said immediately. "What's happened!"

"Extremely sorry to disturb you, Miss Montenero," Yamaguchi said. "Please follow me, my name is Crusty Yama—"

"I know your name!"

"Yes, ma'am."

He ushered her along the main hall.

They passed the Third Living Room.

"There's a phone in there," Lissa said.

Yamaguchi's head shook, guiding her onward, "This way, please, ma'am."

They continued down the marble main hall, their footsteps echoing in the empty stony chamber.

At the cool marble calm and 790,000 volumes of the Checquers Library, Yamaguchi opened the glass door and ushered Lissa inside. She saw the first dozen or so precious Matisses from the exhibit she adored—soon bound for Rio.

She was led past the main desk to a door almost completely concealed in the wall's elaborate carved woodwork. Now she stopped.

"Where are we going—may I call you 'Crusty'?"

"Of course, ma'am. Right this way."

He ducked in through the door.

"Larry, please see to Miss Montenero."

A sandy-haired man in his forties appeared wearing the same military-press khaki twill of Checquers' Security Red.

And Lissa heard sounds inside.

It made her curious.

"Larry" gave her a polite bow: "Miss Montenero."

"Call me Lissa."

"Yes, ma'am," Crusty said. "Nothing to be afraid of—we're here to protect you."

"Protect!"

She shuddered.

"What are you talking about!"

"Please, ma'am, come inside."

A younger man appeared. He was dark-haired, shorter, also in uniform.

Crusty spoke with quiet emphasis: "Please."

Everything she knew of Yamaguchi counseled compliance.

She stepped inside, and the door closed behind her.

The room was long and narrow, a communications center. A table ran along one wall, covered with microphones, speakers, headphones. The walls and ceiling were lined with old Fifties-style dot-drilled white acoustical tile. At shoulder height was a bank of black-and-white video monitors. At the far end, she saw an old-fashioned telephone switchboard—operated in daylight hours, she knew, by equally old-fashioned telephone operator Millie whenever her neuralgia isn't acting up. The Duke adores Millie and Millie adores the Duke. Her job security is immortal.

Lissa knew of Millie as she knew of Security Red—but she was now one of relatively few who had ever been inside.

"They said there was an urgent phone call," she said. "Now you say you're protecting me—I want an explanation."

"We needed to get you out of the Refectory without a disturbance, Miss Montenero," Crusty said. "We're very relieved to have you here."

He held out a wooden chair, but she refused.

"Answer me, damn it!"

"Do you know the man you were talking to?"

"No ... yes and no," she said. "We just met."

"What did he talk to you about?"

"Who knows—life, the big party, a thousand things ... where he grew up—why?"

"Did he ask anything about you?"

"Not really."

Crusty nodded. "He's a very street-smart guy. Did it seem strange that he took an interest in you?"

Her laugh was caustic. "That's a little insulting, Crusty. Do I need to explain it to you?"

"Did it seem strange that he didn't ask anything personal about you?"

"A man like him loves talking about himself—it's not strange at all. He couldn't stop himself, he was having the time of his life."

She met Crusty's eye.

"And so was I."

"He didn't ask anything personal, ma'am, because he already knows all about you."

"Oh I doubt that. He's had a hard time, and he was telling me about it. It was fascinating. What about it?"

Crusty crossed the room.

Several clipboards lay scattered across a table next to a matte-black, typewriter-sized apparatus she couldn't identify. It had a chrome roller for dispensing sheets of paper, but otherwise, it was an enigma.

Crusty picked up a stiffened scroll of sheets from its tray and drew them downwards against the table edge, straightening them. They stubbornly rolled tightly closed again—a series of eight-by-ten black-and-white photos.

"These are from the L.A.P.D., ma'am. Do you recognize anyone?"

She went through them quickly, "No."

She came to the last one.

"Obviously, that's Ski."

"But you haven't seen the others?"

"No."

"Well, you would have."

Crusty's crisp Nisei accent grew precise.

"They're here to kidnap you."

"What!"

The three uniformed men waited, while she went through whatever it was she was going to go through.

"That's insane!"

Crusty shook his head, drawing air through his tightly pursed lips.

Lissa glared back. "They could've picked anyone ... there are hundreds of wealthy people here tonight!"

"But none of them is you. I'm sorry, Miss Montenero, we—"

"Call me Lissa!"

"Yes, ma'am—this is a bit delicate."

She scowled.

"What do they want with me!"

"It's not you—it's your father. He's in some difficulty involving—"

"My father! Who do you think you are, talking about my father!"

She stalked to the end of the room and spun.

"My father isn't in any difficulty—and what's that got to do with kidnapping!"

"We have proof, if you will just let me show you."

"This is completely ... totally—"

She clenched her fists, spiraling out of control.

"You're insane!"

Crusty spoke softly. "We already have three of them, ma'am, and we're looking for the fourth, but he is the most dangerous."

"You don't know what you're talking about! Ski Kobalefffsky is a gentle, deeply hurt man."

"He and the three others work for a man who loaned your father a large sum of money."

"Who told you that!"

"The L.A.P.D."

"And how do they know!"

"Ma'am, it's what they do," Crusty said. "They work the docks in Wilmington, and the loan your father took out has extremely high interest. He can't pay, and they're putting the screws to him."

"Not my Daddy!"

She trembled—rejecting it absolutely.

"He has a thriving import-export business—everyone in Los Angeles knows him! And Ski wouldn't be mixed up in anything like that!"

Her fist smashed down on the table.

"Neither would my father!"

CHAPTER 19

Bobbing Penguins

"RIDICULOUS," IS TWITTY'S best estimate.

Twitty, Proz, and Peevy are standing outside the "Casbah"—Twitty's name for the elegant Ladies Salon. They checked under the stall doors for missing size sixes ... no Lissa!

"Where would she have gone!" Peevy says. "Something's odd—I feel it."

Proz's head shakes dismissively.

"She's out in the garden passing wind."

Peevy snorts.

"She doesn't *have* wind!"

Twitty giggles. "You're an idiot."

But a thought occurs to her.

"Do you think we could go back in and ask Billy The Pirate without getting punched in the boob?"

"You'd get an open palm," Proz glimmers. "Peevy, would you recognize the waiter she spoke to?"

"Of course—Drape. Cute little bugger. Nice hands."

"Maybe he'd give you a punch in the boob!"

Peevy smirks gamely. "Gotta start somewhere!"

But now she's on tippy-toes, straining to see past Proz's tall shoulder.

"Why, Neddy—are you stopping in at the Ladies?"

Proz's tone is sardonic. "What pulled you away from dessert?"

"Your indefinable grace, my love. So she's vanished?"

"And who might that be?" purrs Proz.

He smiles at Peevy.

At Twitty.

"My wife believes Lissa and I are going to elope to Vegas the minute she looks the other way."

He eyes Twitty.

"Maybe Lissa's felon is still at the table—unless he's gone out to steal car stereos. We could ask him."

They're agreed.

Neddy offers Proz his arm, prepared for her to take it in her icy way, fingers hardly coming to rest. Instead, she grasps it firmly. They stroll back towards the Refectory's clattering dinnerware and chugging machine-gun repartee.

But where Lissa and her felon had been, they see two vacant seats!

Instinctively, Neddy seeks his wife's eye—

Just as instinctively ... she seeks Twitty's.

What's the use, he thinks, removing her hand from his arm.

Back at their places, he slides her chair beneath her packet and turns to Peevy. "Drape, you said."

For years, Drape and a hundred of Neddy's closest confidants drank beer on Thursday nights in Casablanca—until his evenings were converted to the amusement of beautiful Proserpina Rutt.

He catches Drape's eye and beckons him to meet at the end of the second table.

"The guy in the ballcap..." he says, and Drape nods immediately. "What was it about?"

"Crusty said, tell her there's an emergency phone call."

"Crusty...."

Neddy thinks it through, but it leads nowhere.

"So?"

"Crusty says, tell her she needs to come outside."

"And what did the ballcap say?"

"He was hustling her. He didn't like it ... you know."

Neddy knows.

"So obviously, I took her out to Crusty."

"What happened?"

Drape laughs. "You didn't see?"

"We were outside looking for her."

Drape's head shakes in disbelief. "Right in front of the whole Refectory ... in comes Doug the Thug and escorts him out!"

"Doug!"

Neddy thinks it through, but it still leads nowhere.

"Okay, thanks, Drape. I owe you."

"Naaah."

It means, yeaaah.

Neddy pulls out a pair of twenties. "Buy a six-pack."

Drape nods, thanks.

"And some chile verde at Casa ... those were the days!"

*****

Neddy hates this—something is wrong ... or maybe nothing is wrong!

Cultivating the unweeded thought, he shoots a quick glance on high. The Duke is reminiscencing ... something about learning the Charleston to please Constance.

Neddy scans his surroundings.

The Refectory contains the richest, brightest, most inventive people currently on parole—yet not one of them has invented a practicable portable phone. Instead of sitting here spinning his wheels, he could be talking to someone he needs to talk to!

At last, he looks where he's avoided looking.

And Proz looks back.

"What do we do?" he says. "Find Doug? Call Crusty? Go to Security Red? We have to do something, before you gnaw off your right thigh!"

"Neddy ... I'm thinking!"

He nods—so what.

"I don't know what to do!" she protests.

"You agree, then ... we should do something."

"Neddy, stop!"

"Exactly!"

Despite everything he knows—everything he can guess—he stands. "Wait here."

"Neddy, sit down, for God's sake!"

"Wait right here, dammit. Don't move—I mean it!"

His tone has an unfamiliar clangor.

It's upsetting.

But it isn't the let's-fight tenor she knows so well. It has a snap no one else hears—meant only for her.

"It does no good if I can't find you when I come back," he says. "Be here!"

It slides her back in her chair—not a lot ... but a little is a lot.

And she doesn't know what to do now, anyway.

"Burtie!" he barks down the table.

His voice is louder, but with the same hard clatter.

Burtie turns away from Ken Stukud as gratefully as if changing the channel from an eczema info-mercial.

Neddy signals him to the end of the table. He's up like a hornet.

"It's about Doug, right?" Burtie says.

"Shut up and listen."

Neddy describes the whole thing so far.

Burtie listens, as if to a prank he really likes.

"Okay," Neddy says, "... let's go!"

*****

Neddy dials the phone in the Third Living Room.

It's the same phone Lissa could've used minutes ago, if Crusty Yamaguchi had been telling the truth.

"It's Neddy," he says into the receiver.

"Good evening, Mr. Lombardo."

"Is this Larry—call me Neddy."

"Yessir, how can I help?"

"I want to speak to Crusty."

"Right away, Mr. Lombardo."

"There you go again..." Neddy says, his chiding tone lifted straight from the Teflon moviestar Commander-in-Chief's most recent State of the Union address.

He hears a ring, and, "Valet." It's Security Red's cover line.

"Neddy Lombardo," he says. "I want to speak to Crusty immediately."

"I'm sorry, Mr. Lombardo, he's not here right now."

"Where is he?"

"I can't say for certain. Is there some way I can help?"

"Who is this?"

"Agent Willett, sir."

"The Duke's daughter and I are concerned something's happened to a guest—Lissa Montenero. Are you familiar with her?"

"Certainly. Agent Yamaguchi just helped her in here."

"Is she all right?"

"We received a phone call from Rancho Palos Verdes—her father has a health emergency. Agent Yamaguchi has notified her."

"Where is she?"

"He's with her."

"And she's okay?"

"She's a little upset."

"Where is her boyfriend?"

"Kobalefffsky?"

"If you say so...."

"I don't know."

Neddy waits a beat.

142

Thinks of his father.

"Incorrect, Agent Willett—you do know! And what's more, you're going to be a lot more helpful! We don't want the Duke disturbed about you—now, tell me where he is!"

"Let me see if I can locate him, Mr. Lombardo."

"You do that. We'll be there in a couple of minutes."

"We, sir?"

"Burtram Balfour."

"Does he—"

"A couple of minutes, Agent Willett. Get Doug—I want to speak to him."

Ned hangs up, feeling something he recognizes from Perth Amboy—cold clarity. He tells Burtie to wait where he is and hurries back to the Refectory.

"Lissa is fine," he announces to the table. "Her father is ill, and she has to go home."

Heads along the table bob and bob like consenting penguins.

"And Billy the Pirate?" Proz says.

"I'm going to find out. Enjoy yourselves ... everything's fine!"

Proz grabs his arm. "I want to say goodbye."

"Crusty says, no—she's upset. She just needs to leave."

His voice has the same cold-steel timbre ... things are under control—stay here.

He hurries out into the hall to Burtie.

They head for the cool marble calm and 790,000 volumes of the now intensely multi-purpose Checquers Library.

CHAPTER 20

The White, The Red, And The Black

YAMAGUCHI'S SMILE GLEAMS like blue chrome in high sun.

"Even Cannizaro broke down and took some coffee."

Doug nods, satisfied.

He and Doug stand outside the scruffy chamber holding Cannizaro, Pulpo and Ski. Checquers' staff, domo to dishwasher, knows it as the Casino Custodian Maintenance Room. Only Security Red refers to it by its core function—the "tank."

But Doug has something on his mind.

"This Montenero dame keeps saying Ski isn't with them, as if he's some kind of innocent bystander. Rich broads ... they want what they want when they want it! Did you get them something to eat—the Duke'll want to know."

"It's coming," Crusty says.

"I told Lombardo Ms. Montenero's gone to L.A.—nobody needs to know otherwise. We have a party to engineer."

"But shouldn't we get her out of here?"

"I don't want her out of my sight till we've got Snake, L.A. says he's bad news. She still won't believe they want to kidnap her ... stubborn as a bull shark. We've got to keep her, but the Duke won't like it."

"You're the boss, Dougie."

"Now I just have to keep Lombardo from burning down the damn Refectory. Can't anyone just take no for an answer!"

Yamaguchi grins.

"Too rich."

*****

Back in Security Red now, Doug serves a gourmet blend of official news and sincere regrets.

"She's gone home already, Mr. Lombardo."

"Alone? With her so upset?"

"Have a seat," Crusty says, trying for an early takedown.

Neddy's having none of it.

"I'd have driven her, Doug—anyone would!"

It isn't the way it sounds. Given the sudden mysterious disappearance of Lissa and her suitor, Neddy's earlier designs on her are as far from his mind now as his Social Security number.

Doug's head shakes. "She wanted to go by herself—I couldn't change her mind."

"You don't change her mind, Doug ... you drive her!"

Doug knows it perfectly well.

"And where is whatssisname, Kobalooski?"

Miserable scrabbling sounds are heard under a moldering headstone in darkest Olde Red Hook....

"Kobalefffsky," Doug specifies.

"Fine...."

"He left, too."

"With her!"

"No, no, separately. His own car."

"I can't believe it," Neddy says. "Her dad's sick, she's upset, and you send her away alone!"

Doug's tolerant tone is wearing thin.

"She insisted."

Neddy is suspended between impotent acceptance ... and outrage! To his credit, he says nothing.

Doug's placating paw comes to rest on his shoulder.

"Ned—enjoy the party."

It's California ... first names have their impact.

"Go to the Refectory and have yourself a time!"

With no apparent option, Neddy nods.

Turns to the door.

"Oh ... listen," Doug says. "Any idea what they're planning for later?"

"No," Neddy says.

But opening the door, he stops. "They were going to go up to the hot springs."

Doug's smile flattens. "It's dense fog and no lights—you can't see a thing!"

Neddy shrugs.

"Part of the allure."

He steps out into the deserted Library.

Behind the closed door, Doug glares at Crusty.

"Blinding fog on the mountain ... Snake on the loose ... and they gotta go up to the fucking hot springs!"

*****

Proz puts a bright face on dark forebodings. It's her legacy.

In crisis, her mother instilled in her stern Rhode Island resolve. Project abiding calm, the firm assurance of a proud woman relying on the good offices of Providence. Proz knows. And she'll do what she can. But given her relative youth, her impetuous temper, and her generation's well-documented defiance, practicing this artifice under stress will be far more uncertain for her than ever it was for her mother.

As for Lissa's father falling ill, Proz is in no doubt ... it's the risk of being Lissa's, and her own, bitterly vulnerable age. Parents go right on superannuating at breakneck speed, just when their children achieve an agreed, hard-earned adulthood. To have this high attainment invalidated by a beloved parent's mortality ... it's the cruelest turning, yet Proz sees it in the best families.

And she dreads the cold hand settling on Daddy's shoulder. If it should—when it does—she feels no small concern for her own deportment ... Barbara Hutton and all that.

She turns to the head table now, indulging her limitless affection for her father. First of his peers, at the peak of his powers, he's nodding, laughing, bursting with vitality. May he ever be so! She wonders how anyone could have lived the eventful life he has lived without showing even a trace of ... no! He's never stopped mourning Mummie! It is his miracle and majesty—he feels it all, the white, the red and the black. He doesn't fear going to Hell ... he's already been! Oh, he is the very best father. She knows too well how grateful she must be!

And she knows how wretchedly spoilt she is—it takes a gala like this to confirm to her her infinite good fortune. But maybe now she'll be more willing to remember.

Neddy and she hiss and spit at each other like bobcats—it's their nature. They know nothing of peace and will do no better until their natures change. But perhaps they can learn from Daddy.

No.

She knows better.

Life is ruthlessly experiential—and in her consummate arrogance, she would have it all handed to her gently and on her terms! It can't be. Its very breadth and depth are its remedy and reward.

But Neddy has something tonight....

A tone.

Maybe it's only her mood.

Or the wine.

In the English manner, Daddy calls cabernet "claret" and his magnificent zinfandel "bull claret." His wine gentles her. Under its influence, she sees her gifts the more clearly. Yes, it's the wine.

Or is it this new tone she hears in her husband? It intrigues her. In spite of her eagerness to dismiss him, she feels an icewater giddiness in her breast for him, she has no clear idea why.

She's seen him look at Lissa—she has eyes.

But even that is changed now!

And please God ... let Lissa's poor father be well.

It's Daddy's zinfandel. That and this giddy icewater thrill inside her! She's glad she shaved her legs.

But isn't that just like her ... thinking only of her advantage—of what she wants and Neddy being convenient.

But he's her husband, why not!

Her secret appetites ... she's like a famished cat, fierce, conspiring, singleminded. She never knows when she's telling herself the truth about sex. Often, she doesn't see the truth until long afterwards—when it hits her with a sudden cold shock! She's so full of sham and trickery. It won't stand still for her to see—and when she tries to see and fails, she feels the fool, and so, stops trying!

She wants to understand how it is for Neddy—but a man is so different.

Unless, he isn't.

What a thought! What if it's no different for him—just as dazzling.

And maybe it's not just him and her ... maybe it's everyone!

Tonight with this pirate fisherman, beautiful Lissa is the most bedazzled of all.

When she stops to think of it ... and, oh, she does ... she knows only to let herself go—let go completely! And thank you, dear God ... she can! When she's in it, it carries her wildly away—she needn't do a thing. Her body flies out ahead of her on rushing torrents, out and out, over the thrilling precipice ... flying, flying ... divine!

Maybe Neddy and she are more alike than they are different!

Maybe from this moment, they need no longer work at cross purposes ... she no longer needs to think she is—

"Pros-ser-PINA!"

Peevy's face is a catastrophe of annoyance!

"Where are you ... my God! You're off in some parallel universe!"

"It's nothing," Proz smiles. "Really ... nothing."

"It's something!"

Peevy glares at Twitty.

Back at Proz.

"Did you sneak an Alice B. Toklas brownie somewhere?"

"There's an idea!" enthuses Twitty. "We need a change of head!"

"You like that stuff?" says "Kenny," as if she had proposed eating raw chicken.

"Don't you?" volleys Twitty.

He weighs the politics ... the Saab.

"... it's okay."

Suddenly, Proz disintegrates in helpless laughter. It's gushing out of her uncontrollably like uncorked bubbly, she can't contain herself! She's bawling ... at Stukud, at Peevy ... the Saab and Twitty ... herself!

"Toklas..." Peevy nods, convinced.

"Almost!" Proz confesses ... keening, straining to rein herself in. She thinks of Billy The Pirate murmuring in Lissa's ear ... of Doug yanking him out of the Refectory ... and her own dire premonitions! Lissa's father is ill—not funny at all—but the rest ... the whole hobo's bag....

Very gradually, her champagne laughter recedes to a parrot grin.

Peevy and Twitty want in on it, but she can't share it—doesn't know how.

Farther along the table now, she admires trim, gleaming Keita Mammady Fallo. He spoons a cut-glass dessert goblet of fresh mango, peach ice cream, and deep amber Vermont maple syrup ... Grade C+, oddly the gourmet choice.

He beams all around, tidy and handsome. Gerald Thermos is regaling him about ... Proz can't quite pick it out ... fireworks or indigestion or both. He follows every word, on the cusp of a giggle—but now his laughing eyes see Proz watching him.

He smiles back delightedly.

"Enjoying yourself?" she inquires, mugging the words extravagantly.

"Oh, my, very pleasant!" he beams, "... so entertaining! It is like an enormous university fraternity party—except with fully grown adults!"

Proz is back to keening, pealing, table-slapping hilarity.

CHAPTER 21

The Lady Of Chillon

KEN STUKUD LOCATES Heaven—a Tequila Mockingbird with lemon sherbet.

"And it's '*sherbert*'..." he says, improving Twitty's pronunciation. "Here, hun, have a try."

She's tried everything everywhere.

But she tries. "Pretty good."

Better'n that!

Tonight, Kenny's a goddamn gourmet!

He looks up presently—and here comes Neddy Lombardo, bounding in like he's lost his Capt. Midnight Secret De-Coder Ring!

"Can't believe it!" Neddy booms to the table. "Her father's ill, she's deeply upset ... so they send her off to L.A. all alone!"

"That's terrible!" Proz declares, in solidarity.

Neddy pulls out his chair.

Doesn't sit in it.

"She insisted, they say! And I say," he declaims, citing stockbroker Chuck "Charles" Peach's view on World Hunger, "... unacceptable!"

"Perfectly right, darling," nods Proz.

"I'd have driven her!"

"Yes," she nods, her smirk teetering on the brink, "... you would!"

But her tone is good-natured. Even warm.

Where did that come from!

"Anyone would!" he confirms, nailing the damn coffin shut!

"And what about Capt. Ahab?" inquires Twitty.

"Ski Kobalefffsky..." Neddy nods for the table's edification. "They say he left separately—and if you believe that, I can prove guacamole is the

149

cure for herpes!"

"You think they left together?" Peevy says.

"They're both gone!"

"Darling," Proz smiles, "did you forget your paranoia pill today?"

But she's smiling ... yes, winsomely!

With no option, he smiles right back.

Swirls the remains of the zinfandel in his glass and tosses it off.

"I don't know what's going on!" he says. "Oh well ... anyone up for the Bijou? *The Maltese Falcon* is showing!"

The grand second table takes its cue and slides back.

"Kenny" ... leaving the sterling silver tableware right where it belongs ... steps in behind Twitty to adjust her wrap, not omitting to brush the soft flesh of her sun-ripened bare shoulder.

In the evening chill and fog, she'll need the wrap ... and mayhaps him.

*****

Jazz singer Anita Rangoon's short, straight black hair gleams like Japanese lacquer.

She's made three fine recordings at Checquers' Bijou, two of them bestsellers. Performances in the Bijou are an occasion. She opens now on Vincent Youmans' bittersweet "Without A Song."

Its heartbeat supplies the Bijou's pulse.

"I love this song," Proz murmurs to Neddy, "don't you?"

He does.

Yet he isn't prepared for her to say so in just this way.

She seems remarkably agreeable.

But life is a minefield....

He'll see.

She takes his hand in hers and nestles against him.

When she's warm like this, he feels a violent surge of reprieve.

On a sudden impulse, like his blind decision at twenty to climb through the stockade fence at Pamplona and run with the bulls ... he pulls her to him and kisses her.

She responds willingly.

Passionately....

He wants more.

But she's nothing if not changeable.

... and life is a minefield.

He releases her before he wants.

"Come up for air, why don'choo!" Peevy complains.

"What for!" says Proz, running her fingers through his hair.

She rests her head on his lapel.

Peevy looks away at Thermos.

At Clive O.E.M. Monogram.

And the table's latest addition, regional poet and U.N. Peacekeeper Gary Larry. He's taking Chester Halimony's place. No lover of either jazz or black-and-white movies, Chester, Peevy notes, "has worse things to do with his time."

Twitty "excused" herself, too—the table resisting drawing graceless inferences.

And moments later, Ken Stukud "excused" himself to follow Twitty.

A whole new set of inferences is not drawn.

All the while, huge Gary Larry slumps mountainously in his chair like a sulking great teenager—doing his best not to block out all view for miles back.

At the next table over, Paw Coggins has hit his stride. Three curvaceously vacant blondes from south of Camarillo—nobody cares where—are all a-glitter.

("Niña, Pinta and Santa Maria," Neddy murmurs in Proz's ear, and she giggles.)

But to the three blondes' distress—it is Paw's curse—an obsequious male threesome now competes with them for Paw's attention. One is Neddy's broker and Tuesday-night poker-victim, Chuck "Charles" Peach ... losing to the Duke's son-in-law is good for the bottom line. The second interloper is legal-eagle Vance Crankenfuss. He boasts a win/loss litigation record even better than Paw's! The third is Fenton J. Pilbeam III. He arrived on a pristine black-with-white-pin-stripe 1956 BMW R50 motorcycle. It's all anyone needs to know about him.

Proz smiles in Paw's direction, and he leans in towards her as if taking signals. "Is Checquers like this every night?"

"No, no," she smiles, "... Tuesday is Gladiator Night."

The three blondes giggle like wind-up dolls.

"'Charles' can tell you," Proz smirks, going native on Chuck Peach.

"But I can't tell you *everything*..." leers Chuck.

"Ooohh-whoaa-ho-hohhh!" go the blondes like three arriving emergency vehicles.

"I haven't seen Lissa," Paw notes now.

"She had to leave," Proz says. "An illness in the family."

"Is it serious?"

"We hope not," says Neddy.

"Certainly do..." says Vance Crankenfuss with Chamber-of-Commerce scrupulosity.

All scan the void ... a scripted pause.

"Speaking of absentees," says Chuck Peach, a player when his wife is visiting Mom in La Jolla, "what's become of Ms. Twits?"

"Gone to the you-know," Peevy says.

"Takes her long enough."

"Gentlemen don't time."

"I'm no gentleman."

"Someone should wash your mouth out with Tequila..." purrs Peevy.

Her suggestive tone has even the gods checking their dance cards.

"Ken Stupid took off, too," she adds. "Wonder what takes him twenty minutes to do!"

"Peevy, really..." beams Proz the Monarchist, skimming the uppermost off her Mockingbird.

As it happens, they are quite mistaken.

Twitty is stealing due east now through deepest shades of Checquers night.

*****

Twitty knows exactly where she's headed.

... then, why the hell doesn't it look more familiar!

Life is a deeply flawed dress rehearsal.

The statues out on the rear lawn beyond the dark terrace are cloaked in dense, dripping coastal fog—until Twitty's progress trips an alert motion-detector.

Instantly, gracious granite statuary glimmers in dewy light.

Nice.

Especially Harpo....

It was one of these stairways down to the lawn, thinks Twitty.

She studies the nearest instance.

But where she dropped the note, the shrubs came right up to the stairs. No shrubs here.

The next stairway has shrubs. She steps down to look.

Nothing.

Unless some damn A.D.D. Checquers groundskeeper has speared it up already....

Crap!

Of course, she doesn't know what she'll do with it, even if she finds it. It just seems ... germane.

But no such luck.

In defeat, she climbs the steps to the terrace and heads back to the mansion, experiencing the scorched belly she gets whenever she tries something dead simple and lands flat on her ass.

Nearly to the house, she sees one last stairway she didn't check.
And the shrubs come right up to the steps!
She studies the shrubs beneath it and—
There!
It fairly glows ... a fat white postage stamp in the gloom.
But she doesn't want to dirty her party dress. She's no goddamn gardener!
Making her way down the steps, she squats low behind the shrub—
strrrretttches...
Got it!
In the terrace's dim light, she reads the sloppy scrawl that brought her down to Gardenia Gazebo ... and disgruntled, dissembling, darkly alluring Neddy.
She slips the missive into the private vault between her twin parcels of prime real estate.
It'll be safe there, until someone ... maybe Neddy, maybe not ... undoes a hook or five, rendering her lusciously, deliciously ... *dee-dee-yump* ... in play!

*****

"I don't need any damn kidnappers—I have you!"
The difficulty is, fit-to-be-tied Lissa Montenero is quite correct ... she's being held against her will, and all the rest is just yelling!
"Miss Montenero," Crusty Yamaguchi says, "we are sorry. We're doing our very best to protect you."
"Stop saying that!"
Her rage is encased in suffocating soundproofing. She can't be heard by anyone but Crusty—and she can't stand it!
Lissa paces back and forth, back and forth, deep in the basement below and east of Security Red.
Immediately beneath the Medieval Dept., under the cool marble calm and 790,000 volumes of Checquers' Library, Lissa's tightly sealed chamber has numerous features in common with that other soundproof facility beneath and south of Bigg Casino—the "tank." The salient difference between them is, the observation port in the tank's steel door is bulletproof glass. Tonight, however, there is one other difference between the two. In stark contrast to Lissa's furious pacing to and fro, once the steel door of the tank swings shut, Ski, Cannizaro, and Pulpo, consulting life experience, serve themselves coffee and donuts, and settle contentedly in.
At least, Cannizaro and Ski do.
Pulpo migrates to the coinless pinball machine provided for transients. (It's still Checquers.) Save for intermittent violent thumps to the

sides of the pinball machine and an occasional "*Shhhitt!*" ... Pulpo is in bliss.

Cannizaro and Ski, meantime, watch the tank's 12-inch black-and-white television.

KBUX-TV Channel 3's "Ten O'Clock & All's Well News" covers the startling strides being made by Dr. Harvey Moonfarm-X, City College's celebrated New-Age Marine Biologist. Against prohibitive odds, and following months of patient instruction, Moonfarm-X has succeeded in coaching his most gifted lab porpoise, Rory, to recite, in porpoise, page-long passages from *Finnegan's Wake.*

The recitation goes off without a hitch.

But farther south and west, Lissa remains inconsolable. Striding aerobically to and fro, she berates Crusty, Doug, and "The Douchebag of Monty Cristo" ... her actual words!

And much like Neddy earlier today, she rails against the laggardly creeeep! of the clock ... Crusty powerless to improve events.

"I can bring you coffee," he proposes. "Tea ... or something stronger?"

He pauses.

"It just isn't safe."

"I insist on speaking to my father!"

"He's on his way."

"What!"

Her outrage goes geothermal.

"You weren't going to TELL ME!"

"Ma'am, I just told you. You will see him the minute he arrives."

"I will, or I'll sue your eyes off! Where is Ski—I want to speak to him!"

"I don't know."

"You ... don't ... know...." she glares, shaming his ancestors.

"Leave me. Get out!"

Yamaguchi bows.

Turns.

Seals the vault.

He stands listening for a moment outside.

Hears nothing.

Just as he should.

CHAPTER 22

Six Million-Five

"YOU'RE A LINCOLN CONTINENTAL—I'd bet the house."

"... even this house!"

Ken Stukud chalks his cue stick, popping his gum like ladyfinger firecrackers.

"You like'em, don'tcha?" he nods. "Sure ... Lincoln Continental."

Stukud sinks the three-ball in the corner pocket.

He shoots pool with the lubricous ease of a Civil War vet playing checkers on the veranda.

"Only the tan-and-navy color combination..." Chester Halimony says, nursing his Henkell Trocken. "I drive a Mercedes ... and am I ever going to get a shot!"

Ken laughs.

"Prolly."

When he's shooting pool, something happens to him. His patter goes straight back to San Joaquin Community College twenty years back.

"We'll see," he says, conceding nothing. He's at home in the biggest way.

"You just keep suckin' down that ginger ale, pardner."

While talking, he's chalked his cue four times and sunk three balls.

The other guy—Payne's the name—doesn't say much.

Odd fella—Larry Payne....

But he's a shooter, Ken Stukud can tell—it's why Ken's working fast.

No time to waste.

The guy might be good, and it's all about winning.

But this Larry Payne—a hard'un to read. Yep, nope ... all that comes out of 'im. Not unfriendly, zackly—but not friendly, neither.

Takes all kinds in this big-ass whorehouse.

"That's two for me—rack 'em," Stukud says, dispatching the eight ball, but very nearly ... *pheeew!* ... dropping the cue and scratching.

He scoops up two twenties off the table, leaves his own down for the next game.

He's feelin' good.

And what the hell...

Instead of playing tournament tight-ass, let's us have some fun!

He lets the cue ball go hard—

Full Blammeeee!

It's an all-skate starburst on the table, balls flyin' every which way!

They go and they go ... missing this pocket, that pocket ... that'un, too. Not a single damn drop!

Okay, now we'll see.

Larry Payne eyes the table, daring it to make a false move.

He drops five in a row.

Draws the cue ball perfectly for the next shot each time.

Oh, boy....

"Like bowling?" Ken says, changing the subject as soon as possible.

"That's my game—just somethin' about it. Good exercise, too. They got a dozen alleys downstairs here somewheres ... the rich guys get together every month and have a tournament."

"Where'd you hear that?" Halimony says, watching Larry Payne.

"Somebody said."

"It's bullshit. They wouldn't be caught dead bowling ... or playing golf."

"Don't know what they're missing. Hell of a game—bowling. Brings out yer inner swagger. Makes a guy walk tall."

Larry Payne runs the table: "Rack 'em."

"Go ahead, Chester, I did it last."

"Got a match?"

Larry Payne's smoking like a chimney fire. He has the smoker's squint, smoke creeping up the barrel of his cigarette right in his eyes. It's why he scowls evil like that. Ken Stukud's studied human nature—there's a reason a guy scowls thataway ... just scowls natural like him. Guys like that—they look like bad-asses, but they're really not. Indigestion, more'n likely, something like that.

He's a Ford guy, too, no Chevy guy—you can bet the world. They're different. A Ford guy sticks out like a Corvette guy—which is *not* like a Chevy guy, no matter what they tell you.

Miles apart.

He's a Ford guy—look at him.

And a hell of a pool shot.

Payne's run the table again....

"Well ... learned *my* lesson!" Stukud beams. Eighty bucks is more than enough to make the case.

"Bowlin' ... there's the game."

"Bowling is for wife-beaters," Payne says.

... first thing he's said, except, "Rack 'em."

"Oh, I dunno."

"You don't have a wife."

"Ya' got me there, ol' buddy!"

Halimony grins over the tip of his cue stick ... and not one warped stick in the whole rack—this is goddamn Checquers!

"Where do you hail from, anyways, Larry?" says Stukud like a sailor on the Greyhound.

"Somewhere else. You guys know plenty of people around here. Ever heard of a babe named Montenegro. Good looking?"

"You'll mean, Montenero," says Halimony, on familiar territory, at last.

"I prolly will."

"She was here—had a family medical emergency. Why?"

"She left?"

Larry Payne's eye is on Halimony.

"She's gone?"

"So I hear," says Halimony.

Larry Payne is still eyeing Halimony.

"Okay," he says.

With not another word, he picks up his twenties, jams 'em in his jeans, and heads down the hall.

"Singular fellow," says Halimony.

Ken Stukud knows the right answer.

He shrugs, instead.

"He's a pool shot—we know that. Takes all kinds in this big-ass barn."

*****

Leon Victor Montenero is enraged. "I insist on seeing her!"

A swarthy man of medium build in his mid-fifties, he has a black mono-brow of profound unruliness.

The Duke looks to Crusty Yamaguchi, his tone stiffening in an early frost. "She is perfectly safe, is she not."

"That's for me to decide!" Montenero roars. "Who the hell do you think you are!"

Doug the Thug ... Douglas Arnold Dwyer, to the trade, it's the middle name that always gives up the precious ground ... steps in behind Montenero. His massive left paw lowers with menacing force on Montenero's shoulder.

Montenero is motionless.

The Duke points to the green-leather club chair in front of his desk.

"Sit, Mr. Montenero!"

The Duke waits.

"Sit!"

The Duke nods.

"And I'll tell you exactly who the hell I am, to within an inch of your cheap miserable little life!"

He gestures to the chair.

"Doug, help him get comfortable."

The chair is at an angle facing the Duke's handsome mahogany desk. The inner office is compact, surprisingly intimate, just as the Duke will have it. Supplicating trousers have settled into this green-leather club chair for decades.

Doug draws the chair slightly back, as if making it more accessible....

Montenero turns—not looking at Doug—and sits.

The Duke follows suit.

"Will you take something? Scotch? Sherry?"

"You're holding my daughter hostage ... it's an outrage!"

"When someone brings outsiders onto my property to kidnap a guest of mine, I make it my business to know all about it."

"That's bullshit, you're—"

"Won't have a drink? Splendid. Now shut your fucking mouth and listen."

The Duke beckons Crusty Yamaguchi forward.

In a courtroom monotone, Yamaguchi recites the entire matter in precise chronology—the L.A.P.D. intelligence report on Montenero ... his bad debt ... an account of the day's security activities, omitting any Security Red measures that are no one's concern. Opening a file folder, Yamaguchi lays out four mug shots from the L.A.P.D., now suitably flattened for easy inspection. These are followed by photos of the same four men, taken at Checquers today. Yamaguchi identifies Cannizaro, Ski, Snake, and Pulpo, noting they've spent the day attempting to locate Montenero's daughter. Yamaguchi recites the L.A.P.D.'s intelligence, that the four plan to kidnap

Lissa in order to impress upon Montenero their intent of being paid all moneys owed and interest accrued, if not on time, on more expansive terms.

A moment passes.

"You weren't even going to come up here, were you..." the Duke says.

Montenero is silent.

"Not until our Mr. Dwyer here told you he would lay out the entire mess in the L.A. morning papers, including a detailed description of your bad debt to the mob. Then, suddenly, you couldn't get here fast enough!"

"How would I know you were telling the truth?"

"By your standards, you wouldn't."

The Duke looks at Montenero...

Out the window.

"We don't choose our parents."

Montenero makes no move to speak.

"You put your daughter in grave danger, Montenero. You brought the threat of mortal violence onto my estate. When told about it, you were going to do nothing—and all you're doing right now is covering your own ass!"

"You think I did it on purpose!"

"It's all your doing—that's all that matters! And it's not hard to see why, you're stupid and a bully and a coward."

The Duke straightens in his chair.

"Do you even care if your daughter is safe!"

"Go to hell."

"What are you going to do!"

Montenero moves not a muscle.

The Duke looks at Doug.

Back at Montenero.

"Guys like you are all the same! You've heard it a thousand times, how it can all go wrong—but no, no, it'll never happen to you, you're too smart. So you take chances ... cut corners ... pull scams."

The Duke's hand fiddles with a sterling silver stiletto letter-opener.

Taps it on his desk blotter.

It makes a tintinnabulous ring.

"Anyone can make a mistake—that's not a sin. But if he's greedy enough, and small enough ... if he doesn't have the balls to face the consequences of his mistake ... it can get really dark."

Montenero is frozen.

"Can't it...."

The Duke pushes the letter-opener aside and comes forward.

"Okay—tell me what happened."

Montenero remains motionless.

"Or let me guess...."

He engages Montenero's eye.

"A shipment of yours got delayed, and you couldn't pay in time. Maybe your goods disappeared—somebody stole them. Come on, damn it ... something happened! You tried to outsmart some sleazeball banana slug down in Ecuador or someplace ... only it turns out you are the sleazeball banana slug and he outsmarted you!"

Montenero looks past the Duke's shoulder. "What does it matter to you? You don't give a shit!"

"I'll tell you what it matters to me—it's your daughter's life! Lissa is a beautiful, magnificent young woman, with all her life ahead of her!"

The Duke's head shakes.

"And now that I've met you, there are only two possibilities—either you have an exceptionally brilliant wife, or an extremely bright pool boy."

"Now listen, goddamn it—"

Doug's palm moves heavily to Montenero's shoulder again.

He remains in place.

"What..." the Duke says, "you think we should be showing you more respect?"

He looks at Doug.

Doug's palm rises.

Montenero slips back deep in the chair—hands clamped to the armrests.

"No worries, Doug. This man is no threat to anyone except his daughter."

The Duke studies Montenero.

"And she can't fight back—so he's not afraid of anything! He's got his tough-guy Wilmington Docks act—"

The Duke leans far forward suddenly.

"It feels good to be threatening, doesn't it ... tough guy. Your daughter is being hunted down by four hoodlums with guns and ropes and an empty car trunk ... but you don't care, because they're not after you!"

"The hell I don't!"

"Oh?"

The Duke waits.

"You care about Lissa?"

"Goddamn right I do!"

"Just a little?"

"What do you think!"

"And you'd give anything in the world, including your own safety, to see her protected—no one stalking her with guns and ropes, ready to tie

160

her up like a hog, throw her in a burlap sack and drive her out to some empty warehouse in San Berdoo!"

The Duke's eye bears down.

"Does that mean anything to you!"

"What do you want from me!"

Montenero's voice is reedy.

"I'm broke! I don't have the money, and they won't take no for an answer! They'll kill me!"

"Better you than Lissa...."

"It's easy for you to say."

The Duke repeats it coldly: "Better you than Lissa."

"I know that!"

Montenero's head drops, his tone paper-thin.

"What do you want me to say!"

"It's not what I want you to say, Leon—it's what you do!"

The room is deathly quiet.

"Do you want to help her?"

Montenero is paralyzed.

"Do you want to protect her? Would you do anything in the world to keep her safe from this shitstorm you put her in! This whole damn mess is on you!"

"I'd do anything!"

"... after you've covered your own ass."

"No!"

Montenero's tone collapses.

"Christ ... no."

The Duke watches him.

"But what can I do!"

"Love your daughter."

The air throbs.

"... love your daughter."

Montenero's breathing breaks.

"Oh, I do ... please, God, I do!"

His head shakes.

"I'm so completely lost!"

He stares at his clasped hands.

The Duke waits.

Looks up at Doug.

At Crusty.

A long moment passes.

He nods once, gravely.

"Give us a little privacy—will you please."

Doug stands stalk still.

"Crusty?"

Yamaguchi turns.

Doug hasn't moved.

The Duke nods again and Doug turns.

At the door, Doug looks back.

"Thank you, Doug," the Duke says.

The door closes behind him.

The two are alone, the Duke's voice deathly still.

"What's the damage?"

Montenero makes no reply.

"Leon ... what's the damage?"

"I know, I know..." Montenero says. "It's everywhere!"

"No, Leon—the money! How much is it?"

"You mean—"

"What did you borrow ... and what is the amount now?"

Montenero is silent.

Finally, he lets it all go.

"I needed five million-five a month and a half ago."

"And now?"

"Six million-eight."

"How much?"

His head drops.

"Six million-five...."

He stares at the carpet.

"I'm sorry. Six million-five."

His eyes come up to the Duke.

"Really. The shipment got delayed, and they played me. By the time it was here to sell, I was underwater."

"Six million-five," the Duke says. "That's the number?"

Montenero eyes the carpet.

"Leon, it's a really bad idea to give me the wrong number—I will find out and it won't go well."

He won't look up.

"Six million-five," he says.

He looks at the Duke, at last.

"I can show you the paperwork. It's pottery, dinnerware, that kind of stuff—from India. I don't know what they thought they—"

The Duke's left hand waves it off.

He's writing a bank draft for the vigorish.

The office is perfectly still but for the pen nub's soft scribbling across the pad. With a sudden flourish of incomprehensible curls and swirls, the cyclonic monogram of blinding wealth ... the Duke tears out the bank draft and comes around the desk.

Montenero comes to his feet, wilted.

"This never happened, Leon."

The Duke hands him the note.

Montenero's head shakes—

But the Duke speaks first.

"We'll get you to Lissa, then we'll put you with the people you need to see—but we need to be quick about it. The fourth man—the bad one—is still loose."

Montenero looks at the bank draft. "I can't take this."

"You just did."

"How can I ever pay it back!"

The Duke holds his eye.

"Love your daughter...."

He points Montenero to the door.

"This didn't happen."

Montenero is too fragile to move.

Expecting it, the Duke opens the door for him, and he steps out.

In the anteroom, Doug and Crusty turn.

Crusty will take Montenero to his daugher.

Montenero is about to speak—

But the Duke shakes his head.

"Don't tell me. Tell her."

Immediately, he's off in the direction of the Bijou and *The Maltese Falcon*. He knows the movie well—he'll be there before Capt. Jackaby of the *La Paloma* is shot. Real life, too, has its false treasures.

Part Four

CHAPTER 23

Slow Boyle

"WHAT DO PEOPLE DO for fun around here?" Vern Jerms whispers, "... anything?"

Proz puts her finger to her lips in the Bijou darkness—hush!

The Maltese Falcon flickers on.

But Vern doesn't like old movies—doesn't like old anything!

For Vern, the evening has been a triumph, and he's at his worst when his evening is a triumph. The jam-packed second real-estate seminar, following swiftly on the heels of the jam-packed first real-estate seminar, was blockbuster. He almost ran out of business cards—almost.

Most of all, he knows it's no accident that in the dark Bijou now he sees Twitty a table away, bathed in intensely flattering klieg lights.

She isn't.

The Bijou is dark as family secrets.

But in Vern's eye, flattering light flows over her for only him to see ... and seeing, imagine.

Is it him—or does she look a little "needy" tonight?

He smiles.

She smiles back, as if at the new boy in camp ... *tee-dee-yump*.

He's going to say something.

And he would, he thinks ... if everyone wasn't gawking wall-eyed at this black-and-white goddamn groaner!

In the same moment, Twitty espies his snazz-o green-and-yellow Madras blazer and big black-rimmed glasses—is it her, or does he look ... "lonely?"

She looks up at the screen.

Back at him.

Smiles her best.

Married men are so grateful!

And she's just a little date palm out here in the middle of the Sahara....

*****

An arm's length—and light-years away—from Twitty, Peevy thinks and thinks about Gerald Thermos.

Gerry.

Zukie....

She smiles at him now—

But why is he always on the other side of the table? They should get to know each other!

Just as Bogie is blacking out up on the screen, drugged by fat, gloating Sidney Greenstreet, Peevy leans far across the table.

"Gerry..." she says in a stage whisper, that to be heard at all—is heard by all!

"Shhh!" snaps Proz.

But Peevy wants Thermos to meet her in the back of the Bijou.

She knows it's gauche—but tonight, she feels gauche!

She engages his eye, feeling it all around her ... foreign intrigue! She's a petite, seductive spy in a danger-filled Constantinople nail salon, and Zukie's her Bogie!

She makes concealed gestures.

Jabs her finger back into the dark.

He turns to look—

What's she pointing at?

She points at herself.

The dark.

Proz hisses, "Shhh!" but Peevy glares right back—

She's not making a sound!

Thermos looks at Neddy...

who knows, but doesn't look back.

So Thermos points at her.

Points back there.

... him?

Neddy whispers hoarsely, "Peevy would have a word."

"Shhhtt!" bristles Proz ... *The Maltese Falcon* clattering on.

Thermos nods, no meat left on this bone.

He rises, at last.

Cripes, thinks Peevy traipsing to the back ... *exhausted!*

*****

"I've seen it a trillion times," Peevy says, "... haven't you?"

She reaches out for Gerald in the pitch black. Her hand finds his olive corduroy jacket. City College model ... suede elbow patches.

"But it's sooo good..." he says disconcertingly.

"We can go back in, if you—"

"What did you want?"

It'd be so easy just to say it.

She looks right through him, instead: "Nothing."

"—I was bored," she puts in hastily—before he can say anything they'll both regret. "Want to talk?"

"What about?"

"Or we could walk. It feels like we've been sitting down all year!"

"Want to go down to the beach?" he says.

She peers out the Bijou glass rear doors at the dense evening fog. The low garden lamps glimmer gloomily.

"Looks a little chilly for the beach, don't you think."

"Atmosphere..." he suggests idiotically.

"Maybe something more, uh ... room-temperature?"

"I know!" he says. "We could ... no we couldn't."

"What...."

"I've got it!" he says, grabbing her hand and opening the Bijou door.

"Oh-my-Gawd Gerry!" she giggles. "What kind of trouble are you getting me into now!"

"You'll love it. We'll build a fire!"

"I love fires!" she says—actually meaning it.

*****

"Name's Larry Payne. Flew in from Chicago—old friend of Crankenfuss."

"Grand," beams State Sen. Pallusian. He gives Larry Payne a politic smile. "Chicago, huh. Sounds more like Brooklyn."

"I live in Chicago," says Payne, "... but you're right—got a match?"

"Don't smoke."

"What's the matter with everybody! Lemme find a light ... right back." Larry Payne knows his way around by now—the waiters all carry matches ... it's fuckin' Checquers! He's back in a trice, taking a deep drag from his Camel—gulping it down like cold Coke in August.

Smoke billows out of him in tatters.

"What's everyone do after dinner," he says, "... get drunk and have car wrecks?"

"That's about it," smiles the Senator.

"A shame about Lissa Montenero."

"You know Lissa? A stunner. Something happen to her?"

"She had to go to L.A.," Payne says, "a family health crisis."

"Dunno how that could be!"

The Senator shakes his head, killing the bill in Committee. "I just saw her old man down by the Library."

"You din't," says Larry Payne.

"I think I'd know Leon Montenero when I see him. Quite a guy in his way. He was in some kind of great rush and couldn't talk ... they can usually talk."

"They?"

"Nothing..." smiles Sen. Pallusian.

"Where'd you say you saw him?"

"By the Library a couple minutes ago. You know Leon?"

"Which way's the Library?" says Larry Payne, suddenly in a rush.

The Senator points along the hall. "Just past the Constance Room."

"Where?"

"Down there a ways," says Sen. Pallusian vaguely. "Oughta have signs in this stadium. Something the matter?"

"I'll find it," Larry Payne nods, snake eyes gleaming. "Nothin's the matter," he says, "... nothin' at all!"

*****

Twitty's trying something risky ... but nothing ventured, nothing blah-blah-blah-ed.

"Vern," she whispers, "... ever wonder what women really think about you?"

In the murky Bijou, she breathes it so softly, Jerms can't hear.

He leans in closer from the next table. "What?"

"I said—"

But she chickens out.

"... ever wonder if movies are really true?" she says—a flimsy phonetic counterfeit of the original question, but the best she can come up with on short notice.

She sells it, nodding up at Bogie and Mary Astor on the screen. "Were people ever really like this?"

"I don't know, Twitty, what do you think?"

"I mean..." she says, "is Mary Astor supposed to be attractive? She looks like a Macy's floorwalker."

"Shhhhh!" snaps Lady Proz, Mistress of Ceremonies. "This isn't a drive-in movie, you know … though I Kind of wish it was."

She smiles up at Neddy, giving it context.

Twitty sasses her right back: "Shh-shhhh!"

What's Proz got to be so smoochy about, Neddy's arm around her like a first date! Everybody knows the truth! And two can play her game!

Twitty leans far over to Jerms. "Come outside with me," she whispers right in his ear so no one—*in hell*—will shush her! "I want to show you something soft and something that isn't."

He draws back.

Scans her head-to-toe, omitting nothing.

She expects it—and is a shambles just the same.

"Come on!" she mouths.

She looks at Proz now and throws her head back brattily, taking her leave.

They vanish into the rear, Jerms' hand around her narrow waist— nudging her intimately, strategically, to the mutual benefit.

She stretches up to his ear, passing out the Bijou doors. "Do you like tennis?"

"No."

"Well, you will!"

He likes the sound of that.

The foggy outdoor chill serves to wrap them even closer together.

They follow the cobblestone path out past Checquers' famed Mansion Of Mirrors. World-class close-up magic will be performed there, starting promptly at the witching hour.

But Twitty strains to see ahead through the fog and drear. At last, she makes it out, but—

Crap...

A healthy conflagration is blazing in there already!

Silhouettes of leaping flame dance high and wild against the de rigueur white-and-pale-green candy-cane wallpaper of the Tennis Pavilion.

No Vacancy!

She signals Jerms to wait here—this is "women's work."

He grunts, half caring.

Slipping through the fog, she peeks around the edge of the curtains. She sees a guy—definitely a guy—and from the sailor suit on the rug ... definitely Peevy.

"What..." says Jerms, back in the fog.

She hears it faintly—the Pavilion's cheesie little Sony transistor radio playing sappy Delius, maybe worse.

Gotta be Thermos.

Peevy, you l'il Dickens!

"Can I see?" says Jerms.

"You don't like tennis."

Twitty, guardian of public decency, blocks Jerms' path ... hauling him back away from the Pavilion like the Volga boatmen.

He resists half-heartedly.

Then not at all.

"I know!" he says. "I have the perfect spot!"

Twitty smiles, as though not fully signed-on ... but just maybe.

She has a better idea now, anyhow, they'll kiss right here in the drippy, duh-reammy fog!

Vern doesn't see the point.

They never do.

And pushy little Peevy ... getting jollied by Thermos to sappy Delius, maybe worse!

*****

Slow Eddie Boyle stomped out of the Grand Refectory dinner, red-ass mad.

He was red-ass mad before he arrived, of course—and he was red-ass mad all the time he was there. But by the time he stomped out, he was also knee-walking drunk. It adds flair.

It's a quarter past eleven in the Pato Café now, and Eddie is in full bloom. So is the Pato Café, banging and crashing through the night like a fast freight, its swoggled clientele hanging on, awaiting events. If you are a commercial fisherman, or playing the part, you're in the Pato tonight and every night—you have your reasons. Located on Calle Casapedo in Pt. Moot, downwind of Santa Lola, the Pato's green-and-yellow neon sign, *bzzzzz*-ing in dense, dripping fog, reads "Ten Minutes From Anywhere."

Candidly, the Pato is no café. Nourishment isn't served, not until pepperoni sticks, pickled eggs, and miniature Vienna sausages form an essential food group. The last mug of coffee crossed the Pato bar one bitter Tuesday twelve years ago, when the afternoon beer truck, lumbering north on Highway 101 from Compton, crashed in dense fog at Seacliff Beach. The holocaust demolished one of the highway's grandest billboards, of 200,000 nationwide, owned and operated by Santa Lola outdoor-advertising magnate Maxwell Marvue. Quizzed by the Highway Patrol at the scene, the beer truck driver could shed no light on the incident or anything else in the preceding decade ... like the Liberty Bell, he'd been rung once too often. Insurance paid all damages—but insurance takes time. The spiritual insult sustained that Black Tuesday by the alkali-dry Pato clientele no regular will ever forget, and just as many can't remember.

Slow Eddie is in the Pato tonight despite the fact that Thursday is a good TV night. It isn't that Eddie undervalues great TV—he venerates it. What he doesn't venerate is Checquers Bullshit, and as night follows day,

Eddie holds only one person answerable—Duke Monty. Eddie has been invited to every Great Party since the Bay of Pigs, yet after decades ... decades ... the Duke doesn't know Eddie from a barrel of chum. In Eddie's view, he has been singularly, cavalierly, intolerably ignored!

And tonight in the Pato, surrounded by simpatico odors and compadres, feelings of abuse fester in Eddie's belly like a swallowed Fourth-of-July sparkler. Cosseted among his brethren, he will dispute to the death the contention that in Santa Lola, commercial fishermen are revered.

In a word ... sharkshit!

What particularly triggers Eddie, duck-walking through a second pitcher of Oly draft, is ... when he was introduced to the Duke's syphilitic son-in-law tonight for the eighth or ninth time, for the seventh or eighth time, Neddy Lombardo nodded, smirked, then scuttled the hell off like the slack-ass *gawwwddammssnobbb* he indelibly is!

(The transcript will show this is not statutorily the Duke's failing ... yet it will serve.)

"Neddy..." Eddie grumbles to himself now on his Pato barstool.

"Neddy!" he re-grumbles, an actionable complaint taking form under his black navy watch cap.

"Who the hell's he think he is ... the Queen of Bolivia!"

Eddie's had enough—except of Oly draft.

And to his eternal credit, up at Checquers, Eddie Boyle made his position crystal goddamn clear! When Neddy scuttled off, just before two billion Block Island cherrystones-on-the-half-shell were rickshaw-ed in by neutered Oregonian slaves, Eddie stomped out! Scroom! He spun on his heel ... pronated instep ... and blew outta goddamn doors, stormed across goddamn lawns, slammed his truck goddamn door! The engine started, third goddamn try, and he drove down the endless, fogbound, blinding, swooping, swooning ... *whoooohah*-Jeeezus! ... mountain damn road back to Pt. Moot, one eye shut the whole way! He could drive that road in blinding fog with one eye shut better than their farting chauffeurs with four eyes!

And top to bottom—for safety—he made sure to straddle the centerline, whether it was single, or double ... or triple!

He kept his high beams on the whole way—let *them* get outta *his* road!

All the way down, what's more, he inflicted unendurable fantasy excruciations upon the entire company of Checquers snotheads. By the time he achieved flat land and the approaches to Pt. Moot, operating all the while on a clinically empty stomach, he had foraged deep into racial memory, mining mother lodes of insensate rage from the most heinous annals of world Divorce Court precedent!

Halting the truck, at last, somewhere within taxi distance of the Pato ... he'll find it later ... a single moral truth was clear—tonight is payback!

A third golden pitcher of Oly stands perspiring on the Pato bar....

Eddie pours two headless, flawless pilsner glasses.

"Mick," he grunts, hunkered down on his barstool like a bullfrog.

Mick receives the proffered glass.

Formally, he is "Mickey Moose," partly because he is huge, partly because he was christened Aloysius Albert Lovely ... but mostly because one Thursday lunch in the school cafeteria, when he was a murderous All-State Prep nose guard on the Santa Lola High football Golden Madres, second-string punter Dub Dolhemus mistakenly addressed him as "Wishy," the unauthorized corruption of Aloysius. At Mick's hands that night behind the gym, Dub Dolhemus was beaten statistically senseless.

Ever since, by acclamation, "Wishy" Lovely is Mickey Moose.

"Gotta do something, Mick..." Eddie says, muttering down the shank of his toothpick like a film-noir hack driver on a meaningless and rainy night.

Mickey plays it back, inspecting its parts. "... do something."

Eddie nods, gnawing his glass. "For the people."

"What people?"

"And our situation...."

Mickey's thick fingers close around his glass like an anaconda preparing piglet brunch.

"Got a situation, do we, Carb?"

"Carb" is short for, "Carbuncle," Slow Eddie's other nickname. It relates to "Boyle" from back in Golden Madre days, when nicknames didn't take a lot of explaining.

Eddie nods slowly at his beer. "Time we did something, Mick ... y'know?"

If anyone in the Pato knows ... it's Mick.

"Hey—Spider!" Eddie says. "Mambo ... Billy, Jiggy, c'mere, I got something!"

Mickey Moose nods for them to get the hell over.

They do, six of them.

They see Carb is serious.

CHAPTER 24

Demon's Eye

"DADDY!" LISSA ERUPTS.

She rushes to her father, clinging to him like a terrified child.

"There you are, my darling," he says, "safe and sound."

"These people said you were in some kind of awful trouble!"

"No, no, darling, everything's fine."

"But Daddy, they say—"

"I know, I know—all a misunderstanding. Everything's fine. Nothing to worry your pretty head about."

"Then, the talk about owing money—"

"Nothing."

"And kidnapping!"

He disengages her.

Holds her out at arm's length, engaging her deep-green eyes.

"Baby, does that sound like something I would be involved in?"

He says it again.

"... does it?"

Sunshine beams in her smile.

"No, Daddy!"

"That's better!"

She melts with relief, hugging him.

He steps back and shoots Yamaguchi a sharp glance. "Now, let's see if we can't get you back to the party, my dear."

"I'm sorry, sir," Yamaguchi says.

"Of course, we can!"

"Nossir—we cannot."

She looks at Yamaguchi.

At her father.

"Daddy, do you know who these people are?"

"Wait here, I'll get this straightened out, will you do that for me?"

"I seem to have no choice."

Her father smiles back, "You're a sweetheart."

He gives her cheek a peck.

Then he takes Yamaguchi by the elbow out into the hall and closes the door. "You can't keep her locked up like this!"

"Would you like to speak to the Duke?"

"No."

"Mr. Dwyer?"

"No, no."

Montenero thinks a moment. Turns back to the door—

"This is locked!"

"Of course."

"Open it immediately!"

"She stays inside."

Adding up unseen columns of figures ... Montenero concedes.

Yamaguchi unlocks the door and Montenero enters.

"Just relax, baby. Don't worry, I'll be back in a few minutes."

She watches him go, her eyes overcast.

He turns at the door.

"Okay, sweetheart?"

Overcast will have to do.

*****

What was she thinking!

She wasn't thinking ... he's an ass!

She wanted to kiss him in the Bijou—her own husband—do it like it's never been done ... and he draws back! She thought they were starting over, all because he began ordering her around. What's that about, anyway!

She's having a relapse, ohhh, she knows it.

And she was doing so well! They both were! He was strutting around like a tin soldier, and she was buying it ... until she wasn't! Funny how they do that, acting as if everything depends on them.

Nothing does.

Such a bad relapse....

But she knows why.

She's afraid. She gets hurt, then she gets mad, then she gets afraid.

She has no courage!

Change makes her so afraid—it's just so hard!

176

If she had just one special thing she did ... something that was truly hers!

If she painted.

Or Tango-ed.

Or went to the bathroom....

That's it—laugh at herself!

And stop being so damn afraid!

Laugh at herself and keep trying hard. It's worth it—

She knows!

But right now, she needs to think about something else ... Daddy should've shown *Casablanca* tonight.

No, he always shows *Casablanca.*

They should've made ten different *Casablancas*, so it would never get old...

And, ohhh ... such a terrible relapse.

She always falls short on commitment. She's so spoiled!

And just when things were looking really good....

*****

Like most nightmares, it was just a fantasy—things went perfectly.

No surprise, thinks the Duke. Doug handled things masterfully. Montenero gave Cannizaro the money just like a bank deposit—of course. Cannizaro's boss likes money, and Cannizaro likes being liked!

The Duke wonders how Montenero explained things to Lissa, certain parts of them, but he has his doubts. He knows Montenero like he knew Big Patsy—except Big Patsy he trusted.

"Montenero just says ... 'Here,'" Doug tells the Duke.

Doug loves telling yarns.

"And so Cannizaro says, 'What's this?' 'Look at it,' says Montenero. 'Don't worry, it's good. Are we done here?' But Cannizaro doesn't even look at Montenero."

Doug grins.

"He looks at me, and I nod—it's good. 'Okay,' he says, 'we're outta here.' I says, where's Snake—but right away, Cannizaro gets all puffed up. 'Mr. Cannizaro,' I says, but he jumps right in like Louie the Lawyer ... 'oh, we're back to *Mister* Cannizaro!' Answer the question, I says. 'If I know Snake,' he says, 'he ain't far.'"

"Where did you leave it..." the Duke says.

"They're all three in the tank."

"I'd prefer they weren't."

"I know, sir—we just missed Snake by two minutes in the poolroom. He can't stay lucky all night."

"Okay. But I want them to call San Pedro and say the money is settled. And Doug, I want you to hear them do it! Then escort them down to the highway."

"That means Snake is still up here by hisself."

The Duke nods. "We have to catch him. Is there some way we can talk the kids out of going up to the hot springs in the fog?"

"They already started," Doug says. "We could make them come back down."

The Duke thinks a moment.

"No. No, no—that's not Checquers."

*****

"So ... shall we hot-spring?"

It was Peevy speaking a few minutes before Doug finished up with the Duke.

And Proz left no doubt ... "We shall!"

To say Peevy was feeling perky after going three sets with Gerald Thermos in the Tennis Pavilion is to say Niagara falls. And Thermos, too, had a bit of the percolator about him. He'd run a half-marathon and was not found wanting—not bad for a slothful thirty-something avant-garde composer with asterisk cholesterol. As for the Charles Stanford on the cheap little transistor radio, what he'd heard of it ... adequate.

In Neddy's mind, given all that is afoot with Doug and Lissa's truck-thief, he was less than sanguine about everyone scrambling up the mountain to the hot springs in dense fog. But he decides he won't trouble Proz about it ... let her enjoy herself. She loves going up to the springs. He and Burtie will go up after finding out what happened to Lissa's bandit.

Yet things are getting strange. Now Lissa's father's turned up!

As Neddy expected, Burtie's been invaluable. After *The Maltese Falcon*, when the decision was made to go up to the hot springs, everyone was clattering upstairs to put on jeans and "grubbies" for the scramble up the mountain, when Burtie pulled Neddy aside. He'd just seen Crusty Yamaguchi going down to the tank with Old Man Montenero ... what in hell is he doing here!

Neddy nodded darkly. "What in hell is Jack Ruby doing here in Dallas Police Headquarters?"

He looked up the main stairs, just as his wife and the others were heading along the hall to change to jeans and sweatshirts for the climb.

"Proz!" he called to her, but she didn't respond.

What's she mad about now!

"Proz—please!"

She waved the others on, Neddy climbing the stairs to her.

178

"Burtie says your father wants a word with me," he said.

She listened, expressionless.

"Proz, what's the matter?"

She said nothing.

"What!"

"Neddy, if you don't want to come up to the springs with me—"

"But I do! We'll be up as soon as we finish with your father!"

"You don't have to—it's fine. Nothing lost."

Without another word, she set off along the hall.

He looked down to Burtie.

Back to his wife.

"Proz, why won't you believe me!"

"It's fine," she said, stepping into the changing room—taking her world with her.

"You don't have to," she said. "Do what you want!"

*****

"A shame Lissa isn't here..." says panting Twitty, her voice muffled in blank fog.

They're struggling upwards—hands and knees clawing into the steep mountainside. Steadying themselves in the gloom, with each new lunge they grip handfuls of grass, clutch at stones, pulling themselves higher.

"She'd love this..." Twitty says breathlessly.

"You're crazy," Peevy breathes, "she'd detest it! Where are you, anyways!"

"Right behind you, silly!"

Peevy feels a sharp prod—a stick poking her stern.

"Okay ... I believe you!"

"You can't see your own eyelashes in this fog!" Twitty says.

"And hers are a foot long..." Peevy grumbles.

"Oh, stop!" Proz says.

She is three leg-thrusts above them, making impressive progress.

"Everyone is so jealous of Lissa. It's not her fault she's beautiful!"

Peevy snorts.

"It's not mine, either."

The hot-springs heroine, Proz knows the way, but as far as the rest can tell, they're completely lost. And at this point, Proz sees Lissa's position with real sympathy. Her father is ill—maybe seriously.

"Poor thing..." she says, "she has a lot more on her mind than finding the hot springs in pitch black."

"That doesn't sound very encouraging," observes Twitty.

Just then, Proz's foot slips.

She laughs, sliding helplessly downwards.

The steepness of the slope and the damp, fog-slickened grass send her crashing into Peevy. Both career uncontrollably lower, shrieking with laughter. They slide to a rude halt in a few feet, their scruffy wear-and-tear jeans earning their keep.

They'll stop for a breather—gasping as much from laughter as exertion.

"Has anyone ever completely disappeared up here?" inquires Gerald Thermos, somewhere off to the right.

"Once," Proz smirks. "Pete Zuria from Laguna Beach. Wolves."

"What!" Thermos gasps.

"There are no wolves," Vern Jerms says. "It's against code."

"Thank you for that, Vern," says Proz.

"There aren't!"

"You're right," she grins, "and when you're right, you're right."

In the blinding gloom, Jerms is somewhere below Twitty—whether far or inappropriately near, Proz won't speculate. Jerms and Twitty spent a fruitless hour hunting a trysting place in the great mansion. Huge as it is, tonight it's jammed elbow-to-kneecap with extraneous humanity. Jerms is in no mood for loose talk of wolves.

"Is Neddy going to be all right?" Peevy inquires, out of the blue. It's an all-purpose query, serviceable at any juncture.

"He's coming up later," Proz says, "... if the wolves don't get him."

"There are no wolves!"

Proz laughs.

"Vern—calm down!"

But why is Proz being so bleeding cheerful, Peevy ponders. Having had her ample serving of Zukie ... a little excess cheeriness from Proz goes a long way.

But Peevy knows Proz dearly loves climbing up to the hot springs. This midnight adventure, scratching up the mountain in blinding fog, is one of her favorite things—a rite she's reenacted countless times.

For Peevy's part, she is less charmed ... and where in this damn pea soup has her Zukie gotten to! During their recent violent mixed doubles, they burned the candle at all ends ... yet already, she feels a restless ember in her flickering back to life. It sparks brightly in the dense fog's sensuous touch-but-don't-look darkness.

Where can his plumpness be!

"Are we halfway there yet?"

It's a new voice in the void.

... but in its way, peculiarly near.

And Proz can't seem to place it.

Well, of course not, she thinks ... is she expected to identify every voice of the thousands she's been battered with at the Great Party!

"Where are you?" it says.

"Here..." informs Peevy, adopting the imbecile's role in every lost-in-the-dark exchange. "Where d'you think!"

"Where is 'here'?"

"Here!"

"Ouch!"

The protest comes not from the stranger—it's Thermos.

Something's done him injury, and not lightly!

"Good Christ!" he snaps. "What's your hurry!"

"You all right?" the voice says.

"Nice of you to not just kick me in the balls!"

"Sorry."

"Gerry, you all right?" Peevy asks.

They hear another query instead from Thermos—"What's that!"

"What?" the voice says.

"In your jacket! It hit me on the head like a hammer!"

"Gerry, are you all right?" It's Proz, speaking for management. "Where are you?"

"Here!" says Gerry ... imbecile number two clocking-in.

"It's a stapler," the voice says. "I had some things to staple driving up."

The silence of Ancient Luxor.

"Gerry?"

Peevy again.

"Here!"

"Ouch!"

It isn't Thermos this time.

"You!" says Peevy.

"You?"

"Who are you!"

"Billie Dumphy."

"Who?"

"Who what!"

"No clue..." says Proz—summarizing for all.

"Billie Dumphy," nods Vern Jerms, doing intake on a new condo client.

"Didn't mean to step on your hand, bud," says Billie Dumphy, struggling higher.

"My name isn't Bud—it's Gerald Thermos."

"Pleeztuhmeetcha. I'm Billie. Yer hand okay?"

"You made me slip. I fell on my ass."

181

Proz's laugh tinkles like a glockenspiel.

"We fell on our ass, too!"

In the wet grass, they hear Gerald, above them now, take a step.

Bump a rock—

"Shit!"

... he's bowling headfirst down into Twitty and Proz.

Down they all go ... whhaaahoooo! ... sprawling in convulsions ... shrieking with laughter ... down and down through muffling fog.

"Y'okay?" says the voice.

They're laughing so hard they struggle to catch their breath ... in order to laugh harder!

Was there ever such a—

... no, never!

They're laughing

... gasping

... snorkeling for breath.

Gradually, like a siren winding down, composure returns, before— another breathless outbreak!

Better now.

Vern Jerms, meantime, ponders Billie Dumphy's housing needs.

He'd hand him a card if he could find an open palm.

"Billie?" he assays blindly.

"Havin' a time, huh?"

A match flares.

Sears an unfiltered Camel.

Zig-zags in the fog...

Out.

The bright orange coal glows in the night.

A demon's eye.

"How much farther," Billie says, "... any idea?"

"Proz knows," Jerms offers.

His hand juts out towards the orange glow.

Fumbles about.

They shake.

Billie inquires, "And where is she?"

"Right here," Proz says.

The demon's eye glows bright.

Billie inhales deep.

Exhales luxuriantly.

"Proz..." he says. "Great to meetcha—at last!"

CHAPTER 26

TAXI!

THE DUKE'S SMILE is brittle.

"I don't know what you're getting at, Neddy—she's on her way to L.A."

"Come on, Duke, where have you got her? Burtie saw her father and Crusty going down to the tank!"

"Tank? What tank!"

"And where's this Kobalefffsky character?"

"Neddy, I—"

"Listen, Duke, I'll go down there myself, if I have to! Try and stop me, and you'll hear the loudest racket since Watergate!"

"Don't threaten me, Neddy."

"Why is her father here—and why is Sheriff Mick here ... Burtie saw him! And stop about the tank, we know all about it! We're not the mindless babaloos you'd like us to be ... come on!"

The Duke considers it.

With the faintest glimmer, he nods.

"You make your point, son ... but we can't talk here."

In silence, he guides Neddy out of the Bijou and down the long broad main hallway.

When they arrive at the cool marble calm and 790,000 volumes of the Checquers Library and step in, Neddy walks straight to the Security Red door concealed in the wall's ornate woodwork. It's no great secret ... but again, the Duke glimmers.

Inside the communications room, Pritchett sits at the switchboard.

(Millie The Old-Fashioned Operator doesn't work nights.) Neddy knows most of the Security Red personnel. Pulling switchboard duty, Pritchett must've gotten himself on Crusty's shitlist. Otherwise, the room is empty.

"I'm going to show you something, Ned," the Duke says, "... on one condition—that you promise to be very quiet until we come back out."

Neddy nods.

But the Duke's eye holds him for a beat.

Now the Duke opens the inner door at the far end of the room. He leads Neddy down the steel stairs to a locked door. The door has a one-way cubby window. He invites Neddy to peer inside.

Lissa is by herself.

Neddy glares at the Duke ... but his word is often his bond.

The Duke waits, eggs being broken, omelets made.

He beckons Neddy back upstairs again to the communications room.

With the upstairs door safely shut behind them, the Duke gestures Neddy to a chair. Neddy scans the bank of video monitors. Nothing he sees on the screens hints at this fiercely uncommon Checquers evening ... but when the Duke's narrative begins, "uncommon" beggars its boundaries!

The Duke recites all the day's events, omitting nothing—the four kidnappers arriving, two by two, the threat to Lissa, her father's bad debt to mob loan sharks, the meeting in the Duke's office. The Duke describes his misgivings about Leon Montenero—reunited with Lissa, he denied all wrongdoing and any danger to her. Three kidnappers, Kobalefffsky included, are being held in the tank, he says ... and the fourth narrowly evaded capture three times.

The Duke shows Neddy the photos—singling out Snake.

Lissa remains massively at risk, he says.

But Neddy's head shakes.

"No, she's not."

The Duke's head nods right back. "She certainly is!"

"The guy's still on the loose, but Lissa is out of circulation, and he knows it."

"We don't know that."

"Come on, Duke! They've been searching for her for hours—this place isn't that big! If she were around, he'd have found her by now! And he's been asking people all day—he knows word has gotten around!"

"What are you saying?"

"Never underestimate a pro, Duke—they're just as smart as you."

The Duke smiles without mirth. "What are you driving at?"

"She's disappeared, and there's talk she's gone home for some phony family emergency. If I were him, I'd know she's out of reach. The signs are everywhere!"

"And?" says the Duke.

Neddy nods impatiently. "His guys have disappeared ... vanished! He knows plain as day the thing's a bust!"

"I don't understand."

"Don't you get it!"

Neddy's demeanor darkens.

"It's all over for him, and he knows it—she's out of reach. But every rich babe in the western hemisphere ... including the very richest, your daughter and my wife ... is swanning around like Jackie Onassis in Central Park!"

Neddy's impatience rises to a boil.

"Use your head, Duke! If he's as dangerous as you say—this Snake guy—he says, hey, there's more to be had! The job's blown, but he's still here, and there's nothing keeping him from going freelance. They think like that, you know!"

He nods.

"Of course, you don't—none of you do!"

"Where is Proz?" the Duke says immediately, jaw clenched.

"Exactly! She's halfway up to the hot springs in blinding fog—they left a while ago! I'm supposed to go up and meet her after Burtie and I unravel the bullshit story about Lissa going to L.A.! If I had any idea what was really going on, I'd never in a million years have let her go!"

"Jesus—this is... we—Neddy ... I'm sorry—"

"Yeah ... there's no time, Duke. Do these guys—"

He nods around him, referencing Security Red.

"Do any of them know the way up to the hot springs in the fog—I mean really know it! Is there any way for them to drive up?"

"Not in this fog," the Duke says. "That was the whole point—to keep it primitive."

"Christ."

"I'm not sure how well they know the way in the fog—not as well as you or Proz."

Neddy nods. "I didn't think so. But whatever you do ... don't have them swarming all over the mountainside getting lost—we're going to need them! Burtie and I'll go up."

"You can't do that!"

"Hell, we can't!"

Neddy is halfway to the door.

"Wait Neddy ... I'll get you some men!"

"No time. Put them on full alert. Keep them down around the bottom near the cars—but have them ready!"

"Neddy, goddamn it!"

He's out the door already.

At the entrance to the Library, he rushes down the main hall.

"Burtie—where are you!"

"Right behind you, Sherlock … what's doing?"

*****

"Likewise, I'm sure…" Proz says to Billie Dumphy.

She gives him an exquisitely ditzy Marilyn Monroe laugh.

It's one of Norma Jeane's signature lines ... and Proz's very favorite. Her mother used it with Marilyn to cheer her up before the final, cruel denouement in 1962—it made her laugh. Near the end, poor thing, she needed to laugh.

"How much farther?" Billie Dumphy says, scrambling up the mountain with the rest, all clawing ahead on hands and knees.

"Don't know, exactly," Proz says. "We'll know when we're there."

"Do we know this is the right way?"

Proz tries to see him.

She sees only the cigarette...

Its demon glow.

"We're on the way, is all I can say—it's always like this," she says. "It's fun!"

No response.

They continue upwards, clutching handholds of soil and rock.

"You sound pretty sure of yourself," the cigarette says.

"I am!"

She giggles.

"Last one there's a Democrat!"

"Keep politics out of it," Thermos gasps—huffing and puffing.

"It's not politics," she laughs, "... it's Darwin!"

"Oh-ho!" Thermos booms, squandering precious oxygen.

"Gerry, be quiet ... silly fool," Peevy snaps. "You'll give yourself a heart attack."

"If you don't give me one first!"

"Now, what could that mean..." purrs Proz.

She's moving upwards with impressive force, making good progress, when—

They hear it far, far below ... an almighty *scccruffffling*!

It comes bashing upwards towards them with shocking velocity.

Proz stops to listen.

The others stop now... the great *fuffling, grabbllling, grrrrrufffllling* racket drawing nearer.

Dirt clods are thrust astern.

Disturbed rocks *clack!*

186

It's either a powerful new military all-terrain vehicle...

Or beloved no. 78 of the Golden Madres—Garrett Lowell Larrold!

He churns violently straight up the mountain, a threshing machine gone tribal.

"Who's there!" calls Proz ... to avert a mortal impact.

"Me!"

In lethal exertion sufficient to make even Gary Larry breathe hard...

He surges ever closer, his mighty upward struggle no more discomfiting to him than screeching at the top of her lungs hailing a cab in the rain would be for Judy Garland!

"Gary?"

"Proz?"

"Here!"

"Ahhhhh...."

He comes to a halt—

Downing no trees.

"Found you!"

"For God's sake, stop running!" pleads Thermos.

"Are we halfway up yet?" Gary Larry says.

He hopes we're not.

"Are we?" says Thermos—almost crying.

"In this beautiful fog ... who can say?" Proz beams.

She shows a limitless exuberance exhibited nowhere else but in Bergdorf's. "Let's find out!"

"Great!" barks Gary.

Crud ... meditate Thermos, Peevy, Twitty, Jerms, Billie Dumphy, and the Vietcong, hovering just beyond the perimeter.

Laboring grimly higher, Thermos gasps... "Taxi!"

Peevy giggles at her Zukie—dim bulb.

"We're getting there..." Proz says, in a motivational role.

The vertical aggression grinds higher and higher, Gary Larry accomplishing an effortless end-around. He pulls in alongside Proz.

Being only a regional poet, though a published one, he will defer to her to lead.

*****

Angus Cannizaro glares at the wall of the tank.

"Lennie," he argues, the phone riveted to his ear, "do wild bears fart on Tuesday—of course, it's good! Rutt signed it himself ... Montenero was right there!"

He waits.

Nods.

"Yes, the whole amount."

He nods theatrically: "Bank draft—cash!"

He doesn't look at Doug...

Won't look at Doug.

"Well, if you don't want it ... I'll take it!"

Sheriff Mick and three Deputies stand by, witness to felony extortion. But they're irrelevant. Leon Montenero is irrelevant now, too. He stands in the corner like a floor lamp.

Cannizaro nods and nods at the phone, as if his boss can see.

"Lennie, we're not playing *Hollywood Squares* up here. I'll explain it all later, it's everything you want, neat as a nickel."

He looks at Doug—just a glance.

"Well, not all," he says into the phone. "Everyone except him."

Cannizaro frowns.

"Nobody knows where he is!"

He scans the room.

"Rutt just wants you to know the cash is settled—right?"

He bears down.

"*Right?*"

He nods at Doug now—all okay.

Suddenly, Doug wrenches the receiver out of his hand ... but Cannizaro's free hand deftly cuts the connection.

Doug glowers.

"Now, what'd you do that for!"

"He don't wanna talk to you."

"Is that right...."

Doug places the receiver in the cradle, and in one gliding thrust, lifts Cannizaro up against the wall like the catch of the day.

"You're leavin' now—hear?"

He sets him down and turns to Pulpo and Ski ... "Questions?"

He nods. "Ditn't think so."

Doug gestures to Yamaguchi.

By now, all of Security Red carries radios and sidearms.

"Get Mr. Montenero and his daughter," he says. "Take them to the office—the Duke wants to see 'em. Allison and Cortez, you stay right here. Prichett stays on the switchboard."

Whatever Prichett did ... he shouldn'ta.

CHAPTER 26

Hot Water

IN DRIPPING GLOOM, Proz's hand searches blindly above.

Comes upon a low course of cinderblocks.

"Wooo-hooo!" she French horns.

From here on, it's an easy stroll over the ridge to the hot springs ... and blessed repose.

"Great," grunts Thermos.

"At last..." grumbles Twitty, as if the dishwasher finally stopped.

"Yay..." croaks Peevy miserably.

... she's getting too old for this shit.

One by one, majestically now, as once did Mankind at the Dawn of Everything, they rise to vertical. Proudly on hind legs, forepaws liberated, thumbs cunningly opposing, they stride forth, naught else to consider but the steaming mercies beckoning ahead.

"Is it really hot tonight?" Billie Dumphy says. "Or is my head just on fire."

Not a word.

In the silence, Proz steps in willingly—the tour director: "The springs is hot at one end but cooler at the end away from the pipes. You'll love it."

They stride on a longish while, when—

"Whoa, *Sheeyyittt*—"

PPppllassssh!

But then—

"... *ooooooooomm.*"

189

"Gerry!" Proz laughs. "You're supposed to take your clothes off first!"

"Certainly are," Peevy confirms, taking a proprietary interest in all his affairs.

"*Oooooooooomm...*" he repeats—no need to say more.

No one except Proz knew they'd find it—it's the hot springs' risk and reward ... that and the sublime 120-degree sulphurous mist rising above the broth. In night chill, the water is so hot ... yet so perfect! One inches in pore by pore, pausing at intimate threshholds, until—

Ooooooooooomm.

Bliss.

Except for its rugged stone bulwarks, the hot springs is sandy-bottomed, rustic, raw, exactly as old Cyrus Rutt prescribed back in the Twenties. Fourteen feet by twenty, its milky contents are uniformly five-feet deep. Hot-springs tradition holds that long before Cyrus' rough-cut masonry was laid down, outlaw Joaquin Murrieta and his band—between legal indiscretions—stopped here often. It's no more or less true than any other Santa Lola lore passed down from keg party to keg party.

Close enough for California.

Old Cyrus willed that his beloved hot springs should remain forever unchanged—suitable only to those who will appreciate a bit of Olde West grit with their bliss. The open grasslands of the mountain saddle enclose the springs' rough stonework like a snug turtleneck, with no pretense of a deck or clearing. You're either in the water enjoying life, or knee-high in grasslands getting dressed again for the long, sated return down the mountain. Enjoying the springs' blessed heat and repose in all-consuming blackness is everything a worthy pilgrim will require.

Squishy slogging is heard now, Thermos' wet garments flying off into the surrounding grass, one piece after another. Multiple drier disrobings occur in the middle distance. Later, all will cooperate in intimate ways, retrieving blindly their most personal items one at a time, exchanging this for that, until all are fully reconstructed, a hot-springs legacy reaching back centuries.

But now—

Ploops! of bare feet.

Plups! of bare ankles

Swawwwshes! of circling open palms

and

... *oooooooooomm.*

A giggle.

SSSSsssss ... the hot-watery bubbles hiss.

But not Proz—she's the queen!

Tall, slender, nude as an Easter lily, she strides invisibly through night and fog ... she would stride just as proudly under a full moon ... straight to the hot end and—she's in like a seal.

They hear her sensuous female *Ooowwoooo*.

La Proserpina...

First Lass of "the planet."

Twitty listens to her friend.

Smiles with reverence.

For twelve long years at Cañon Perdido, they explored, tentatively at first, then avidly, the fast-multiplying mysteries of finesse and young womanhood.

Twitty loves it ... the luxuriant music of Proz's pleasure.

But Billie Dumphy is waiting for something.

His clothes remain firmly fastened.

"This is great!" Thermos booms—repaid in full for the struggle up.

"Come on in!" yells Gary Larry, aware of the intransigent Dumphy.

No reply.

They only sense his presence—

Just as he only senses their nakedness

... girls too!

It's like Tijuana!

He's never felt so conflicted!

"We won't look," says Proz.

She laughs.

"We can't look!"

But she has an elegant edge—the sensuous playfulness Twitty loves most in her friend.

It heartily contradicts her words ... she will look!

"We can't even see you!" Gary Larry says.

"And we don't care to," snaps bratty Peevy.

After an hour and more of pelvic matchplay in the Tennis Pavilion, Peevy feels extravagantly confirmed.

But Billie Dumphy doesn't move.

They aren't sure of this, but they hear no movement—evidence enough.

"Oh, come awwn...."

It's Proz again—her voice a taunting purr. No one, not even the tree frogs, knows if it's by design.

But the tone has a deft aggression—she'll look...

Or cosmically worse ... *not* look!

He takes a step.

They hear his rubber-soled shoes, feeling the way along the rough stonework cap of the springs ... he doesn't want to fall in.

Inching ahead, he moves towards Proz at the hot end—walking a highwire in the infinite foggy void.

"You won't like this end," Proz cautions. "You should start down at the cool end."

He keeps coming.

Stops.

"Don't know what you're missing..." she murmurs.

He imagines her grin.

"I don't swim."

"No one's swimming," she says.

"I don't like the water."

"It only comes up to your—"

She pauses teasingly.

"... boobs."

A match flares in the void.

Dies back.

Touches the tip of his unfiltered Camel.

Nobody talks.

The cigarette coal inches closer.

Right above her, he squats down.

Waits a moment.

"Get dressed."

"What?" she says.

"You heard me—get ... dressed—do it!"

"Why!"

He kneels down and grabs her under her arms!

She struggles. "Let go!"

The stapler in his jacket comes out in his right hand now, its cold muzzle pressed hard against her temple ... a Walther PPK 7.65.

"Hey!" Gary Larry yells into the void.

"Shut up!" he roars.

"All of you!"

He has his left arm locked under Proz's shoulders, paralyzing her— the gun tight against her head.

"You're going to get dressed—now!"

"What are—"

"Shut *THE FUCK up!*"

Peevy screams.

Jerms grabs her forearm in the dark to silence her.

Instead, she screams twice as loud!

Snake's arm locked under Proz's shoulder ... he fires straight up in the air—

BLAAANGGG!!!

"I said SHUT ... *UP!*"

No sound.

"LISTEN to me!"

"What do you want?" It's Thermos—nothing bad can happen ... he's certain … just can't!

"Shut up asshole!"

They listen, no one breathing.

"You're staying here—all of you! She comes with me ... understand?"

"You wanted us to shut up..." Thermos says.

"*UNDERSTAND!*"

No answer.

They understand.

"If I hear one sound, I shoot every fucking one of you!"

"Where are you taking me…."

Proz's voice is quiet, almost calm—except for the terrible quaver at its heart.

Snake's voice goes low ... more threatening still: "I'll blow your fucking heads off."

Everyone sees it.

"That's it..." Snake whispers, icy-cold. "Don't piss me off, bitch."

The water is silent—no motion.

"Out of the water," he says.

"I will, I will. Let me go, *please*—I can't move!"

"You'll move like I tell you!"

He yanks her straight up and back out of the water.

"Ouuuwwwooo!" she yells, her naked back scraped raw against the stonework.

Gary Larry's lips hiss with empathy.

"Shut up! She'll live."

"*That hurt!*"

"Yeah…."

Her voice breaks, in grievous sobbing.

"Shut ... UP!"

"What do you want!" she wails—in pain.

"Put on your clothes."

"I don't know where they are!"

"Now! Make trouble and you'll hate what happens next!"

"Please—I will!" she sobs. "Help me—I can't find them!"

"It's all right, Proz," Thermos says softly.

"Quiet!"

"Trying to help..." Thermos says.

"Fuck you."

A beat passes.

"Here..." Snake snaps at Proz. "What's this?"

He shoves a pair of jeans at her.

"Put them on."

"These ... they're not mine!"

"PUT — THEM — *ON!*"

She struggles in his grip.

"But they're huge!"

"Do I give a shit! Roll them up!"

He grabs a piece of clothing draped over the grass—a shirt the size of a trenchcoat.

"Put it on, dammit ... we're leaving!"

She's struggling to get into the huge jeans.

She pulls on the enormous shirt, but has to tie the jeans' narrow black leather belt in a knot at her waist.

"HURRY!"

He looks out into the dark.

"You assholes move, I blast her away!"

"I need shoes, at least!"

"No, you don't."

"How can I get down the mountain without shoes!"

"Find them—WE'RE LEAVING!"

"I'm doing my best! Here ... here they are."

She has one of her jogging shoes.

Now the other.

Then, her own pants must be somewhere here...

But she mustn't provoke him.

Maybe it's best—

... *how to know!*

She has to let go!

... but what's he going to do to her—she isn't that kind of pretty!

Does he want money ... or something *really crazy!*

She can't even see his face!

"Let me put them on," she says, "... please!"

"Roll up the pants so you can walk. FAST!"

He holds her arm like a chicken drumstick. She's doing what he says. But he knows all about times like this—nothing ever goes good ... he hates every second!

"If I hear anyone move...."

Nothing.

"Come *ON,* dammit!"

"I'm tying them!"

She pulls on the second shoe.

"How can I tie the laces—you're holding my arm!"

"You're rich. Make someone do it for you!"
She finishes tying the second shoe, sobbing softly.
Yeah, he thinks … yeah—tough.
"*Roll up the fucking pants!*"
"I am!"
She wipes her eyes with her free hand—she can't see!
The jeans are elephantine...
Rodeo-clown pants
Gary Larry's.
Ridiculous!
He'll have to come down the mountain with no pants.
No shirt.
Nothing is funny...
She only wants to *live!*

CHAPTER 27

Mona Lissa

"ANYONE HERE..."

"*ANYONE!*"

The shout in the blackness is blanketed in muffling fog.

"Quiet..." Vern Jerms whispers to them under his breath.

It comes closer.

"Anyone ... *HEAR ME?*"

The group at the hot springs is dressed—everyone except Gary Larry and Peevy Palmtry.

Peevy is too scared. She sits nude on the rough-cut stone at the edge of the hot springs, hugging her knees—rocking back and forth, back and forth, on her bare, trembling buttocks.

Gerald Thermos huddles next to her ... he no longer has any influence over her.

Gary Larry isn't dressed, either.

If he tried, he would find only shoes, socks, underpants.

"*ANYONE!*"

They hear footfalls come nearer in the grass...

A two-finger whistle fierce enough to shatter glass!

"It's Burtie..." Thermos whispers to Jerms.

"*Neddy!*" he shouts immediately.

"*HERE!*" bellows Gary Larry.

Neddy and Burtie have flashlights—a significant breach of hot-springs etiquette. But in the deep fog, they're no use.

"WHERE!"

The five at the hot springs see phantasms on the air.

Glowing lights dart in ... out.

"Over here!" shouts Jerms.

Ethereal glimmers evolve to flares...

196

Flares with white centers.
A direct blinding light suddenly beams—
Illuminating Gary Larry's full-frontal manhood.
He doesn't flinch.
Peevy's eye follows the beam...
anatomically correct.
... more than representative.
Neddy and Burtie hover in the glow ... spectral holograms.
"He took Proz!" Thermos says.
Neddy moans, "... *nooooo*."
"Are you all right?" Burtie asks.
"He has a gun," Jerms says. "He's crazy!"
"N*ooooooo*...."
"It's all right, Ned," Burtie barks. "We'll get her!"
"How long ago," Neddy says.
"You passed them coming up," Jerms says.
"He saw our flashlights!"
"Not in this fog," Burtie says, "... not necessarily."
"You said crazy."
"Like a bad Doberman…" Twitty sobs ... rocking, rocking.
"Don't worry, Ned," Burtie snaps, "we'll *get* her!"
"Come on!" Neddy says.
They're gone.

*****

The full frontal image of Gary Larry is imprinted on Peevy's brain.
She comes to her feet.
Peevy appreciates Gerry.
... he is a sweetheart.
But with all that's happened ... in order not to think—she *mustn't* think ... she steps forthrightly ahead.
"Gary," she says into the fog, "I need to talk to you."
She addresses the others—no nonsense.
"I have something to say to Gary."
She reaches out blindly.
"Where are you?"
In sensuous blackness, she finds Gary's palm.
His massive shoulder hulking unthinkably high over her ... she leads him off into fog and tall grass.

*****

Leon Montenero strides in.

His daughter turns.

"All settled, dear."

Crusty Yamaguchi strides in behind him, closing the soundproof door under the Library's Medieval Dept.

"We need to pay our respects to the Duke," Montenero says. "He's waiting."

"What do we owe him!"

"He's gone out of his way to keep you safe."

"Locking me up in this dungeon! Daddy you haven't told me anything!"

"Come along, dear, I'll explain the whole thing—it's all over."

"What has he done with Ski Kobalefffsky?"

"Who?"

She glares at her father. "I want to say goodbye to him."

Montenero looks at Yamaguchi.

The Nisei agent shakes his head.

"Daddy ... who are they!"

"They thought I owed them—"

"They were going to kidnap me—it's true!"

"You're completely safe. They've left."

"Crusty, I insist on seeing Ski!"

"I don't know if that will be possible, ma'am."

"Why not!"

"He's gone," her father says. "I told you!"

She looks at Yamaguchi.

Her father.

"I don't believe a word you say—either one of you!"

"You're not seeing him," Montenero says. "I forbid it. We're going to go and thank the Duke—we owe him that. Then we're leaving."

"I owe no one anything!"

*****

"Hear anything?" Neddy mutters.

Burtie makes not a sound.

"Either it's good," Neddy says, "... or it's really, really bad!"

"We're almost down, Ned—almost there."

They resume the mad slide down, the broken soil of the mountainside giving way beneath their feet. They're trying to move quietly, while descending at full speed—impossible, Neddy knows.

But *everything* is impossible—and Snake has a gun! The only hope is the fog and hearing something.

Then they hear it—a muffled gunshot far below.

"Christ, Burtie!"

They scramble headlong downwards now, abandoning all caution. Sliding and traversing the loose soil, on the ragged edge of control, seeing only a yard or two ahead, in minutes, they reach level ground ... on the dark side of the moon.

Neddy's never made it down faster, no falls, unhurt ... good ... but what did they miss!

What if she's gone!

Irrelevant thought—a luxury of stupider times!

On flat grass in the huge Checquers car park now, they're somewhere near the Automotive Service Lanai ... *the goddamn garages,* Neddy thinks now—sick to death of this Checquers horseshit!

They hurry past dripping-wet Jaguar after dripping-wet Jaguar—but these are no threat. In the fog, Snake needs a car that will start!

And if he takes Proz to the garages, maybe Tipton has a gun.

He stops Burtie to listen.

Nothing.

"What do you think?"

Burtie peers into the void.

"... ask Stevie Wonder."

When they hear a distinct—*Pop!*

"What's that?"

And nearer by—

... *Pop!*

FFFFsssssss....

"What the hell!"

"Search me..." says Burtie.

FFFFsssssss....

*****

Proz is a haute-couture scarecrow.

Bunched up madly in Gary Larry's hulking blue jeans, his long skinny black-leather belt cinched tight and knotted at her waist, she's slender, stark, striking. The legs of her jeans are rolled up in gigantic triple cuffs, like Sing Sing dungarees in a Thirties Cagney convict drama. Her huge, blue chambray regional-poet workshirt, gathered-in dramatically at the waist, blouses out puffily above the belt like an old-fashioned chef's hat—yet she's still recognizable by the acute registering of her dark eyes on her mad-eyed captor.

When they first started down the mountain, he released her arm— he needed both hands free to prevent him from tumbling down the mountain. He put the gun away in his pocket, too, but it was readily available, exhausting that topic. She asked him where he was taking her, but he said, shut the fuck up ... exhausting that topic, as well.

One pace ahead, she obediently made her way lower in the gloom—but halfway down, he grabbed her arm suddenly.

He pulled her up short, took out the gun, and fired it straight up into the fog ... no reason, just do it ... BLAAANGGG!

Crazy!

Without a word, he put it away again and forced her the rest of the way down....

In the car park now, the gun is out again.

He grabs her arm like a billy club.

"Please..." she says, "I'm not going to run away."

"Goddamn right, you're not."

They hunt along the level ground, crouching among dripping cars, line after line of them. He's looking for Ski's black Ford ... but fat chance. It's like getting a cab on Park Ave. in the rain. He hates this!

When—

Pop!

He clenches her arm viciously.

"Oww."

"Shut up!"

Pop!

"What's that!"

"You're hurting me!"

"Quiet!"

It's a cruel whisper ... and it's carrying a gun.

Pop! FFFFsssssss....

"What *is* that!"

"No idea!" she says.

He pulls her back the other way—

Pop! FFFFssssss.

It's over this way, too—it's all around them!

He stops.

For the first time since the hot springs, he straightens upright from his crouch.

She does, too.

It feels good to straighten her spine.

"Where do the cars end?" he says.

She points in the direction she believes leads to the Automotive Service Lanai.

"You're not lying...."

"I swear."

He pulls her arm sharply, exerting fierce command.
He's still hoping to find the black Ford.
Sure...
Fat chance.

*****

The Duke's inner office is empty.

Yamaguchi ushers Lissa and her father in and shuts the door to call the switchboard.

"Where's the Duke, Pritchett," he says into the phone. "What's happening?"

He listens.

But his demeanor jells like FDR hearing the first reports from Pearl Harbor.

"The car park!"

He nods sharply.

"Pritchett, get our people down there pronto—and find the Duke!"

His head shakes.

"I don't care what you have to do ... find him!"

He slams down the phone.

"Mr. Montenero, if you will please wait here—we're finding him."

"We're leaving...."

"Daddy, just stop!"

"We're leaving!"

"Please, sir, wait here—it will be just a few minutes."

Yamaguchi hurries out the door.

Lissa glares at her father.

"Why are you even here?" she says. "Why did you come all the way up to Santa Lola to lie to me?"

"I didn't lie to you!"

She looks straight through him, "I don't want to be here anymore."

"I told you—we're leaving. It's insulting!"

"No, Daddy—I don't want to be here anymore with you!"

She stalks to the door.

"Come back here, Lissa!"

She slams the door behind her and rushes down the long office hall.

CHAPTER 28

Flat As Grace Kelly

Pop! FFFFsssssss....

    Burtie straightens up.

    Stands stalk still.

    It's happening all around them!

    "Shit, Burtie," Neddy says.

    Pop!

    "Tires..." Burtie nods.

    FFFFsssssss....

    Even closer!

    "Gotta be."

    They hear sniggering.

    Haw-haws.

    Neddy yells ... "HEY!"

    "YEAH?"

    They aren't bashful, either....

    "WHAT ARE YOU DOING!"

    "WHO WANTS TUH KNOW!"

*****

"Make a sound—one sound—and I'll pistol-whip you!"

    "I won't!" she breathes.

*****

"I SAID, WHO WANTS TUH KNOW?"

"NEDDY LOMBARDO!"

"AND BURTIE BALFOUR!"

Pop! FFFFssssss....

"JUST WHO WE WANNA SEE!"

A pause.

They hear it, low and garbled in the gloom.

"... hey Mickey!"

"Wait—"

Pop!

Haw-haw-haw.

"Where are you?" Neddy says.

"Over here."

It's Mickey now. "Neddy wants tuh know what we're doin'."

FFFFsssssss....

Neddy and Burtie move towards the nearest voice.

"Do I tell 'im, Carb?" Mickey says.

"Dunno—do yuh?"

A beat passes.

"Where in hell are yuh ... NEDDY LOMBARDO!"

"Right here," says Neddy.

They're within spitting distance of the voice.

"What are you doing!"

They move closer, peering into the fog without seeing.

"Letting a little air outta the Great Party!"

The voice is on one knee—just there!

"Who is?" Neddy inquires.

The figure stands ... after a teeter-y sort of fashion.

"Oh, you don't know *me* ... not the Queen of Bolivia ... NEDDY Goddamn LOMBARDO." He emits a gurgling little laugh. "Not after getting introduced twenty-nine fucking times!"

"I know the voice..." Neddy submits into the gloom.

He takes a step closer.

"Least, I think I do."

He completes the thought.

"... Eddie Boyle."

Oooks ... nearly said, Slow Boyle.

"Yeah?" says Eddie, measurably flummoxed. "Well ... shit."

Eddie doesn't know what to say, except, "Umm ... thassright!"

He snorts at himself now, considering events.

"Right out here in the middle of the fog, without even seeing me ... he knows my voice!"

Eddie will go a long stride farther.

"I give you credit ... Neddy Lombardo!"

"What do you mean?"

Neddy takes a step closer.

"I don't know!" says Eddie—speaking the unvarnished truth.

"I saw you at dinner," says Neddy, the observant huntsman.

He can make out Eddie vaguely now—a wavering misty silhouette.

"Then you disappeared! Shoulda stayed. You missed a helluva steak."

"Yep..." Eddie nods now, mulling the indisputable evidence. "I shoulda ... shouldn't I."

Neddy steps in. "Listen, what's that you've got there?"

He refers to a church-key-like device in Eddie's hand—the object making all the musical *Pops* and *FFFFsssssss*-es.

Eddie hands it right over.

To Neddy, it makes no more sense than a Piltdown slide-rule.

But Burtie recognizes it immediately—and bursts out laughing. At USC on Friday nights, he and the "brothers" used to yank valve stems out of lesser fraternities' tubeless tires—rendering entire rival parking lots flat as Grace Kelly!

"You mean you're..." Neddy begins—

... and breaks down in dumbstruck laughter.

"Eddie, I don't understand! Why are you—"

But he pulls himself up short...

Proz!

"Listen ... never mind about that right now, Eddie," he says in earnest. "We've got ourselves a situation here, and I wonder if you and Mickey and whoever else could maybe stop what you're doing and help us out?"

Eddie squints at Burtie.

At Neddy

... who knows him out here in the blinding fog ... BY VOICE ALONE ... screwed if he don't!

"Yeah, I s'pose we could."

Eddie smiles cordially.

"Don't know why not ... tell us what it's all about?"

*****

Snake pulls Proz back sharply...

Don't budge!

... stay put!

She will.

Ski's sinister hulking black Ford Gran Torino is parked right next to a sacrilegiously British Racing Green 1954 Porsche 1500 Super Cabriolet. As always, Ski left the keys on top of the Ford's left-rear tire, just in case.

Snake fumbles around under the dark fenderwell, grabs the keys ... but now he sees it—the tire is flat!

He sees the front tire, too.

Flat!

How'd they know—the sons of bitches!

"Where's your car?" he growls.

"Our car?" Proz says. "In the Automotive Service Lanai."

"The what!"

He spits on the grass.

"Never mind, never mind ... we're goin' there! And pull up yer damn jeans!"

*****

Mambo says his name is Mambo.

Fine with Burtie.

Mambo even has an extra Oly in his beer belt ... it's a bigger-than-life cartridge belt that holds six stubbie beer bottles, three on each hip—for travelin'.

Burtie twists the cap off.

The beer isn't cold and champagnes all over his wrist from getting shaken up yanking out tire stems ... but it's honest work, Burtie knows.

He and Mambo clink bottles.

Jiggy, Mickey Moose and Eddie raise their beers.

Neddy explains now about the guy with the gun. Nobody should do anything they don't want to, he says, it might get strange. But the guy with the gun took away Neddy's wife, and now he has to get her back again, they know how it is.

They do.

They drink Oly.

The question is, says Neddy, what should he do?

And he says it right out, he doesn't know—it's the first time anyone ever took away his wife! More than that, he doesn't really know where the guy with his wife is ... whether he's down here getting a car, or what, though it makes the most sense. But since he's probably down here somewhere, everybody should be a little quiet and try not to spook him ... since he has Neddy's wife and a gun, and all.

Right now, Neddy admits, he doesn't have any good ideas—it's all pretty new to him.

"Sure," Eddie nods.

They all nod.

205

Jiggy reaches to his beer belt and draws Neddy a bottle—his last one.

It champagnes all over Neddy's wrist.
They clink bottles.
Drink Oly.
Listen to the night.
Nothing.
Dead quiet...
It's not like Proz.

*****

It's too quiet—
... no *Pops!*
No *FFFFsssssss*-es—
What're they up to?
They're all around him in the dark, but where?
Snake jerks Proz to a stop and listens hard.
He hears muffled voices out in the fog—but whoever they are, they're not up to much.
They don't even have the sense to be quiet!
Good.
He'll get away—work his way to the garages.
"Which way?" he says.
Proz nods to where she hopes the Automotive Service Lanai is.
But she can't see a thing. She's afraid she might have lost her bearings, and she's deathly afraid of what will happen if she's wrong—he's so crazy!
They're back to crouching.
They pass car after car.
Come to the end of a row—but still no garages.
"This way," she says, no idea if she's right.
She leads him straight across the grass anyway—moving on from the end of the cars.
But now he stops her in pitch black and reaches into his pocket for something. It makes a light-metal *clink!* against his jacket zipper. It's a fresh magazine of cartridges. She's seen them in movies, but it looks different when it's right in front of her ... different and terrifying!
Clutching the Walther with his left hand, he ejects the old magazine, inserts the new one, chambers a round.
He's ready...
She sees it in the slits of his eyes.
She hates his eyes.

206

Hates them!

"I can get the keys..." she whispers.

Her voice is just breath forming the shapes of words.

"There doesn't have to be any shooting," she says, "... really, I'll do it!"

"I'll decide that. And if we don't get there pretty damn quick, I'm gonna get real angry."

"I know the way—please!"

She leads him over close-cropped grass. She hopes she'll see something—anything—indicating where they are.

They take step after step, moving deeper into the void.

Nothing.

Suddenly, they can go no farther—a weathered barnwood wall stops them—

She was wrong!

No...

It's the rear wall of the Lanai!

They have only to inch their way along the wall and around the side of the building...

Into the light.

*****

Burtie sees the glow of lights.

And he hears it distinctly, the tinkling water of the Spanish fountain in the Constance Room ... but no, he can hold it.

Through the fog in the dim entrance, he sees a genteel circle of party guests. He approaches them, Carl and Judie Boynk surveying his scruffy hot-springs jeans.

"Well, where have you been!" Carl B. says.

"Up the mountain. Seen the Duke? Or Doug?"

"Doug?" says Judie B.

"So *serious* Burtie..." puts in Carl. "Did you lose a dime?"

"Have you seen them!"

"My, my..." Carl chides. "Doug was here moments ago with a small group. They headed down towards the Automotive Lanai. Why? What's it all about?"

"A group, you said."

"Strangers ... L.A. Nothing much to recommend them."

Burtie turns.

"Hope you find your dime!"

Must've been the three bad guys, Burtie decides, Doug taking them down to the Service Lanai to put them on the bus.

207

"Doug!" he yells out into the fog ahead now, running along the ghost-lit walkway.

Not for the first time ... he wishes Checquers wasn't so damn huge!

*****

Far ahead of Burtie, three men stride through the miasma—Paw Coggins chief among them.

Paw's arrangements have changed materially. Spiritually modified by Chief Barman Battle's good offices, the diaspora of Niña, Pinta and Santa Maria leads in all directions. Niña decided to boogie-down at Checquers' famed Disco dynamo—Studio 55. Pinta, her station rising measurably, is entertaining BMW motorcyclist Fenton J. Pilbeam III in a fourth-floor linen closet. And Santa Maria, in a brave display of independence, elected not to be dazzled by baseball's greatest living magician—Paw Coggins—choosing, instead, the close-up magic in the Mansion of Mirrors.

She asked Paw to join her, but Paw's view is that magic, like any well-constructed used-car transaction, always rests on some measurably depressing deceit.

He gets enough of that with his knuckler....

At this late hour, Paw's "dates" are the unshakeable Chuck "Charles" Peach and foursquare Vance Crankenfuss Esq. Statutorily married, with 3.2 children and other amusements when traveling, Peach and Crankenfuss make swell company. Paw is content talking baseball with anyone who has a sense of humor and his own ride home.

But what, ho! Who here cometh highballing through the fog!

Paw's 20/10 eyesight is the first to perceive peripatetic Burtram Balfour—

But Burtie has no time just now for the ol' bawgame.

"Vance!" he booms.

"What?"

"*Where's Doug!*" he gasps, struggling for breathable mixture. "Or the Duke ... *it's important!*"

"I'm sure it is—slow down, for Godsakes!"

"*Gotta find'im!*"

"Catch your breath—"

"*No ... where!*"

"He was at the house," Peach offers. "He couldn't talk."

"Proz is *hostage....*"

"What!"

"He's got a gun ... *down here somewhere*—find Doug! You see the Duke ... *tell'im!*"

Burt sprints on.

The three follow suit—Paw already neck and neck with Burtie.

"Go back..." Burtie yells. "*Tell the Duke!*"

Out of breath immediately, anyway, "Charles" doubles back now to Checquers in search of Duke Monty.

The other three run on towards the garages, Crankenfuss keeping pace effortlessly. He runs ten miles every morning, before appearing in court to win his case.

*****

Lissa is rushing out along the Duke's inner hallway...

No idea where.

No matter.

Just rushing.

"Come back here!" she hears far behind.

"Leave me alone!"

After two turns, she finds her way out into the mansion's public regions.

Crowds are scattered about in circles, talking, laughing, admiring the oxygen. The Duke is nowhere to be seen, but for her purposes, anyone will do who might say where Ski is. He's obviously involved—they were going to kidnap her! Her father wouldn't be here otherwise.

But she isn't clear on exactly why her father is here. He lied about everything ... she doesn't know him! He's the man she sometimes wondered about, but never fully acknowledged. He had a facile way of changing positions when he saw advantage, a way she chose not to examine ... he was her father and she loved him. She knew he sometimes made decisions that were "unusual"—but she would let him remain unusual. If she knew all the details, she'd reach the same decisions ... it was fine.

But that was past....

He is what he seems.

And, ohhh, how will she live!

She will, though, she has the strength. He gave her that.

Without him now, though—how will it feel!

Ohhh ... how could he!

In the entrance to the Constance Room, she sees Patricia Pending, Lena Shay, Moreton Fig. They're standing by the Mont Ste. Victoire—of Cezanne's several, the one truly great one.

Lena Shay smirks ... but no, not at her, she's quick to think. In her present state, she must be very careful of her thoughts.

She'll ask.

"Are you all right, dear?" Lena Shay says immediately.

"Yes, yes. Have you seen the Duke—it's very important."

"He was with his uniformed people," Lena says, "... the Oriental—you know."

"Yamaguchi," Lissa nods.

"What's going on?" Patricia Pending says.

"Where were they?"

"Headed to the Library," Moreton Fig says.

Lissa smiles, thanks.

"No hints?" says Patricia.

"Don't know myself!" she smiles, pure as the driven snow.

She crosses the huge Constance Room into the far hall. Entering the Library, she goes straight in through the cryptic Security Red door.

"Ah, here she is!" beams the Duke—modulating immediately to the minor. "Lissa dear, we're very busy just now, do you mind?"

"Where is Ski Kobalefffsky?"

"Yes..." the Duke nods. He turns to Yamaguchi, "Call Doug and see if they've left yet."

Yamaguchi grabs his radio.

"Where are they!" Lissa demands.

But in the same instant, "Charles" Peach—escorted by Agent Cortez—bursts in, gasping breathlessly just four tattered words.

They begin with "Proz" ... and end with "hostage!"

CHAPTER 29

Cannonade

FLOODLIT FOG DAZZLES the front plaza of the Automotive Service Lanai.

Miasmas of blinding light and deep shade glow under top-lit gas pumps. Swirling mist and shadow cloak the low utilitarian service structures ... slanting off into film-noir gloom.

Snake Sneave, his back tight against the garage front wall, grips his Walther. His arm clutches Proz's slender waist.

She stands motionless. Her regional-poet blue chambray workshirt billows out in volumes over her Jack & The Beanstalk blue jeans. In this extravagant light and shade, her face is a mask of Greek tragedy.

"Tipton," she orders, "... the keys to the Tucker—I could not be more serious."

"Very good, ma'am," the Lanai factotum nods.

"And snap it up!" Snake growls.

"Larry," Tipton orders, "the Tucker."

"Try anything smart," Snake says, "and she gets it first!"

Larry moves along the extended row of individual garage portals. Next to Tipton in the murk stand two Lanai staff, Henry and Trayvon.

Their arms hang limp ... abandoned marionettes.

Seven garage stalls down, the Tucker engine turns over.

Doesn't start.

Turns over again.

... starts.

Its wide whitewall tires crackle on the concrete.

The turquoise sedan rotates slowly forward towards them in the fog. Its twin headlights, plus the central third beam above the low grille, glare ... triple halos broodingly advancing.

"Stop!" Snake orders before the car crosses in front of him.

His eye is on Tipton.

He waves the gun at Larry. "Move around the front of the car—unless you want her to get splattered all over the fog."

Larry obeys.

Snake looks at the car. "What is *that!*"

"A Tucker," Proz says. "It's a classic."

"Sure it is…."

He looks again.

"It doesn't need to be warmed up, sir," Tipton volunteers.

"I see that."

"I mean, sir, it is air-cooled. It's—"

"Never mind that—has it got brakes!"

"Yes, sir."

He nods to Proz.

"Outta luck, sweetie. Get in—*very carefully.*"

"Please don't hurt me."

He shoves her the last two steps to the driver's door.

She gets in, the Tucker nodding at her ingress.

"Classic…" Snake mutters, hating the world. "Slide over!"

In three motions, she moves herself across the front seat.

But before he can climb in, a hard ceramic impact explodes on the concrete out in front of the Tucker—*Klonkk!*—followed by a messy *spraaassshhh!*

Particles of shattered brick smithereen across the concrete.

"Hey!" he roars.

Tipton and the others stand motionless—innocent of blame.

Another hard *Kronkk!*

Shards of disintegrating brick splatter the concrete on the far side of the car.

"God-*dammit!*"

Snake lunges for Proz's arm but she cringes—shrinking to the far end of the passenger side, covering her head.

Klllonkk! … *spraaassshhh.*

It's on Snake's side this time, deep in sightless fog—he can't see where.

"*FUCKERS!*"

He kneels on the concrete below the driver's door and fires backwards into the fog.

BLAANGGG!

On the far side, another brick crashes in … *Krrronkk!*

212

... sprrrrrassshhh.

He hears it in the fog now, a low whispery voice—

"... how dead you wanna be, asshole?"

It comes from just there on the right.

"How dead you want *her* to be!" Snake rages.

"Please—*no!*" Proz screams, pressed down tight against the passenger door.

"See!"

"... but after that—Snake."

The voice is low and quiet.

It comes from just behind the car.

"... how dead?"

It waits.

The Walther spits fire back into the gloom—*BLAANNGG!*

"Missed again ... asshole."

"If you give a shit about her!"

"... cold dead?"

Proz knows the voice. It terrifies her.

Krrronkk!

Sprrraasshhh....

And she sees it—

Snake jumped!

He makes no sound.

The Tucker engine idles moodily.

"Hey—dead guy."

It's around behind the car now.

Snake fires blindly in its direction.

BLAANNGG!

BLAANNGG!

But suddenly, far forward beyond the garages—

BLAMMM!

And deafeningly—

BLAMMM!

BLAMMM!

The new gun spits raw flame!

Fat slugs rip into the Tucker fender right in front of Snake.

The gunman is a dim form behind yellow fire.

Snake crouches low behind the door and fires back, *BLAANNGG!*

... an insignificant sound.

BLAMMM!

The bullet ricochets on the concrete past Snake's knee.

Proz scrunches down low behind the dashboard—

But at her back ... the passenger door!

It *moves....*

The sensation freezes her.

Pinned on one knee behind the driver's door, Snake fires at the cannonade beyond the garages—BL*AANNGG!*

... and the door behind Proz opens more.

She feels a hand at her arm!

She *jumps*—

But its firm squeeze gentles her.

BLAMMM!

BL*AANNGG!*

Neddy pulls her out the door forcefully—out and down and away ... tugging her back and back ... past the dark side of the car.

They scramble on hands and knees past the rear, far around behind ... going and going back and away from the light—she doesn't know how far ... *still going!*

Forcibly now, he presses her flat on the pavement, descending over her like a cloak ... holding her deathly still.

Panicked—

PROZ GONE!

Snake dives up into the Tucker—he has to move!

Crouched low, he depresses the clutch.

Grinds the shifter on the steering column.

Crashing the transmission into gear, he races the engine.

The Tucker chugs into blinding fog—its sudden acceleration slamming both doors shut!

The right-front wheel bangs over a splintered brick, the glaring triple headlights blanking all forward vision.

BLAMMM!

Snake's driver-side window explodes ... a shower of safety-glass nuggets pelting him.

Catching a glimpse of pavement in the bottom corner of the Tucker windshield—he veers hard right. Throttle floored, he sees two rows of dim, glowing lights out the shattered window.

The front walkway to the huge mansion...

YESSSSS!

The Tucker heels far over—sliding across loose white pea gravel.

Carving a wide arc...

It slams up onto smooth pavement.

... the long, winding main drive under the trees—he remembers!

HE'S GETTING AWAY—

as fast as this craphound will go!

He has the dumbass front gate to get through ... but—

God he hates this!

*****

The damp concrete is dank.

Stale.

Like mildew.

She lies pinned beneath him, quaking.

His arms are tight around her.

"Dear Proz."

He combines their bodies in hugging, safe warmth.

"I'm sorry, baby," he says. "I didn't know."

"What...."

"About *them!*"

"Who?"

"They planned to kidnap Lissa—then they took you."

"You didn't know."

"They weren't telling anyone ... they had to keep the stupid party going!"

"How could you know?"

"But you're safe."

He gives her a squeeze—packing courage into her.

"Your car..." she says now. "I know how much it means to you."

"I don't know what I'd do if anything ever happened to my baby."

Her body shudders violently.

He clutches her hard—overwhelming it.

"But you're fine, aren't you," he says.

He nods.

"You're fine."

"God..." she breathes, as if to herself.

Neddy hears footsteps now.

"Is she all right?" Tipton says.

"She could be better," Neddy says.

"No..." she says, her voice tremulous, warm. "No, she couldn't."

Tipton waits.

Neddy kisses her temple.

"Do you think you can get up?"

She makes a half nod, "Let's find out."

He releases her, at last, climbing to a knee.

His arm slips under her shoulder—but she hisses suddenly, in pain.

"Are you hurt?"

"It's pretty badly scraped," she says, her voice reedy, "... up at the hot springs."

"The son of a bitch!"

"It's all right, dear."
She uses his arm to steady her, climbing to her knee.
"Here, let me," says Tipton.
"We're fine, thanks," Neddy nods.
She's to her feet...
But it will take a moment.
"Hold me," she says.
"Give us a minute, will you, Tipton."
Tipton nods. Turns towards the floodlights.
"Hold me, baby," she whispers.
"Me, too," he says in her ear.
They enwrap each other—bound in a desperate embrace.

*****

The emergency call to seal Checquers' Front Gate arrives at the Security Red switchboard...

But Pritchett is in the loo, and he has his dignity.

Two ticks later, the Tucker Torpedo is bowling through Checquers' wide-open granite arc.

Snake crash-dives down the narrow, steeply writhing cliffside two-lane towards the coast.

But just 300 yards astern, a single Security Red contestant is in hot pursuit. The puny little red four-banger Dodge Challenger import driven by Deputy "Don't-Call-Me-Dog" Dodd is no road warrior.

Yet on the plus side, Dog knows this road like his hammertoe.

They're brilliantly handicapped.

A mile farther back—just now roaring past the great mansion—the main force consists of Doug the Thug's black '82 Chevy Camaro and Sheriff Mickey Bunt's massive, green-and-white Ford Crown Victoria Police Interceptor. On form, they hold all the cards. However, Doug, leading, is a native New Yorker. His Camaro slides heroically sideways at every turn, squandering precious velocity like a Coney Island bumper-car.

Right on his rear bumper, Sheriff Mick wants to get past—but Doug won't be bested by some country-gravy sheriff!

They're having the time of their life ... and Deputy Dog, who's done time racing Formula Fords, is pulling steadily away.

At the front, Snake is no match for the Tucker. Another native New Yorker, he slashes tight curve after tight curve down the steep descent, his reaction times *centuries* behind the needs of the suffering Torpedo. Traversing its increasingly warm bench seat with every curve, Snake grabs at the passing wheel, stabs at the gas, suffering painful velour burns with each slide.

In the tightest turns, the Tucker slows almost to a walk—and the little Dodge pulls right alongside!

Resenting this, Snake nails the Tucker's throttle and bashes straight into the Dodge's front fender, kayo-ing its nearside headlight—

But now the Tucker is...

careening straight out to the cliff!

Snake hits the brakes.

Regains his steering.

Motors bitterly on.

Jeans smoldering...

He must pull himself together.

He grips the wheel now with both hands.

Braces his left foot on the Tucker's deluxe gray carpeting.

He will take careful note of where he's pointed, applying throttle not yet ... not yet—okay ... *YET!*

The Tucker gains pace immediately...

Requiring more braking at each turn.

But this is great—*he's pulling away!*

BRILLIANT!

The Tucker moves faster and faster.

After several turns, the little one-eyed Dodge is...

GONE!

But so—increasingly—is Snake's brake pedal.

Turn by turn, it sulks more

droooops

STRAIGHT DOWN TO THE FLOOR—

No brakes at all!

And Snake's downhill velocity increases madly.

He battles through a steep right.

A hard left.

A plummeting right—

tires *SHRIEEEEKING!*

And just now, far underneath, a huge, essential black Tucker stovebolt, the mate to the stovebolt Neddy lost this afternoon on the drive up...

Breaks free!

The rear suspension collapses with

AN INDESCRIBABLE ROAR!

Sparks propagate like Macy's 4th of July.

Snake is surrounded in *chain lightning!*

He tugs the wheel manfully—

no response at all!

On casters, the Tucker slews

wide
WIDER...
right out to the cliff!
Momentarily, all goes quiet
the Torpedo on soft dirt.
Its nose rises on the roadside earthen berm
lifting...
grading...
grinding...
to a wobbly—
teetering
STOPPPP!

Nothing moves.
Fine.

But if Snake *blinks...*
He'll go smashing, crashing, bashing
straight down to Hell!

*****

Deputy Dog's Dodge Cyclops hounds around the last bend—
    To see the Tucker Catastrophe dead ahead.
    Dog executes a boulevard stop.
    His single high beam studies the sedan...
    Hanging over the cliff.
    No movement.
    Well...
    a teeter.
    Dog considers the soft dirt berm under the Tucker—
    All that keeps Snake Sneave in the known universe.
    But now he hears raging V-8s
    yowling sirens
    caterwauling tires
    ... the NASCAR Special Olympics!
    First comes Doug's Camaro—
    and not a rear bumper later
    Sheriff Bunt's Crown Vic Police Interceptor!
    Seeing the little Dodge directly in his path,
    Doug spins one-eighty degrees.

His high beams now blinding Sheriff Bunt—
Bunt locks his brakes!
The boxcar-sized Crown Vic grinds straight ahead,
cue-balling Dog at the teetering Torpedo.
... faintly heard out on the precipice—
"*noooooo....*"
The little red Dodge ploughs haplessly forward—
coming to a halt...
one taco short of sending Snake to a Higher Authority!

Before the dust settles, Bunt, Doug and Dog are crouched behind their fenders and service revolvers.

Bunt aims the Police Interceptor's blinding spotlight at the tippy Torpedo, its powerful beam ready to nudge Snake straight off to Infinity.

They await events.

None occur.

Sheriff Bunt will open with a deuce.

"Snake?"

"Yeah?"

"You in there?"

"Oh, fuck you."

"Toss out the gun and come out with your hands up!"

Nothing.

"Or take up sky-diving."

The clock is ticking.

"Snake?"

"If I move, the car goes over!"

Silence.

"So, what'll you have for breakfast...."

Pregnant pause.

"We can help, Snake," Doug offers, on a constructive note. "We'll steady the car while you get out."

"After we have your gun..." Bunt stipulates, restoring the chain of command. "Or we can wait for an earthquake."

The Silence of the Incas.

"I can't move—*can't talk!* How am I going to get my gun out!"

"A problem," the Sheriff concedes. "But the berm isn't getting any stronger You have no cards to play."

"Never did...."

All take a moment to review life's lessons.

"Tell you what..." says the Sheriff, practicing Platinum Coast *realpolitik*, "you slide the gun across the seat—we'll have to trust you on that. Then hold your hands up so we can see 'em. We'll hold down the back of the car, open the passenger door, and you slide out!"

No sound.

"Gotta move, Snake..." Dog says.

"I know."

"It'll go any second..." Sheriff Mick says.

"I know."

"You don't want that..." Doug says.

"I know," repeats Snake, in solemn Canticle and Response.

"Slide the gun across the seat," Bunt says. "Remember, we got three guns."

A beat passes.

"I did it."

"Hands up!"

They see two hands.

Guns trained, they stand.

Step forward.

Snake moves not a muscle—hands up.

At the side of the Tucker, where its 1948 coachwork bulges voluptuously outwards, the Sheriff peers in.

The gun is on the seat. He nods, okay.

"Smooth and quick now..." Doug coaches. "Ready to scoot."

"They'll bear down," Bunt counsels. "I pull the door ... when I say, go."

The Sheriff touches the door handle.

Feels it teeter!

"Snake—"

"*Yesssss!*"

Dog and Doug weigh down the rear bumper.

The Sheriff opens the door—

the berm crumbling!

"Go-go-go!"

Snake slides across the seat, the hood already dipping—

BUT HE'S OUT!

The Tucker noses over...

SLIDING...

taillights and sleek low tailfins RISING!

It inches forward.

GRINDS over the precipice

a great turquoise sea monster DIVING

LUNGING

PLUMMETING

down and down

TO INFINITE BLACKNESS!
Silence.
They hear it in the fog now…
   unthinkable CRASHING … glass SHATTERING, steel beams
SNAPPING, body panels mashed in MADDENED, BRAWLING
DISASTER!
   Quiet….
   They peer over the brink—
   No fire.
   Thank you God.
   But only Snake sees it now…
   The Walther on the dirt.
   It slid out ahead of him.
   He waits.
   They'll see it.
   He has no cards.
   Never did….

CHAPTER 30

Hero

PROZ BURIES HER FACE in Neddy's shoulder.

"All right?" he says, squeezing up her courage.

She makes the least hint of a nod.

"It's okay, baby," he says, "you're safe."

"Really?"

"Promise."

He looks through the murk to the front of the garages.

"But what *was* that!" he says, half to himself. "It was deafening!"

They hear voices in the fog beyond the garages now, the talk low and all business.

"I have to know," he says.

She looks doubtful—afraid of anything she can't see clearly.

And why not!

He presses his cheek against her. "We're fine babe, it's all over."

"Not all," she submits quite correctly.

"I know. Come on, let's find out."

They walk through the vaporous glow. Figures begin taking shape—deputies, and farther back, a suit. The suit is talking with his hands, but the Deputies are having none of it.

Tipton and his men stand off to one side.

Behind him, Neddy hears the commercial fishing fleet, emerging now from the fog. Jiggy and Mickey Moose appear first. Mickey still has a brick in his massive fist—just in case.

One by one, Eddie and Spider and Marty and Veal and Mambo

materialize. Everyone wants to know ... what *was* that!

Neddy beams to all: "You guys are the best!"

"Naaah…" says Jiggy.

"You were great!"

Mickey laughs. "Really got him, din't we."

"Just like you said," Eddie nods.

"It's all thanks to these guys heaving bricks!" Neddy says to Proz.

She looks at him—at them—piecing it all together.

"Tell you the truth," Eddie says, "I thought it was nuts. How'd you know it would work?"

Neddy's smile is spookie.

"I didn't."

"It was *crazy!*" Mickey Moose says, highest praise.

"It *was* a little," Proz says, pressing against Neddy adoringly.

"Crazy like a bull shark," Jiggy confirms. He lost two fingers one day boating a bull shark, but they sold the steaks that afternoon to Roman's Sea Quest as swordfish—tastes better anyway, Jiggy reasoned.

They stroll on, Proz visualizing the bricks coming in from all directions in the fog!

She presses tighter against Neddy, speechless.

"Whoever *he* is," Neddy nods ahead, "... we couldn't have done it without him!"

In the floodlights, they make out two Deputies ... Crusty ... other forms.

But the suit—Neddy can't make out the dark face in the dim light. He's short, slight, arguing bitterly, "But he flatten-edd thee tires from my beautiful Lagonda ... I *revenge heem!*"

"Motha!" Neddy exclaims—

But instantly, he recants. "Apologies … *Ahmed!*"

"Not to call me Motha!"

"I *am* sorry, Ahmed. That was *you?* Fantastic! You saved my dear Proz's life!"

"I was," says Ahmed confusingly ... putting matters momentarily on hold.

But Crusty Yamaguchi glares at Neddy. "What do you mean, fantastic!"

"His gun!" Neddy enthuses. "It was *so loud* ... he saved everything!"

"A lot more than loud." Crusty's tone is hot with indignation. "A snub-nose .44 Magnum … Mr. Lombardo, a Ruger Red Hawk with no carry permit ... it's just a murder weapon—the worst kind of illegal! He's under arrest!"

"For defencing thee pair-sonal haw-nor! He destroy-edd my vee-hickle—one cannot!"

Motha appeals to Neddy.

"Thee same one has been taking *your vee-hickle* … ee-vil!"

"If only you knew…" Neddy beams, giving Proz a joyful squeeze. "Crusty, he was kidnapping my wife!"

"Kidnapping!"

"Mr. Lombardo," Deputy Evans objects, establishing order, "he was down here slashing tires!"

"Not at all! He took my Proz hostage at gunpoint up at the hot springs!"

"He damage-edd my Lagonda!"

Neddy shakes his head, smiling all around. "Tell them, Tipton!"

"Perfectly correct, Mr. Lombardo," Tipton confirms. "He had a gun on Ms. Proz. He stole Mr. Lombardo's car to take her down the mountain at gunpoint."

Neddy's laugh is delirious. "And Ahmed—you prevented it! You saved everything!"

"I do," Motha says disconcertingly … again putting matters on hold.

But Neddy carries right on.

"Without Ahmed, my wife would still be racing down the mountain with Snake! Ahmed's Magnum scared the crap out of him. Scared you, didn't it? Scared me! We were trying to shake up Snake by throwing bricks out in the fog to get Proz back. Then Ahmed started shooting. It froze Snake, and I got her back!"

"He not damage-edd my luxury car?"

"Ahmed, you are a hero!"

He nods firmly, "Yes."

"Yes!" Neddy gushes.

"Yes, indeed, Ahmed…."

It's a booming basso, resonating forcefully from deep in the fog. All identify it immediately.

The Duke strides forward into the light.

He gives Proz a mighty hug, tears of relief and release streaming down her cheeks.

He gives Neddy the same mighty hug.

"Well done, lad!"

He turns now to Motha. "And we are blessed to have you here tonight, my good friend … I say blessed—you may be sure of it, Mr. Fakhr!"

Neddy hears it—a hint of hilarity in the emphatic pronouncement of Ahmed's surname.

"It's been a desperate evening, I think we will all agree," the Duke declares. "Yet it ends with this wondrous rescue of my dear daughter, all thanks to you, Ahmed."

Ahmed nods solemnly—confirming all.

"And thanks to Neddy and his wonderful fishermen friends! I'm sure Sheriff Bunt recognizes our extreme gratitude to everyone present!"

"I revenge heem!" Motha says.

"Certainly did!" the Duke confirms.

He lets it hang there an extra moment, to good effect.

"But as someone once said," he beams, "all's well that just bloody ends!"

The entire company indulges a unanimity of relief.

"And now that it's behind us, we are obliged to see to the needs of our guests' immobilized automobiles," the Duke continues. "Tipton, will you look into that?"

"Very good sir."

"Splendid."

Supplying countless missing valve stems, reseating detached tire beads, and installing sufficient compressed air to refloat the entire spectator fleet ... it's a Checquers-sized undertaking. Trayvon and John will determine how many deflations are in play, while Larry and Henry look into the availability of valve stems and compressed air in Greater Santa Lola—and if necessary, the reputable sectors of Santa Barbara.

"Meantime," smiles the Duke, "we have a party to accomplish!"

With the greatest ebullience now, he proclaims it: "Tonight more than ever—we got it plenty!"

*****

Refloating Checquers' scuttled personal transport proceeds apace.

In the interim, the party faces the prospect of partying still deeper into the night. At Bigg Casino, this is received with good grace. Even those not formally accumulating the "bacon" press agreeably on.

To guests hampered by the car-park mischief, it seems only fitting to book an overnight at the mansion ... and Checquers cheerfully welcomes others who were *not* so hampered. The tedious few insisting on honoring first-thing-Friday obligations will be provided rental cars while their vehicles are being resurrected, all courtesy of the duchy. In the spirit of Commander Whitehead (sadly, recently departed this mortal plane), those staying the night will, in the ayem, be greeted with Chef Rodant's nonpareil Eggs Benedict.

The Duke, nothing if not a realist, must hold the Fishermen's Grange answerable for the many instances of personal transport laid low in the car park. Even the esteemed black-with-white-pinstripe 1956 BMW R50 motorcycle of Fenton J. Pilbeam III was reduced to its rims—by Jiggy, a Harley man. Yet in the same breath, Duke Monty feels measureless gratitude to the same Fishermen's Grange. Its brave brick-launching services at the Automotive Service Lanai were indispensable in liberating Proz.

Having served him so rudely and so well, Duke Monty gladly prescribes for them the re-stoking of mesquite coals and a gala late dinner seating. The Grange will get in amongst the Duke's Double, amply buttressed by whatever liquid offerings these "men of the soil" ... we have City College's word on it ... deem fitting.

*****

"We'll show you the way," Doug the Thug nods almost politely.

And just now Angus Cannizaro is inclined to comply with whatsoever Doug propounds.

Backed by Sheriff Bunt and his Deputies, and for good measure, the assembled Security Red staff, Pritchett included, Doug invites Cannizaro to drive himself and Pulpo down the mountain to the freeway, availing himself of the onramp marked, "101 South – Los Angeles."

There, he will proceed on its smooth concrete surfaces ... "not looking back."

In due course, Sheriff Bunt's Ford and a second Deputy's car escort the black Lincoln Continental Town Car from the mansion down the steeply twisting mountain road. As fortune would have it, the Town Car, a late arrival at the Great Party, was stationed at the western extreme of the car park, cloudlessly escaping the ministrations of the Fishermen's Grange.

At Highway 101, the two county Fords idle quietly on the shoulder, the black Lincoln Town Car slipping off silently into night and fog....

Snake Sneave, by the by, is to remain up on the Platinum Coast, awaiting Santa Lola Justice. It's reasonable to assume he won't be strolling Avenida Sabado Bingo munching a fish taco anytime soon. The precise term of his absence is in the hands of Vance Crankenfuss Esq., consulting with the great man himself. Generally, the Duke practices moderation in his legal decisions, though a degree of firmness may attach to the current matter. It was his own daughter, after all, who was abducted. Odds on the street have Snake joining one of the Duke's sprawling, low-recidivist Eastern Oregon cattle spreads for a suitable stay.

But after not too grotesquely long, things going well, Snake will soon be at liberty again to make his own choices. A marked improvement is devoutly to be wished ... all credit to the abiding wisdom of Lex Checquers.

CHAPTER 31

Alyeska

UNDER THE GRAND ARCHWAY, opening onto Checquers' Third Living Room, beloved Golden Madres No. 78 Gary Larry stands before cheering throngs like John The Baptist.

Survivor of extraordinary events up at the hot springs, Gary wears athletic socks, size 18½ sneakers, pale-blue underpants—and not a thread more. The underpants, washed-out regional-poet Penney's briefs, are not flattering, but no matter. They are sign and symbol of Checquers' triumph this night over fiendishness and ill intent. In manifold ways, Gary Larry is on top of the world.

The hot springs will do that.

Further contributing to Gary's, and the general, high spirits, it is confirmed by Sheriff Mickey Bunt that Snake Sneave, miscreant, is in custody far down the mountain. Justice, however, has its price. It is also confirmed that Neddy Lombardo's much-admired 1948 Tucker Torpedo is, alas ... "somewhat farther down the mountain."

Mere moments after blameless Gary Larry, underpantsed victim of blackguardism, achieves the Third Living Room, decorous Doug the Thug appears, furnishing him with a big-and-tall, fluorescent-green-and-navy polkadot terrycloth bathrobe. All well and good. But like the diva, asked to cut short her wildly importuned curtain calls, Gary will not hurry to hide his light under a hayrick with Doug's robe. His multitudes of Third Living Room wellwishers, he knows, mean him only the best.

Among these are fellow victims Twitty Conway, Gerald Schmidt Thermos ("The March King"), Vern Jerms, and Peevy Palmtry (she looks positively beatified). They are joined by wellwishers Clive O.E.M.

Monogram, Burtram Balfour, Julian Axel, Chester Halimony, Fenton J. Pilbeam III, Moreton Fig, Patricia Pending, the Boynks, Pasadena's May Wong and Leslie Wight, and varied hundreds.

It should be noted, further, that laid-back "Gerry" Thermos has graciously endorsed Peevy's "playing the field" with Gary Larry up at the hot springs. In fact, Zukie extends his dispensation to all other sportsmen this evening "in stirrups" ... tally-ho!

Meantime, he busies himself embellishing his All-State All-Skate Marching Band ... it will be "awesome!" And on a related pedantic note, debate rages among Golden State Histrionologists over whether Thermos' use of this exclamation is, or is not, the very first recreational use of that pandemic modifier. A vocal minority from Hermosa Beach in the South Bay claims USC surfer Havana Bob, tasting the pastitsio at Greek 2 Me on the Manhattan Beach Pier, uttered the first-ever "awesome." Trojan balderdash. Greek 2 Me will not open until March, 1985—months after the Checquers Great Party! To Thermos, then, all credit, and enmity.

As Gary Larry, at long last, avails himself of Doug's polkadot bathrobe in the Third Living Room's north entrance ... through the Third Living Room's *south* entrance saunter Chuck "Charles" Peach, Paw Coggins (his Aston Martin has three flats—won't start anyway), Lance Crankenfuss Esq., Ken Stukud, Councilpersons Carbon, Varp, Mudhutt and Vindik, Ski Kobalefffsky (surprise!), Duane Snit (fists heavily bandaged, pain pill-induced cockatoo grin), the convened Fishermen's Grange, and Niña and Santa Maria. (Pinta is entertaining Keita Mammady Fallo in a fourth-floor broom closet.)

... while, meantime, waaaay back again at the *north* entrance ... in she strolls, quite alone—the destructible-after-all Lissa Montenero.

She stands glumly next to Gary Larry, inspecting his neon big-and-tall bathrobe.

"What's the matter, Lissa?" he says.

"You're saying, something is the matter?" she inquires.

He nods annoyingly, yes.

Lissa would put words to her annoyance, but before they can bond farther—

A deafening commotion is heard far down Checquers' cavernous polished-marble main hallway.

Lissa and Gary turn.

The twin honorees of this raucous demonstration ... supported by new hundreds, coming in now from the tumultuous Hunt Room & Grille ... are the ever-remarkable Proz and her newly remarkable (and then some) Hubby Neddy.

Preceded by hosannas, they promenade the great hall like newlywed bullfighters. Advancing in majesty, Proz still wears her bizarre scarecrow outfit, just as when she was so cruelly forced down the mountain ... good grief, at gunpoint!

She strides on Neddy's arm, the celebration building rapturously, as they achieve the arched entrance to the Third Living Room. The costume of her shocking ordeal ... hooligan jeans and bloused-out blue chambray workshirt—more suitable in every way on the very hairy Gary Larry—has a devastating impact, inciting an immediate, drop-everything rush.

Yet in this supremely galvanic moment, Proz bespeaks a finely simpatico fatigue ... the more poignantly visible entering the Third Living Room's hovering beneficent glow. The strain on her brow combines with a sweet smile of careworn peace ... tonight's events she will need time to learn.

For the moment, she seeks only affection and concern.

The women, drawn irresistibly, surge to her like water through a narrows.

But seeing her from the midst of the crowd—and freed tonight of his lifelong awkwardness—Gary Larry bellows, "*Give back my clothes!*"

She laughs from her belly ... inciting loud cheers!

"No wonder!" she shouts, gesturing at his polkadot bathrobe. "Shall we change right here?"

"Why not!" snips pesky Peevy. "We've all seen your curlies."

"Not in the light..." stipulates creepy Vern Jerms.

But the women surge closer—Neddy consumed in the rush. He mugs comically to Burtie for rescue, carried helplessly along, making no effort to escape.

With all attention on Proz now ... Ski Kobalefffsky steps across the great room to Lissa. She makes no move to meet him.

And seeing this, Chester Halimony follows Ski, three paces behind. Lissa gives Chester a grateful nod—it's fine. Just the same, he stands protectively nearby.

"You okay?" Ski says. "This whole thing stinks."

"Yes," Lissa says, "it does."

"I wanted to tell you, I'm sorry. The old man said you asked to see me, so he agreed to let me stay. Funny place ... Checquers. I've decided I'm done with all that stuff, thanks to you. You made me see."

"You saw for yourself."

"No, I feel awful. There's no way it will mean anything to you, I know—but I'm really sorry. Everything changed, talking to you. I'm not going back to L.A."

"Really?"

"I don't know what I'll do, but it's going to be completely different. I was hoping ... can we maybe talk sometime?"

"Sometime."

"Yeah..." he says with resignation. But his tone softens. "I wouldn't hurt you for the world."

She nods.

He takes her hand. "You're the most beautiful person I've ever met."

"Take care, Ski."

Releasing her hand, he turns and walks out into the night....

She looks back to the Third Living Room. To Chester Halimony ... Neddy and Proz ... the multitudes she knows, and who know her.

Tears well up.

She isn't as strong as she'd hoped.

*****

The little laugh of the Duke's is comical—an unguarded cackle not heard from him in decades.

"And he's a poet, too," he grins. "They always are."

Moments earlier, Gary Larry and Proz left the Third Living Room. At last, they would realign their wardrobes.

At the Duke's invitation now, Neddy and he have adjourned to the large, comfy leather chairs in the Constance Room's far west end. The great manor hearth rages before them—a bawdy conflagration, popping and crackling in the low light.

Audible in the distance, the Great Party in the Third Living Room rumbles on. Except for one couple in the distance at the Constance Room's eastern end, negotiating quietly as couples do at one o'clock in the morning, Neddy and the Duke are alone.

"She looked exquisite, didn't she," the Duke beams. "She's never looked more precious to me than in that ridiculous outfit. I do treasure her!"

His head shakes.

"And you ... getting the fishermen to do all that, then threatening the guy out in the fog. Tipton told me the whole thing—extraordinary! You are your father's son, in all the very best ways."

Neddy's toes curl ... like listening to Peevy gush about her deplorable little dog.

"But then..." the Duke says, "it's how men do such things. They don't think about them, or they wouldn't do them."

Neddy says nothing.

"I know," the Duke nods, "... an old man talking. But you make me feel young again. My father would've liked you, and that's saying something. He was no easy man to impress—I never could."

"Oh, come on," Neddy says.

The Duke nods. "He'd tell me, you keep on trying, you might learn something—as though I never did anything right my whole life. It's what fathers do with sons, do you think?"

"My father did." Neddy waits for it to stand still in his mind. "I didn't hate him, but I barely knew it till he died."

The Duke nods off into the distance. "Did I ever tell you about Alaska? My father had a hell of a time getting out, you know. He told me not to talk about it—which is exactly why I'm going to tell you now."

He holds Neddy's eye. "But don't tell Proz—she might not see it for what it is."

Neddy smiles. "She was pretty good tonight."

"Yes, she was—but even still."

The Duke goes on. "You've heard most of it, I'm sure, how he got out his ... he called it, his 'dirt' ... the last few days and made his way up the Yukon for Skagway and the ship home. By then, everyone around Fortymile Creek knew he'd done pretty well, no way to hide it. And not everyone wished him well. Turkey Bill Everett, Shaney Nichols, and Mick Dixon were goldminers who did their mining without picks and shovels, if you take my meaning. They knew Billy Kilgore in the trading post had brokered a string of horses to Father, and that didn't take a whole lot of explaining."

The Duke settles himself in his chair, looking into the fire.

"They went out into the forest around Father's claim and watched him load his 'dirt,' making sure he got everything he'd hidden away. It was June and midnight sun, and they watched him for probably three days.

"On the last morning, when he was all ready, he said, he figured they'd decided to wait until he got well up the Yukon—it would be less likely for anyone to know something had happened. They trailed him upriver, things playing right into their hands—but what they didn't know was, he'd heard one of their horses. Something must have spooked it, a wolf or bear or something. Father knew they were there.

"By the middle of the next day, with mosquitoes eating him alive, he found what he was hoping for—a semi-circular granite outcropping where he could hole up and make a stand. He tied off the horses, as if everything was just fine, took out his rifles and two pistols and ammunition, and waited behind the boulders under the cliff, his guns all laid out. He'd done a lot of shooting up on Elmira Creek, so he knew what he was doing—but this wasn't target practice anymore. He said he made himself pretend he was playing hide-and-seek with Franklin, his big brother back at the farm in New York—it was the only way to keep himself calm, he said ... hide-and-seek behind the barn.

"But he didn't have long to wait. In a while, he saw one of them run through the trees on one side—Dixon. He had no shot, but he was in good cover. Dixon didn't have a shot, either. He waited some more, swatting mosquitoes, sweating with the heat and a whole lot more. Then he heard a yell. Next thing, they were all three shooting at him like the cavalry, bullets glancing off the stone all around. He moved behind another boulder—he couldn't see anything—when a shot rang out right behind him! He wheeled with his rifle—Dixon was aiming again—and Father only had time to point and shoot. He was crazy lucky, his first shot hit Dixon's rifle and knocked it out of his hands. He pumped the lever, and the second shot dropped Dixon where he stood."

The Duke looks at the fire.

"One of the others saw Dixon go down and yelled—but no answer. So the other two opened fire, angry as hell and wasting ammunition. Father just waited. When they stopped, he yelled, 'Come on in, boys, we've got all day!'

"Nothing happened for a long time. He knew they'd try to swing around on both sides, but he couldn't see them.

"Then he saw Everett running behind some trees on one side. He took a shot and missed. Nichols fired from behind him on the other side and missed. He could see Nichols' position—but Everett could be anywhere behind some rocks on the other side. Nichols fired, but when Father looked that way, Everett fired. The first shot tore into his left forearm and made him yell out—which they heard. Tucked in out of the line of fire, he looked at his arm. The flesh was pulled open below the elbow, but his luck held—it missed the bone. He had a lot of luck that day.

"So he made the best of it and groaned out loud some more.

"'Didn't hurt yuh, did I?' Turkey Bill Everett yelled to mock him ... you know.

"Father didn't answer.

"So 'Ohhh, nooo,' Everett yelled, 'doesn't sound good....'

"Father stayed quiet and waited. He knew they'd come in. Everett would take a shot, and he'd hear Nichols move. Then Nichols would shoot, and he saw Everett move. He waited and waited. When Everett fired, he saw Nichols duck out from behind a tree. Steadying his rifle on the rock with the bad arm he got Nichols in the belly and he went down yelling.

"'Shaney!' Everett called out, but all they heard was gurgling.

"Father waited a minute or two.

"'Just you and me now, Bill,' he yelled, 'and I'm going to kill you!'

"'Son of a bitch!' Turkey Bill yelled back.

"Father had only one position to watch now, but his arm burned like open flame. He couldn't pay it any attention—he just thought about Turkey Bill. He didn't want a standoff, and he didn't want Turkey Bill to leave. He wanted to kill him! But where Turkey Bill was, behind a lone tree, he couldn't move without Father seeing. Nothing happened for a long time.

"'Hey, Bill,' Father yelled at last. 'You want the gold, and I'm going to kill you!'"

The Duke's eye brightens.

"Everett said, 'Yeah?'

"'Well,' Father said, 'how should we do this?'

"'Go to hell!' Everett yells.

"'Not yet, Bill—I'm going to kill you first.'

"So they sat there thinking. Then my father says, 'Tell you what, Bill ... I'll put both hands in the air, with a pistol in my right hand, if you do the same. We can both stand up then, walk out like grown men and get the thing done, what do you say?'"

"He said that?" Neddy says.

"That's what he told me. He peeked out from behind the rocks so he could see, and said, 'Deal?' And Everett says, 'Deal—you bastard!'

"So, one by one, they peek out from behind the rocks. Each one sticks out his hands—only a little, at first, really cautious. But both see the other's hands—one hand with a pistol.

"Father says, 'Okay, we stand up now, both hands in the air.'

"They do.

"They move towards each other, step by step. When they're in range of each other, Father stops. 'Going to kill you now, Bill.'

"But before he finishes, Everett's gun comes down.

"Father's comes down, too.

They fire at the same time, and Dad feels something buzz past his face—that close! His shot misses, too. They take a second shot, and Everett misses again—but Father's goes straight through Everett's chest. Kills him instantly!"

"Wow!" Neddy says.

"Dead. Father checks him to be sure. Dead. He checks Shaney and Mick, too. All dead, and his arm is way too shot up to think about digging graves. Besides, it's Alaska.

"He does what he can to clean up his wound with whiskey. The pain, he said, was like open flame with a heartbeat. It was a while before he could do anything else. Then he made up a clean bandage and rested. After a time, he mounted up again, took his horses over the pass and down to Talya Inlet."

The Duke nods. "He boarded the packet and sailed out to Seattle."

The Duke smiles at the great hearth's blaze.

"You don't know how good it feels to tell it, at last—that's just the way he told me. You've got to break some eggs, Ned."

He stares into the fire.

"Welcome to the family."

CHAPTER 32

Asses

NOTHING DAMPS THE pilgrims' progress.

Checquers' Third Living Room at one-thirty in the morning is like the stroke of midnight New Year's Eve. The result of the exciting derring-do in the fogbound car park, bearing witness to a just universe in fine working order, is electrifying. The Great Party's spirits, charged by crisis ... released in triumph ... gyre now in pagan pandemonium. Society circle after society circle mixes and matches in manic spontaneity, the amassed exuberance like jubilant mobs flooding out of a brilliant Broadway comedy.

In the frenzy, Julian Axel, feeling much better, thank you, zooms in on Twitty Conway—his timing couldn't be better. Until hearing of Axel's fistfight with Duane Snit, Twitty hasn't given him a seventh, sixth, or even fifth thought ... but all that's changed. In like manner, Vern Jerms, breadwinning for the wife and 2.5 children—and ever aware of the sensuous pleasures recumbent in fevered sales lust—markets to red-eyed Pinta a condo in far, forlorn Guadalavista.

He stands ready to perform all duties required for an immediate, and intimate, close.

Elsewhere, the collective Smart Sets of the Greater Southland compete accomplishment for accomplishment, locked in mortal combat. The Pasadenans, captained by Leslie Wight, Paige Turner and May Wong, duel a chic squad from Newport ... but the Newporters establish a commanding lead—they're "into" falconry!

When suddenly, irresistibly...

Heeeeere's Proz!

Emerging sublime from her final costume change, she is a vision!

Carelessly casual in elegantly embroidered, fitted, flawless Jordache jeans, a simple beige silk blouse and rule-breaker periwinkle pumps, she is a firestorm sucking the air out of the room! Those previously dizzied by Neddy's swoggling *richesse* sprinting into the Grand Refectory banquet almost late, now beholding Proz ... are struck idiotic.

She is supernaturally post-horror.

A miracle of spiritual regeneration!

Before all, she parades her divinely slinky jeans and impudent periwinkle pumps—on a victory lap.

She moves with supreme ease.

Mythic grace.

To the fragile of soul ... she is cause for urgent self-reappraisal.

"Look at her!" babbles "Charles" Peach...

But we're looking!

Nymphlike, her steps barely reach the ground.

And she commits something timeless now.

Her cheeks coloring ever so slightly in an endearing wee blush ... she wiggles her bottom deliciously, throwing her willowy arms skyward—taking a transcendental grand bow!

"Wooo—Hooooooo!" whoop the maddened throngs.

Quintessence is come home to roost!

*****

The Third Living Room tumult gushes out even to the deepest reaches of the far Constance Room.

Hearing it, Neddy nods knowingly ... "Proz."

The Duke smiles, quite so.

They rise.

Straighten.

Stroll east.

But Neddy will tie up one loose end...

"He never heard anything more about it?"

The Duke's head shakes.

"There are bears.

"Wolves.

"Eagles.

"It's Alyeska...."

*****

Rusty Arms and the Orchestra render a lilting City-Billy reading of Willie Nelson's winsome *Always On My Mind*.

235

Deftly style-neutral, it would cause even the Duke to rise and dance, were he in the mood—which he is not.

But no ... he is!

He ushers Proz onto the floor now.

They dance playfully, gracefully ... grandly close.

Proz radiates the repose of Garbo in love. The Duke is Father of The Bride.

At the same time, Neddy steps straight to the only noncommittal face in the packed Third Living Room. Lissa Montenero stands motionless, her expression a smile in name only.

With not a word, Neddy whisks her out into the hall. It triggers a lightning-bolt of annoyance ... will she be whisked anywhere by anyone!

Yet Neddy's grip is firm.

Startling.

And given tonight's brave exploits, he's not just "anyone."

Two steps into the hall, though, she tugs back her hand.

"All right Neddy ... what!"

He smiles, making no reply.

"What do you want?"

"I have to tell you something, Lissa, and you have to listen."

"No, I don't."

His smile is placating, "... try."

He maintains his smile, but her annoyance makes it burdensome.

"I know the whole thing, Lissa."

He's buying every possible second.

"People are asses ... I'm a complete ass!"

"Neddy, I've had a long night and—"

He grasps her hand. "Shut up and listen—we all do completely asinine things without any idea why ... because we are asses. When someone does something asinine to you, you think they're doing it on purpose—just to hurt you!"

"What are you talking about!"

He would hold her still, but he knows he can't.

"I'm talking about me and you and Ski and Proz."

He pauses.

"And your father."

He holds her eye.

"I'm talking about everything that's happened to you tonight—and not happened to you tonight. I know how it looks to you, and I know how you feel."

"You know nothing, Neddy. I'm going back inside!"

"You need to hear this, Lissa! You think people do bad things and it makes them evil—and you're right, some of the time it does. But most of the time, we do bad things without any idea we're doing them. We're blind! I said I'm a complete ass, and I'm going to prove it to you—just listen. Would you believe I had it all worked out today that I was going to seduce you?"

"What!"

Her laugh is caustic.

He laughs right back—but a softer laugh.

"Well, I hoped it wouldn't be quite that repugnant!"

His smile persists.

"But let's pretend, just for a moment, that you found it infinitesimally, imperceptibly, unsatisfactorily flattering!"

Her face gentles.

"Proz and I have been having a terrible time," he says. "It's no secret, to you or anyone else. But today, I was going to do what a lot of married people do when they're in trouble ... people who are asses. And now I'm going to tell you something else that is in strictest confidence— I'm trusting you, now, Lissa."

"You already said it," she says, "you're an ass."

"No, no, that is well-known—in the public domain."

She hints at a smirk.

"I had it all worked out," he says, "... really. But this is the part that's strictly between you and me. I left an unsigned note in your Jaguar that I wanted you to meet me in secret this afternoon—except the car I left it in wasn't your Jaguar ... it was someone else's!"

Her laugh is genuine.

"Oh, God, Neddy!"

He nods.

"She still has the note. It's in my handwriting. Now politics are involved! I have no idea how to get it back—no idea what's going to happen next!"

"And, of course, you won't tell me who it is...."

His finger wigwags in a profoundly Gallic *non-non-non*, like Cañon Perdido's Headmistress Pimblitzer.

He invokes the school's solemn motto, *"Toujours La Finesse."*

Her laugh comes from the belly.

"I told you" he says, "... an ass!"

She takes a little step to one side, savoring it.

"Of course, after all the craziness tonight," he says, "I'm everybody's hero—a star. Yet all day long, ever since Proz and I arrived, I've been talking myself into this scheme about you! I was dead set on it! Then I screwed it up massively with the note, and God only knows how I'm going to make it right!"

He nods sharply.

"We're asses, Lissa—all of us! We don't mean to be, we don't plan it ... we just open our mouths! The Duke gets by better than most of us—but tonight, even he had his moments! I'm telling you all this for a very specific reason, and you need to hear it."

She doesn't budge.

"I know better than anyone but you that your father didn't come out looking great tonight—and I know just how much that hurts. Trust me. My dad was a pretty good guy some of the time, but I didn't have to look far for the times he wasn't. I was used to it, but you're not—and it hurts. The point is, most of the time, none of us knows what we're doing! We scheme and plot, we think we're being brilliant, and it's all because, in our asinine ignorance, we think we have no other choice! My father was like that, and so am I—do you see?"

He takes her hand—his tone bearing down.

"And so is your father!"

He holds her eye.

"We're asses. We don't try to be—we're born to it!"

She says nothing.

"Do you see what I'm trying to say?"

"You have a very good heart, Ned."

"If you say so. But don't noise it around, I have a reputation to protect."

Her eyes gleam.

"Grant me this much," he says. "When I get a really bad idea, at least, I choose a genuinely beautiful woman."

She leans in and kisses his cheek.

"Thank you for this, Neddy."

He holds her hand in his. "Okay. But if I see you start to forget—asses—I'm going to remind you!" He grins. "And just think, maybe you could've had more from me than holding hands."

She smiles right back.

"Maybe you could've, too!"

He laughs. "... don't play with matches!"

She laughs back—a wonderful laugh that warms his chest.

He releases her hand.

"Your Dad is just like my Dad," he says. "I know all about it. It doesn't make him good—far from it. It doesn't even make him okay, and I know exactly what I'm saying. But I promise you, he doesn't want to lose you—even if he deserves to!"

He smiles into her gleaming green eyes.

"But you'll be fine—I see that. You're very strong, and that's a wonderful thing. Okay ... ready to go back?"

She shakes her head, no.

"That took a lot of courage, Neddy."

"That's the way with us asses—tons of courage. It gets us into unbelievable messes!"

"Well, thank you. You're a dear." She touches his cheek. "You're very sweet."

"You deserve it."

He offers his arm and she takes it, smiling.

They enter the Third Living Room, just as Proz and the Duke are finishing their dance.

"Duke," Neddy says, "... meet the second-most beautiful woman in the room."

Lissa beams.

The Duke gives him a crinkled aluminum-foil grin.

"Son, you have the makings."

"He gets what he's after," Proz says, a light in her eye, "no matter who he's just been out in the hall with."

She hooks her arm in Neddy's and nibbles his ear.

*****

"We're honored to have you," the Duke beams.

"The honor is all mine."

Paw Coggins shakes the Duke's hand.

Lissa smiles ... coolly indestructible again, after all.

Paw's eye narrows. "I was hoping you might convince Lissa to give me a dance."

"She shall," the Duke decrees.

Lissa nods happily, let it be so.

"Well, now," says the Duke, "what did you think of our little side-show?"

"Haven't had this much fun since the Series."

The Duke's smile modulates, turning to Neddy. "I'm sorry about your car."

"It was a heroic end," Neddy says. "My father would approve."

"What car?" says Paw.

"A Tucker," Neddy says.

"Is that a sports car?"

The Duke's clattering laugh is answer in full.

"At least, it wasn't like in the movies," he says, "... it didn't explode in flames. The whole mountainside would've gone up!"

Proz glimmers mischievously. "We're putting a roadside cross up at the site. Or maybe a flashing neon sign ... something tasteful."

"On that note..." Paw says, leading Lissa to the dance floor.

"Handsome couple," the Duke observes. "Second-most attractive pair tonight."

"Oh, Daddy..." Proz says, her golden smile like late-afternoon sun.

CHAPTER 33

Coda

HE WON'T TELL her.

He may be an ass—but he's not a fool!

She's right next to him at the bar now, shoulder to shoulder—alluringly close, in every way.

But not a word.

He orders a Mount Gay and tonic. He'll take a moment to collect his thoughts....

He won't try to explain it to her for a thousand reasons. The first, and least relevant—he got no argument on it from Lissa—is, he's an ass. Not to be trusted. Tonight, he deposited heavily in the First National Bank of Neddy. He is a man of exploits. Only a complete imbecile would squander all that the very first night!

He savors his Mount Gay.

His wife has never looked better to him ... not even that breathtaking first night.

And she's never looked more confirmed.

More in love.

They've never felt closer.

But he wants to explain—he needs to! He doesn't want a secret standing between them.

Maybe, after all that's happened, things between them really have changed. Maybe he'll take her up to the room tonight, believing all is going to be fine—and it really is going to be fine!

But he can't tell her.

No.

Lissa will, of course. Women talk.

But he had to tell Lissa—had to tell someone!

And Lissa's a good sort, she may not.

Never try to explain the inexplicable....

It brings him to the crux of the matter—Twitty. She's listening now, even intimately, to every word from Julian Axel. It's what women do with Axel ... listen. They're huddled together on the purple loveseat, Axel busy plotting the Eastern Campaign. Twitty nods and smiles, and Axel is enjoying himself. She's overdoing it a little, but the hour is late, after all. They need a resolution.

Good.

It keeps her from doing anything filthy with the note.

"There's an oddity," Proz says, nodding to Twitty and Axel. "But after a night like this...."

She lets it trail off.

"And you, my sweet," he says, "... after a night like this, you've come through like—I don't know what!"

The warmth of her smile would open sunflowers. "Then, we're even, dear."

He smiles back.

Going to be fine.

But if he told her—right now—she might understand...

Is he nuts!

*****

Clive O.E.M. Monogram has waited...

And waited.

Now he has his opening.

He's standing behind Neddy and Proz with Burtie and Halimony.

The perfect lull....

He taps Proz's shoulder, nodding to the Pasadena ladies.

Proz smiles.

Nods.

"You know..." he says, in a stagey tone, "it's so dark and foggy out tonight...."

"Pardon, Clive?"

"I said—"

He's playing to the third balcony. "... it's *sooo* dark and foggy out tonight—"

She glimmers.

Her eye slides to Neddy.

Back to Monogram.

"Okay, Clive—just how dark and foggy out is it?"

He nods to the Pasadenans.

"It's so dark and foggy ... you can't tell Wight from Wong."

Stricken grimaces all around.

Burtie retches.

"... been waiting all night for that, haven't you," says Halimony.

Clive beams.

Nods.

"Longer."

*****

Crunch time.

Ken Stukud loves this ... the very best part.

"'Course, I'd take less for cash..." he allows. "Might be best, all-around-wise."

"I'll have to see it first, of course," Julian Axel nods.

"Natch. Why don'tcha bring Twitty."

"Can't do that," Axel says. "It's a surprise!"

"Ah..." Ken grins. "Depends how things go tonight."

"Nothing of the sort! It's only a trinket!"

"And the top goes down..." Ken winks. "She'll love it!"

"Well, now ... here she is!" Axel beams cordially—Twitty returning from the loo.

She smiles back ... tee-yump. (No strings now—the lateness of the hour.)

"Still burning the midnight oil, Kenny?" she says.

"That's what it's for, id'nit! But I'll be needing some shut-eye right soon—Friday's a big day on the lot ... especially after this hoedown! Bargain Friday, I call it!"

"Speaking of which," she says, "I'm still interested in that cute little Saab convertible."

Ken smiles like the Fourth of July—all options open.

"Say, Kenny—" Twitty says.

But she smiles now to Axel, "... pardon us a moment, Julian, I have to talk to Kenny."

Axel bows out graciously and turns to the bar.

Christ, thinks Ken—she's gonna make an offer.

He loves his life!

She draws him back a step or two, creating a space.

"You know Neddy Lombardo," she says, "right?"

"Like my own socks!"

He nods along the bar. "... sittin' right there!"

She smiles. "Will you do me a favor?"

"Anything t'all!"

"You're sweet, Ken. It's a surprise for Proz, but she can't hear anything about it—promise?"

"I'm yer man."

"Top Secret!"

"You don't gotta beat me up, darlin'—I get it!"

She nods.

"Tell Neddy for me to go to the men's all by himself."

"Check—all by his lonesome."

She nods again, getting this straight. "And when he comes back ... he's to look in the hall underneath the small Brancusi."

Stukud makes a face. "The what!"

"Brancusi," she says. "It's like Jacuzzi—except 'Bran.'"

"Bran-coozy."

"Think you can remember that?"

"I'm not an idiot!"

Twitty smiles like all outdoors.

"He'll know what I mean, Ken. Just tell him—he has to do it all alone, nobody around!"

"Secret—gotcha. Hun ... that little Saab's down there's just pinin' away, y'know."

*****

"Wellllll, now...." Proz luxuriates.

She releases her breaths in gently subsiding waves.

It's four a.m., and she's in the Checquers bedroom, where she came into this world, where she came of age—and now a very good deal more.

"Darling..." she sighs, "where on earth have we been!"

He says nothing. Nothing needs saying.

She nuzzles his chest. "We've been setting the table for this for ... it seems like forever!"

She laughs, a gushing, self-congratulatory chuckle.

"There are feasts," she says, "... but then, there are feasts!"

He strokes her elegant high cheekbone. "Was rather good...."

"Rather!"

She kisses his chest, indulging God's Own Secret Joy.

"Let me see now," she says, a thought taking form, "... how did it go again?"

Her hand slides around his waist, her tone softly mischievous.

"I believe we begin right ... here."

*****

He pads softly along Checquers' gleaming marble main hallway in dressing gown and slippers. The pre-dawn gloom is relieved by only one lamp.

Proz fell gently asleep. It took all his discipline not to do the same—

But this comes first.

And he must be quick. With all that's happened to her tonight, difficult dreams may come. If not tonight ... they will come.

Beyond the Third Living Room, he goes straight to the wondrous, shining bronze object on the low marble table. Its form thrusts vigorously skywards from the base ... a gunshot's—*bang!* ... dynamic, exquisite.

Gently, he slides it sideways on the mahogany base, surprised at its heft. In the low ambient light, he finds ... nothing.

But he moves it farther—disclosing a tiny sliver of white.

Moving it more, he uncovers a nest of white paper shreds.

Twitty's thought this through.

If stumbled upon, the shreds will be indecipherable.

But are they?

Gathering up the shreds, he centers the precious Brancusi again on the mahogany base.

Under a lamp on the coffee table in the Third Living Room, he identifies the elements of his scrawl on the shreds of paper.

But assembling them ... pieces are missing! What remain are meaningless hieroglyphs. It's the Egyptian enigma without aid of the Rosetta Stone!

Sweet Twitty—he is forgiven!

Toujours La Finesse....

He scatters the bits of paper across the embers, still glowing red in the Third Living Room fireplace.

The papers crinkle.

Writhe.

Exult in cheery wee licks of flame...

Expire.

Sweet Twitty.

In love as if for the very first time, he pads back along the hall, up the stairs again, to his wife, to their bed, to the consolation of deep, healing, redemptive sleep.

It's Checquers....

Finis

ABOUT THE AUTHOR

Ted West published his first two stories in *Road & Track* in his senior year at the University of California at Santa Barbara. With the help of *Road & Track* Editor James T. Crow, in 1968 he was hired as Feature Editor at competing *Sports Car Graphic* in Los Angeles, where he wrote monthly columns, feature stories, road tests, and racing coverage. In 1970 and 1971 he went to Europe for *Road & Track* to cover the Porsche 917s and Ferrari 512s in the World Manufacturer's Championship, returning to America each summer to cover the Can-Am and Formula One for *Sports Car Graphic* and *The Motor* (London).

In 1976, he moved to New York to become Articles Editor for *Car And Driver*, where he wrote a monthly column, road tests, and feature stories. In his first year in Manhattan, he won the International Motor Press Association's prestigious Ken W. Purdy Award For Excellence in Automotive Journalism for a story on a gathering of grand-prix immortals Juan Manuel Fangio, Phil Hill, Rene Dreyfus, Carroll Shelby, Dan Gurney, and others. In the Eighties, he won two more Purdy Awards for *Road & Track* coverage of the Indianapolis 500. West is the only three-time winner in the Purdy's 60-year history.

As a Contributing Editor, first at *Road & Track*, then *Car And Driver*, he wrote features and covered professional racing in North America and Europe. His work has been featured in *The New York Times, Motor Trend, Town & Country, Outdoor Life, Boating, Pan Am Clipper, Motorboating & Sailing, The Motor* (London), and others. He is a select contributor to *000 Magazine*, an exclusive publication devoted to the history and traditions of Porsche, and he contributes regularly to *Porsche Panorama*. He also served as Editor In Chief of *Hard Card*, a NASCAR website associated with Richard Petty Motorsport and Stewart-Haas Racing.

ALSO FROM TED WEST

This is the first in Ted West's *Diddly* series of novels that plunge us into the special challenges of the richest family in the world.

West made a name for himself as a motor-racing writer and reporter. Prior to the publication of *The Seven Diddly Sins*, West's most recent book – and his first novel – was the Unabridged Edition of *Closing Speed*, a riveting look at the 1970 World Manufacturer's Championship in Europe immortalized by Steve McQueen's *Le Mans*. An earlier edition appeared in 2010, but the Unabridged Edition restores material originally intended by the author. *Closing Speed* is a complex, adult, intensely personal novel of professional racing during its most dangerous time.

The Seven Diddly Sins will be followed by West's third novel—a prequel to this book. The same cast of *Diddly* twits, knowing still less about life, but willing to guess, take the stage again, remembering not a word of their lines, bumbling their way to a not-so-logical conclusion.